Within the Skin

by

Zara West

The Skin Quartet

Within the Skin

Cover Art by *Kristian Norris*

The Wild Rose Press, Inc.
PO Box 708
Adams Basin, NY 14410-0708
Visit us at www.thewildrosepress.com

Publishing History
First Crimson Rose Edition, 2018
Print ISBN 978-1-5092-2073-1
Digital ISBN 978-1-5092-2074-8

The Skin Quartet
Published in the United States of America

Toro extracted the gold-bordered engraved card with her name on it. She ran her finger across the raised letters—Alba Vargas—an apparition from another time, another world.

Alba Vargas had been a timid, frightened child who'd spent her nights huddled at the bottom of a closet with her hand over her baby brother's mouth, hoping that whoever was beating her mom didn't start on her next.

She was no longer that girl. Tonight she would be the new Alba Vargas, reborn and rebaptized as a woman with power. Tonight she would be one of the movers and shakers in the art world. Tonight she was a winner.

The glass door loomed in front of her. She drew to a halt and peered into the museum lobby. It was like watching a ball scene in one of those boring chick flicks. Overly skinny women in glittering gowns gathered in small groups, their manicured hands moving like flighty little birds.

Men stuffed into black tuxes hovered over them, claiming ownership with carelessly placed hands on an upper arm or on the curve of a waist. Others stood in animated pairs conversing about whatever denizens of the art world talked about.

A slight breeze ruffled the edges of her cape and a chill swept across her exposed skin. She didn't belong here all alone, wearing these too-revealing clothes and flaunting false femininity.

Toro gripped her purse tighter. Didn't matter. She had to do this. For herself. For Hanger.

Praise for Zara West

"I can't recommend this book highly enough to any romance reader. You have to like your dangerous bits, too, though; because there's the thriller part of this book as well. Try it, you'll love it!…Such talent. I hope she never runs out of ideas now that she's gotten started."

~Blue Cat Review

"I tend to think of the romantic suspense genre as being full of rich and/or successful people and exotic locales or exotic careers. Ms. West turns this stereotype on its head and makes it do handsprings. - a compulsive page turner."

~5 Star Goodreads Review

"This suspense-laden love story will appeal to readers of many genres and leave one satisfied as they reach the conclusion to this intriguing and entertaining read."

~InD'tale Magazine

Dedication

In memory of my mother who loved Brooklyn as much as I do.

Chapter 1

Scritch.

Something scraped against the outside of the building. Pharaoh lifted the pencil from the tattoo sketch he was working on and listened.

Scritch.

There it was again.

Crap.

He pressed his palm against his pounding temple, then tossed down the pencil, and staggered to the front door, nearly tripping over his boss's latest rescue kitten. With a groan, he swept it off the floor, kissed the tiny thing on the top of its head, and set it gently down on the sofa.

He unlocked the tattoo parlor door. Toro's brother had better not be spraying graffiti on The Siren again.

He stuck his head out and squinted through the glare of the morning sunlight. The throbbing in his head increased. Yep. It was Hanger.

The teenager stood in front of the shop, his faded Yankees' ball cap tilted back on his forehead, a spray can in hand, surveying his work.

Pharaoh glanced up at the wall. The kid had talent. The mermaid with her long swirling red hair and silver-scaled fishtail was a graffiti masterpiece.

But it didn't belong here on the outside of Williamsburg, Brooklyn's most renowned tattoo studio—not with its huge naked breasts and certainly not with the much too familiar face.

His boss wasn't going to be happy seeing herself portrayed so graphically on her place of business. He stepped out the door. "That's it. I'm calling the cops."

Hanger's head jerked around. "You wouldn't."

Pharaoh slipped his cell out of his back pocket. "Watch me."

"Toro will wring your neck."

His finger hovered over the phone. He really didn't need Hanger's brother any angrier with him than he already was. They used to be best buddies. Now they barely talked. "How about I wring yours instead?"

Hanger grinned. "You'd have to catch me first, Fur Tree."

Pharaoh glared at him. "I ain't Fur Tree anymore. Name's Fernando Pharaoh."

"Fur Treeeee. Fur Treeeee. You can't catch meeeee," Hanger chanted in the singsong voice that drove him crazy. "Not with that hangover, you can't."

"Try me." Pharaoh lunged at him.

The kid danced back on his toes. "See. Bet you're seeing double."

Hanger was right. After boozing all night, he was in no condition to catch anyone, especially not a wily street kid. "Look. Just promise me you'll stop putting Bella's face on these naked sirens you're throwing up all over Brooklyn."

"Give me a tattoo and I'll stop."

"Don't be an idiot. You know you have to be eighteen."

"Yeah. Right. Wait three more years? Knew you'd say that." Hanger stuck out his tongue. "Did one myself."

Pharaoh's head roared. "*Stupida*. You can't tat yourself."

"So can. Put a nice big T-Crew crown on my leg."

Pharaoh swallowed down the bile creeping up his throat. He sure hoped the kid had used a sterile needle. "Let me take a look." He moved toward him.

Hanger slung his duffle over his shoulder and edged back. "No way, *amigo*."

"Could get infected."

"What would you care? You stopped caring about me and Toro and T-Crew long ago."

Then Hanger took off running, zigzagging in and out between parked cars, hopping up and over trash cans, and dashing past the early morning rush hour commuters plodding their way to the Bedford Street subway entrance on the corner.

But Pharaoh had been a graffiti kid, too, and knew all the tricks. He just wished he hadn't buried his troubles in a whiskey bottle last night. Cursing his aching head and roiling stomach, he ran down the street in pursuit.

****

By the time he reached the East River, Hanger knew Pharaoh would never catch him. He looked back and gave his once-upon-a-time hero the finger, then dove around the corner of the elegant condo where the person he hated most in the world lived. He stopped short in his tracks.

The bastard's garage door was open.

He peeked inside. No guard. He could hide in the garage, maybe even leave a few tags on Kiro's stolen car collection while he waited for Pharaoh to get bored and go back to The Siren.

Four minutes later, Hanger was scrunched between the cement wall and the shiny red Spyder that should have belonged to his lady idol Bella happily spraying his version of Jaws on the gleaming surface.

He stood back and narrowed his eyes. Oh yeah. Shark Tooth Man Kiro was gonna shit his pants when he saw it. He took out his favorite silver cannon, pressed down on the nozzle, and aimed at the windshield.

Now for the finishing touch. In broad strokes, he sprayed his tag—MV for Micea Vargas—his real name. He leaned back and surveyed his work. Perfect.

Crunch. A footstep sounded behind him.

He whirled around.

Whack.

Something hard smacked the side of his head, and everything went black.

****

"*Idiota.*" Pharaoh gazed around the corner of the smooth white facade of the condo. The driveway stood clear, the garage door partially open. He rubbed the close-cropped hair on the top of his head that had earned him his street handle, Fur Tree. The kid wouldn't have gone inside. Would he?

He let out a huff of air. Nah, Hanger wasn't stupid. Probably made it look like he'd snuck into the garage. Little imp was slipperier than the green soap he used to prep his tattoo customers.

Tattoo customers? Hell. What was he thinking? He had no time to play rat chaser with a kid. He had clients waiting.

He turned in the direction of The Siren, then peered

back over his shoulder at the building. The kid was going to get himself killed if he hung around that place. The bastard crime boss living there had no use for anyone associated with Bella or her husband.

He loped back up the street toward The Siren. He'd have to speak to El Toro and tell him his brother was running amok. That is if he could face the T-Crew King and actually have a conversation.

They'd been inseparable once. Now the leader of their little band of street artists never seemed to be around. When they did meet, Toro turned away and refused to look at him.

The other T-Crew members, Solo and Neto—now they were another story. His former friends were on the warpath, and he was their intended victim.

After what he'd done to Bella, Pharaoh didn't blame them.

He recrossed Bedford and raced down the sidewalk. Forget the kid. What he had to worry about was getting back to The Siren in time to open up and prep for the first customer.

Someday he'd have a tat place of his own. But for now, his boss Bella relied on him, and he wouldn't let her or anyone else down—ever again.

Chapter 2

Toro yanked the dress over her head and winced as the zipper caught in her hair. She tugged it off and tossed it to the floor. Forget it.

She toed the crumpled garment. Alba Vargas, *Hot New Artist*, indeed. If only the contest application hadn't required her social security number and real name.

Now, to appear at the gala and claim her award money, she'd have to show up as a woman. She'd never manage it. A girl didn't live six years disguised as a boy and then instantly turn into a beauty queen.

She lifted another gown from the black plastic bag and held it up. The filmy cloth was some kind of satin or was it sateen? What she knew about dress fabrics would fit in a marker cap.

Tentatively, she brushed her open hand over it. The rough pads of her fingers caught on the fine threads. Hands that could haul her up the side of a building and wield a spray can for hours weren't meant for such finery.

And then there were these idiotic undergarments. She plucked at the lace barely covering her breasts. The tiny panties and bras Bella helped her buy made her feel naked.

Besides, she'd lived too long on the down fringes of Brooklyn society. Exposing all that skin was a recipe for attracting the wrong kind of attention from the males of the species.

Ugh. Give her body-concealing men's tees and sweats any day.

She dropped the dress and sank down onto the bed. Bella had been generous to lend her these beautiful things to try on, but none of them worked. The slim skirts hobbled her ankles. The full skirts tangled around her legs.

She'd begged, but Bella refused to let her wear something sensible like jeans. It was time, the tattoo artist said, for El Toro to embrace her feminine side.

Right. What feminine side? She liked herself the way she was.

Mierda. She cradled her head in her hands. She just wouldn't go.

Toro flicked the invitation off the nightstand and caught it as it floated down: *Gala and Awards Ceremony for the Winners of the First Emerging Young Artists Competition.* She'd done it—won the recognition for her art that she'd always dreamed of.

The first-place award was five thousand dollars. Not only would that keep her in paint and canvas for months, it would help send her brother to college. Let him escape a life on the street.

She shoved the bag of clothing off the bed. It landed with a plop. A rainbow of colors tumbled out onto the threadbare Oriental carpet she'd rescued from a trash can. She poked at the dresses with her toe.

Sure, she could hole up in her apartment and have them mail her the check. But she'd never be able to propel her career forward if she didn't go. Professional artists needed to interact with their public. They had to meet clients. Contract with gallery owners. Get patrons. Face the press.

That's why she entered the competition in the first place—to get recognition, attract media attention, become a name in the art world, and sell enough paintings so she and her brother would never go hungry again.

If she didn't go to the awards ceremony and socialize with the people who'd selected her paintings as the best in the city, they'd probably write her off as a reclusive freak. Without contacts, she could paint from dawn to dusk and never make a sale.

Besides, she'd promised her mentor, Ari, she'd go. She couldn't disappoint him. Toro rubbed the back of her neck. If Bella's brother hadn't paid for the treatment for her neck fracture, seen that she'd gotten physical therapy, and given her time to heal on Eudokia, that wonderful Greek island of his, she'd never have walked again, much less painted. Somehow, she had to pull this off for his sake, if nothing else.

With a huff, Toro swooped the plastic bag from the floor and yanked out something stretchy in green. Using her gentlest grip, she maneuvered the clingy fabric over her head, wiggled the dress past her hips, and tugged the hem down.

She adjusted the neckline and studied herself in the mirror. The slightly flared skirt came to mid-thigh, and way too much of her chest and legs showed, but otherwise this one kind of worked. It moved with her body and didn't constrict her movements.

She jumped up and down and did a cartwheel. Tried a few ballet poses. The dress revealed a heck of a lot of skin, but at least it didn't trap her arms or cinch her legs.

Toro slithered out of the dress and held it out in front of her. Yep, this one might work. If she had to, she could shimmy up the side of building in it.

But *cielos*, the color was ugly. The bilious chartreuse reminded her of one of North Street Deli's half-sour kosher pickles. She'd stand out in the crowd for sure.

She tossed it on the bed. Too bad it wasn't black. But then Bella never wore dark colors.

Toro gathered up the other dresses and shoved them into the bag. She'd take these back, and then get Bella to teach her how to put on the makeup. She hadn't the faintest idea what to do with all that girly stuff they'd bought at the drug store.

She glanced at the clock. Nine forty-five pm. If she hurried, she'd get to The Siren a few minutes after closing time at ten. With the shop closed, Bella would be free to give her some tips.

And by then, Pharaoh would be gone. He never hung around after hours. Too busy drinking and whoring.

A heaviness settled over her. Why had her best friend turned out to be such a hateful person? She'd thought he cared about her. With his height and strength and quick reflexes, she'd always relied on him to watch over her and Hanger when they were attacked by rival crews or ran into a street gang set on violent mischief.

But when she'd been injured, it was like she'd turned into some pariah. He hadn't come to the hospital. He hadn't sent her one single letter or email while she recuperated on Ari's island. And now, the minute she showed up at The Siren, he acted like she wasn't there.

And the hell of it was, she wasn't the one who had done something to feel guilty about.

When she was in Greece, he should have taken over as the King of T-Crew. Instead, he turned his back on Solo and Neto and their new Big Bad Street Art tourism business, and became a tattoo artist.

She didn't have anything against him wanting an artistic outlet that paid money rather than an illegal one that would land him in jail again, but then he'd turned traitor and stolen Bella's sketches and her TV job.

Big-hearted Bella had forgiven him. But Toro couldn't. Not when he couldn't forgive himself and thought drinking himself to oblivion, just like her mother had, was the answer to his problems.

But damn it, she missed having him around. She missed the smell of him, the way his powerful muscles moved as he ran and leaped.

Her body warmed at the thought of him climbing behind her, hoisting her up onto a window ledge, standing next to her as they spray-painted a throw-up they'd designed together on some unsuspecting merchant's wall.

Dios mío. Why did such a gorgeous-looking guy have to be so rotten inside? She pressed her palm against her chest. Merely thinking about him made her heart beat faster and heat build between her thighs. And she knew what that meant.

She may never have slept with a man, but she was no naïve girl. She lived amongst guys. Ogled the hotties with them. Slapped their backs at their conquests. Leaned in when they shared how they brought their girlfriends to orgasm. Oh yeah. She knew exactly what happened between men and women.

So hell yes, she was attracted. Her female parts worked fine. That prickle of desire was almost enough to make her think about revealing her secret to him. But she wouldn't.

Pharaoh had made it perfectly clear he wanted nothing to do with her. No way would she waste her virginity on him. Plenty of other good-looking men were out there. She'd find her prince yet.

She glanced over at the battered volume of fairy tales lying on her night table—the only belonging she still had from the time before all the bad things happened. Before her father disappeared. Before her mother died. Before she and her brother were left to survive on the streets.

Toro gave herself a don't-be-a-fool shake. The idea of dressing as a woman after all these years was messing with her head. Once upon a time, she had a papa who called her his little princess. Once upon a time she foolishly believed fairy tales came true. But she knew better now.

Life wasn't a fairy tale, and she had more important things to do than think about princes and sex.

She shucked the girly underwear and snapped on the skin-tight elastic binding she'd devised to flatten her breasts. Then she pulled on her oversized men's tee and sweatpants. She picked up the bag of clothes, slung it over a shoulder, and then dropped it back on the floor.

Drat. Focused on the dresses, she'd completely forgotten all about the back-to-back graffiti piece she was supposed be helping her buddies, Solo and Neto, spray paint that wonderful new plywood construction barrier over on North Third.

She'd have to send her brother to tell them she wouldn't be coming. The awards ceremony was tomorrow, and she was far from ready. Grabbing her sweatshirt, she opened her bedroom door and peered out.

Uh-oh. No TV blared. No slobby kid raided the fridge.

She gave a yell. "Hanger."

No sullen kid answered her back.

If her brother wasn't home, she'd ground his butt, for sure. She stalked into the living room. Yeah, it was summer. But out there on the street, danger lurked. Drugs. Gangs. Guns. Pimps. People who would love to get their hands on a pretty young boy.

For six years, she'd faced down all those dangers to keep him safe. She massaged the back of her neck. Had the scars to prove it. She wasn't going to lose him to the streets now. Not when it looked like she might be able to pull them up and out. Not when she could start thinking about sending him to college so he could make something of himself.

She tugged the sweatshirt over her head and then headed to his room. Hanger knew he was supposed to be in at dark unless they went out together to tag.

And he'd been good about it, especially after that Kiro character kidnapped him and Bella. Nevertheless, Hanger wasn't perfect. How could he be? He was fifteen and thought himself invincible.

She peeked through his half-open door, hoping he was using that invincibility to crush an online video game opponent. Dirty clothes blanketed the floor. Sheets lay heaped in a pile on the bed. Some god-awful mermaid with bare breasts the size of watermelons was spray-painted over his headboard.

She wrinkled her nose. Ugh. That would have to go. *Pronto.* Bad enough they all breathed in the paint fumes outside tagging. But graffiti inside was forbidden.

She moved farther into the room, knelt down, and peeked under the bed. Nope. No curled-up teen battling demons on his tablet or reading one of those Riordan books he loved so much. Just another heap of stinky socks and underwear.

She stood up and put her hands on her hips. Not here. Damn the kid. She would have to call the twins and see if her brother was with them.

She really shouldn't. Graffiti artists hated to be interrupted in the middle of a throw-up. The idea was to get the painting up as fast as possible, then scram before the night guards or cops showed up.

Still, a prickle of unease crept through her. Hanger should have been home by now. He knew the rules. He knew she'd worry.

She slipped her cell from her back pocket, swiped it on, and tapped Solo's icon.

"*Que pasa,* Toro?" Solo's voice was murky, barely louder than the street traffic in the background.

"Hanger with you?"

"Haven't seen him. Not since yesterday. Gone AWOL again?"

Toro stomped out of Hanger's room. "Yeah. Should have wandered in over an hour ago."

"So, you still coming?"

"Look. Sorry. Can't make it tonight. Got to see Bella about something, then find my stupid brother."

"No prob, man. We'll miss ya. We need you doing

the high parts."

"If I can get there later, I'll give you a call. Be a shame not to finish. Bad for the rep."

"Yeah, do that. Someone coming. Got to go. *Adios.*"

The phone went silent. Toro tossed the cell from one hand to the other. She was letting her team down again, missing a slam, lying to them about who she was. But she couldn't tell them she was a girl or that she was skipping tagging to learn how to put on makeup.

They had no idea that tomorrow she was going to be hailed as a great new artist by the New York City art critics and highbrows. The same people who looked down on graffiti artists and did nothing when they were thrown in jail.

Still, her betrayal of the twins' trust hurt all the way to her core. The guys were loyal. Had been ever since the night she'd rescued them—two twelve-year-old runaways—and shown them how to survive on the street.

They did everything and anything she asked even though over the years they'd grown taller and stronger. *Cielos.* They looked more like her bodyguards than her best friends.

Someday she'd let them in on the secret, but not yet. First, she had to make sure she had money enough to make a normal life for Hanger and her. Because one thing was for sure. Once they knew she was a girl, they'd never treat her the same way again.

She tucked the phone in her pocket and headed back into her bedroom. Tossing the makeup case into the bag of clothing, she knotted it closed and hefted the sack over her shoulder. Keeping the truth from them might hurt now, but in the long run she knew she was doing the right thing for her and for her brother.

Chapter 3

Pharaoh watched the light in El Toro's apartment flick out. He wedged himself farther into the heavily shadowed niche in the wall opposite T-Crew's building. It would not do to be seen.

But he couldn't stay away. Memories of the happy days, when he'd been part of the graffiti crew, drew him back night after night like a homeless man to a hot grate. He took a swig from his hip flask, then wiped his mouth with the back of his hand.

Those days were over. Solo and Neto had warned him to stay far away.

He knew what they were afraid of—Toro taking him back under T-Crew's wing. El Toro was like Bella. The Graffiti King stood up for his friends; witness how he risked his life to protect Bella's brother from that bastard Kiro.

Pharaoh sucked in a breath of the humid air, heavy with the taste of diesel fumes and spoiled garbage. Crazy fool. Toro'd nearly ended up paralyzed trying to free Bella and Ari.

He scuffed the toe of his sneaker along a crack in the sidewalk. Sure, his friend would forgive him for stealing from Bella. The problem was he couldn't forgive himself.

He glanced up and down the street. Better this way. Wondering where the twins were. When the next attack would come.

And they would get him. Of that he was sure. He was pretty well matched with either one of them. Same towering height, same strong limber muscles from their night-time gymnastics on the city's roofs. But when they were together, the twins were smarter, stronger, and definitely more vicious.

Not only were there two of them, but they had a spine-chilling way of knowing what each other was thinking, allowing them to move as a coordinated unit of terror.

He rubbed the scars that slashed across the tattooed sleeve on his lower arm. The thing was, they didn't intend to slit his throat, merely cut out pieces of flesh. One notch for every sketch he'd stolen from Bella and sold.

He pressed his scarred arm against his side. Three down and twenty-four to go. Hell, but he wished they'd kill him outright.

Bang. The door across the way slammed open. Toro bounced down the steps and took off up the street. Pharaoh followed behind. He couldn't help himself. Stalking his used-to-be best buddy was better than lying awake feeling sorry for himself all night in the dank little apartment he rented.

And it was too early to get falling-down drunk. He couldn't get through a night without downing a bottle or two to wipe away the guilt enough to sleep. If he were smart, he'd get a job as a night guard and get paid for not sleeping.

With enough money, he could leave this freaking city and all the bad memories behind and start his own tattoo place—somewhere south, where it was always warm.

Ahead of him, Toro stopped at a traffic light. Pharaoh caught sight of the black plastic bag over his shoulder and frowned. The King never went anywhere without his satchel of spray paint. So what was with the bag? Not garbage. T-Crew's building had plenty of trash bins.

The light changed, and Toro cut across cattycorner and hustled down North Eighth. Pharaoh came to an abrupt stop. Damn it, Toro was heading to The Siren. Not a place he wanted to be right now. Bella would insist he and Toro be polite to each other. No way that was happening.

He shoved his hands into his pockets. That left drinking for his evening's entertainment. Doubling back, he headed for his favorite hidey-hole, The Top-of-the-Day, which despite its name, was dark, empty, and off-the-beaten track—a bar and grill for serious drinkers and bottom-feeders who wore guilt like a skin.

The perfect place to drown his demons in a bottle of rotto whiskey.

****

Ten minutes later, he was inside the long, narrow barroom with its battered oak counter and sitting at his usual table way in the back. He signaled the barkeep to bring him his regular rotgut. He'd never liked the taste of alcohol and hated how it burned going down, but it was the fastest, cheapest, legal way to blank out the bitter voice in his head.

He might have chosen drugs. The glassy-eyed dealer sitting on a stool at the bar had made him some enticing offers. But after watching his brother die of a drug overdose, he'd rather go slow from a bad liver or fast from a suicidal leap off a bridge.

The bartender slapped the tumbler on the table and went back to staring at the ball game. Pharaoh picked up the glass, careful not to rest his arm on the table top. The gouged wood was sticky with spilled beer and littered with peanut shells—the only food he'd ever seen offered at the Top-of-the-Day.

His belly growled, reminding him he hadn't eaten any dinner. He studied the stained hand-lettered menu above the bar listing the expected hamburgers, wings, and fries and wondered if he'd end up with stomach poisoning to go along with his pounding head if he ordered something. A quick glance at the sullen bartender, polishing a glass with a dirty rag, decided him.

He'd stick to alcohol. Drinking until everything blurred into nothingness was what the place offered. So drink he would. Oblivion would come faster on an empty stomach than a full one. He raised the glass in an ironic toast to the air.

He gulped down the whiskey. It was raw, bitter, and seared his insides. He swallowed hard and ordered another. Then another.

Pharaoh was well through the third glass when a skinny dude with a twitchy eye sat down at his table. What the hell? People usually knew to stay away from a six-foot-four black man sitting in the shadows.

He lowered his eyebrows and showed his teeth like the half-civilized animal he was. "*Scram.* Not looking for company."

"Heard you do tattoos." The man's voice was low-pitched and syrupy.

Pharaoh looked the guy up and down. Baggy suit,

well creased, stained on the lapel, smelling faintly of a cologne sweet enough to be a woman's. Not the tattoo type, but then you never knew. Maybe he wanted a Love Mom heart on his ass.

The twitchy eye bothered him though. Made him think of crooked lawyers, for some reason.

Pharaoh put his hand on the table and then regretted it. It came away covered with gunk that stank worse than sour beer. He wiped his hand on his jeans. "Not in bars. Come to The Siren, and I'll see what I can do for you."

"Heard you were looking to leave that joint. Might be able to offer you something a bit more rewarding—if you know what I mean. Good pay. Side benefits." Twitchy-Eye tapped the glass. "Better whiskey."

Pharaoh sat back. He'd been trying to find another tattoo studio to take him on for months. He hated being beholden to Bella after what he did to her. But no ink shop in all of Brooklyn would rent him a tat station. All the local tattoo artists loved Bella.

Then again, her husband had probably spread word through the grapevine that he'd betrayed Bella, and no one would gainsay the former crime boss. Vernon Newell might not have a criminal empire behind him anymore, but he still had some nasty friends.

The guy across from him pulled his coat collar higher around his neck and started to rise. "Suit yourself. Some other tattoo artist will do it."

Pharaoh drained his tumbler. He had nothing to lose. And he sure could use the money. Every little bit extra added to his escape fund. "Might be interested."

The man thumped back down and fished a paper out of his pocket. "Can you tat that?"

"This?" Pharaoh spun the scrap of paper around and blinked his eyes to clear them. After three whiskeys, everything was a blur. Usually at this point, he started for home while he could still find it.

He blinked again and studied the drawing. Looked like a simple rose design you could find in any tattoo coloring book. Even a two-week apprentice could tat it. "Sure. But—"

"Five hundred dollars. Come along if you're interested. I'll take you to the shop. You can give it a look over and decide."

He didn't trust the guy or the offer. But he found himself getting up and following the man out of the bar. Later, he would blame everything that happened on loneliness.

Chapter 4

"Hey, Bella." Toro pulled open the door and stepped inside The Siren. The lingering scents of ink, disinfectant, and sweaty bodies assaulted her. She pinched her nose.

The sample designs on the wall might be beautiful, but tattooing was not the art form for her. Give her the smell of spray paint on a clear night or oil colors swirled over a fresh canvas any day over working in this fug.

She let the door close behind her and dropped the bag of clothes. She glanced around to make sure Pharaoh was gone for the day, then called, "I found a dress to wear for tomorrow."

"Wonderful." Bella came out of the bathroom wiping her hands on her jeans. "Lock the door and turn off the sign. I want to see you in it. Which one did you pick?"

"The pickle one."

"Pickle? Oh, the green A-line. I thought it would fit you well."

"I didn't bring the dress. I'm here because I need help with the makeup. Teach me how to do it."

Bella clapped her hands. "So fun. Never had the chance to play make-over artist before."

Toro handed her the cosmetic kit. "You can do it, right?"

22

"No problem. I do my own makeup every day. Really no different than tattooing. Except it all washes off. Come along. I can't wait to try out all those eyeshadow and lipstick colors." She moved toward the tat station in the back. "With your olive skin and black hair, we can go very vibrant. Should have brought the dress though so we could see how it all worked together."

Toro trailed after her. "Whatever. As long as I look like a woman."

Bella looked over her shoulder. "You're not still worried about that, are you? Don't you know how gorgeous you are? Now sit. Take off that yucky ball cap and the sweatshirt and pretend I'm your fairy godmother, and you're Cinderella."

"Bah, never happen." Toro stripped off the shirt, then flopped down in the tat chair, her heart fluttering in her chest. Cinderella had been one of her favorite stories when she was a kid living in the filth and terror of the projects.

She pulled the elastic band from her ponytail and tossed back her head. Usually, she kept her hair greased down and plastered to her skull. But to please Bella, today she had washed all the goo out.

Let loose, her hair fell to her shoulders in a cascade of waves. She shoved the thick, unruly ringlets behind her ears. "I can't stand all this mess on my head."

"It's absolutely beautiful. You'll get used to it," Bella said with a smile.

Toro glimpsed herself in the mirror on the wall and yanked herself up from the chair. "This isn't going to work. I know it isn't. I'm used to looking like a boy."

Bella's lips winked up. "A twenty-one-year-old

guy without a beard, no stubble showing? How do you explain that to your buddies?"

Toro scrubbed at her cheek. Her lack of facial hair was a problem. A big one. It was another pressing reason to sell her art and get off the streets. "I wear a hat. Keep my face dirty."

Bella laughed. "Lovely. Now sit back down. And let's get that dirt off." She rummaged in the cosmetic bag. "Your eyelashes are thick and dark so no mascara is needed, and your skin is clear so you don't need foundation or anything. Just some color. Let's start with the eyeliner."

Toro sank back down in the chair.

Bella moved in with the brush. "Hold absolutely still."

A key turned in the lock. The shop door opened. Toro grasped the arms of the chair ready to fly if it were Pharaoh.

But it was only Vernon. Bella's husband knew all her secrets.

Vernon Newell called in, "Hey, time to take a break, Bella. You've been on your feet too long already. Baby's due in a month."

"Busy."

"What the hell. You should have come upstairs half an hour ago." He slammed the door behind him and pushed through the shimmery gold and emerald green beaded divider that separated the waiting area from the tat stations.

He stopped in front of the tat chair and frowned. "What's going on here?"

Bella finished lining the other eye. She tipped her head up. "I'm doing a makeover."

Vernon squinted. "Of Toro?"

Bella pressed her fingers right below Toro's eye. "Big gala is tomorrow."

He waved a hand. "You know this is all unnecessary. Gender is as gender does. Put him in a suit. Stick some lipstick on. No need to pigeonhole the kid."

Toro glared at him through narrowed eyes. She was already pigeonholed. Poor. Uneducated. Grubby. The kind briefcase-toting passersby gave a wide berth, and storekeepers watched with eagle eyes.

She knew it was selfish. Foolish even. But for one night, she wanted to be the girl she might have become if her childhood hadn't fallen apart one winter night. She opened her mouth to defend herself, but her she-tiger friend jumped in first.

Bella put down the liner and straightened up. "Toro is not a kid. She didn't choose to be a boy because she wanted to. It was forced on her by circumstances." She wrapped her arms around Vernon's neck and rubbed her baby bump against him. "There are distinct advantages to being a woman."

Vernon lowered his mouth and kissed her. "Yeah. There are."

"Now move aside and let me finish. Wait till you see the difference." She turned back to Toro and finished lining the other eye. She tilted her head one way and then the other. "I think the emerald eye shadow. The green will bring out the gold flecks in your eyes."

Toro wrinkled her nose. "What gold flecks?" Her eyes were brown—plain ordinary brown.

Bella handed her a hand mirror. "Take a look."

She peered at herself and then tossed it down. "Just the reflection of the lights."

"Whatever. Now close your eyes and hold still." Bella swiped on the eye shadow.

The brush tickled. Toro bit the inside of her lip and grasped the arms of the chair to keep from jerking away.

Bella massaged her shoulder. "Relax already. You're more tense than a newbie getting his first tat. A little color on the mouth and we're done." She put down the eye shadow and picked through the lipsticks. "Ah, yes. This coral will be perfect. Now hold still a little longer."

The lip brush flitted over Toro's upper lip and then her lower one. All her focus zapped to her lips. Her toes curled. Her stomach clenched.

She squeezed her eyes closed. If putting on lipstick made her tingle everywhere, what would a kiss feel like?

How pathetic. Twenty-one-years old and never kissed. She gripped the arm rests tighter. Never would be. Not by the one man she wanted.

"You can drop your death grip. I'm done." Bella handed her the mirror again. "See what you think."

Toro gazed at her reflection and sucked in a breath. "*Cielos?* That's me?" The girl in the mirror didn't look anything like her. The face looking back at her had huge eyes and a pink pouty mouth like some model on the cover of those girly magazines sold on the newsstand.

Bella laughed. "It is—unless an alien took over your body when I wasn't looking. You like it?"

"It's amazing." Toro stretched her lips and blinked

her eyes several times. "Still, all this stuff on my face doesn't feel like me."

"You'll be so busy getting your award you'll forget you're wearing it."

"And I'll pass as a girl?"

"You *are* a girl." Bella put a hand on her arm. "Come over here, Vernon, and tell Toro what you think."

Toro settled her hands in her lap and interlaced her fingers. She'd forgotten Bella's husband was still here, standing behind her, watching.

Vernon circled round. He stopped in front of her, jaw slack, hands on his hips, and stared.

Toro looked down at her white-knuckled fingers. Bella was one of the kindest people she knew. She'd say anything to make her feel good. But Vernon? Before he'd married the flamboyant tattoo artist, he'd dated models and movie stars, and he wasn't known for his diplomacy.

She peered up at him. Hell. He was still staring. "Didn't work, did it?"

"It worked all right. No one would ever recognize you." He glanced at Bella. "She's goddam beautiful."

Toro straightened back in the chair. Beautiful? Vernon thought her beautiful? Bah. He was just making nice for Bella.

Vernon circled around her. "You know self-defense?"

"Huh? Yeah."

He put a finger under her chin and lifted her head so their eyes met. "You go out on the street looking like that, and you're going to have to fight to keep the men's hands off you."

Bella elbowed him in the side. "Not helpful."

"What? I was serious. Kid needs to know what she's in for if she does this. She's going to attract attention. The wrong kind."

"You let *me* out on the street," Bella said.

"And I don't like it."

She whacked his butt. "Stop being a caveman."

Vernon rubbed his rear end. "Okay. Look. You know how to behave, sweetheart. You know what to do as a woman to keep yourself safe. Toro here—he's run wild for years. Fearless. He has no idea what women face out there."

"Enough of this." Toro yanked herself out of the chair. "I'm only going to this awards thing. One night. Three hours. Besides"—she whipped out the knife she always carried against the small of her back—"I'm wicked good with this, Mr. Vernon. I may not have flaunted my stuff before, but I've been protecting my little brother and me for years from the filth."

With electric speed, Vernon grabbed her wrist. All her defenses snapped into place. Fiery, hot adrenaline flooded her body. Her knee flew up. Her fingers jabbed for his eyes. And she found herself tumbled to the floor and straddled, her knife hand still in his grasp.

Vernon squeezed until she dropped the knife. "Good. But not good enough," he said, huffing. "You haven't got the weight to fight off a determined man. I suspect you usually do a quick knife dance and then run up the side of a wall."

"Get off her, you big oaf." Bella yanked on Vernon's earlobe.

"Ow." He rubbed his ear and got up. "Toro needed a lesson. He won't always find a building to climb."

Bella put her hands on her hips. "*She*. That's no way to treat a lady."

Vernon's eyebrows rose. "He-*she* nearly took out my balls. The kid's no lady."

Toro half rose. The last thing she wanted was to cause friction between Bella and her husband. "It's okay, you two. I got the message.

Vernon offered his hand.

Toro took it and hefted herself up, slipping the folding utility knife back into its sheath beneath her waistband. "I'll watch myself. Stay out of sight. I'll wear a hooded cape and take a cab there and back."

She touched the hard bump of her blade. The dress had no waistband. She'd have to figure somewhere else to hide the knife. Because one thing was for sure, she was going armed.

Bella wrapped an arm around her husband. "You should go with her. Be her bodyguard."

He shook his head. "No can do. I was a major art collector. Too many people who know me will be there." He took Bella's hand. "If you want me to stay clean, I have to avoid temptation, baby."

Toro looked from one to the other. No way would she risk these two people's lives. They'd been staunch friends ever since her injury. "I'll be fine. By the way, have either of you seen my brother today? He missed dinner."

Bella pursed her lips and made a low noise in her throat. "Didn't see him. But he sprayed another bare-breasted mermaid on the front wall of the shop early this morning. Pharaoh went after him, but said he lost him over by the river." She rubbed her forehead. "I know how hard it is. But you must get the kid to stop.

The breasts are getting bigger and bigger and while I'm broad-minded, and I doubt my clients care one way or the other, I can't have voluptuous naked ladies sporting my face painted all over the shop front. My fellow merchants don't like it one bit."

"Sorry, Bella. I don't know what to do with him. The kid thinks he's Superboy. I'm afraid he's going to end up in juvie." Or worse. She touched the knife at the small of her back. She wasn't the only one out on the streets carrying a weapon.

Vernon laughed. "They have to catch him first."

Toro grabbed a paper towel, wet it, and wiped the lipstick and eye shadow off her face. "Right. And the kid's gonna wish juvie caught him when I get hold of him." She turned to leave.

"Wait." Bella held out the cosmetic case. "Don't forget your makeup. All the colors I used are inside. You going to be able to put it on by yourself?"

Toro took the case from her. "I saw what you did. No different than painting on canvas."

Bella nodded. "Remember use the emerald green on your eyes and the coral lipstick."

"Got it. Now to find that crazy brother of mine." Toro waved goodbye and then stepped out on the street.

She looked both ways. Where would a fifteen-year-old be hanging out? Best start where Bella said he was last seen. She turned and headed toward the river.

Chapter 5

By the next morning, Toro was totally exhausted and more than worried. She'd spent the entire night searching the neighborhood with no luck.

Now and then, her brother disappeared without telling her where he was, but never for a whole night. The kid was always hungry, and his stomach brought him home no matter what mischief he'd been up to.

But it was going on twenty-four hours since he was last seen. Out on the street, anything could have happened.

She threw on a change of clothes and raced out the door of the apartment. Much as she hated it, she had to go back to The Siren and question Pharaoh.

He'd been the last to see her idiot brother. Her old buddy might avoid her like the plague, but maybe he would at least deign to tell her exactly where he'd abandoned Hanger yesterday morning.

With a last look around the silent apartment, Toro took off, running full tilt the eight blocks, every thump of her sneakers on the pavement mirroring the racing of her heart. She couldn't lose her brother. She just couldn't.

He was all she had in the world.

By the time she reached The Siren, every worst scenario had tumbled through her head. Hanger had been arrested. He'd fallen off a roof. He'd been run over. He'd been snatched by some gang.

Pulse pounding from the run, she pulled open the door and charged in. Pharaoh stood behind the counter working on a sketch. His head jerked up, and a strange expression flashed across his face on seeing her.

He thumbed toward the back. "Bella's setting up for the day."

Toro rested her hands on her thighs and took two deep breaths. "Not here for Bella." She sucked in another breath. "Hanger didn't come home last night. Vernon said you chased him off yesterday. Did you see where he went?"

Pharaoh looked everywhere but at her. When he spoke, his normally soft baritone sounded rough and whiskey burned. "I lost him down on River Street near the condo where Vernon used to live."

"What's this about Vernon?" Bella came through the beaded curtain carrying her customer sign-in clipboard.

Pharaoh rubbed his forehead. "Toro says Hanger didn't come home last night. Last I saw him, he was down at Kiro's place—near his private garage."

A shiver ran down Toro's back. There was something Pharaoh wasn't saying. He looked miserable, eyes puffy, his broad shoulders slumped. Sure, he drank too much, but this was something else. He looked broken.

She softened her voice. No sense enraging the guy. "Where exactly did you lose him?"

He sucked in his lower lip. "By the garage entrance. Thing is—the overhead door was partially up. But he wouldn't have gone in, would he? I figured he ducked past and hid out of sight. Maybe headed up to

McCarren Park." He slid his hand across the wood counter top. "That's when I gave up and came back here. I had a customer coming in for a consult."

"No." Bella put a hand on Toro's arm. "He wouldn't have—"

Toro stared at her. "Wouldn't what?"

Bella gripped her arm tighter. "Gone into the garage."

Toro's whole body tensed. She glanced at Bella and then Pharaoh. "Never. He knows Kiro's a bloodthirsty bastard."

Pharaoh's expression darkened. His head came up. "Of course. The cars. The *freaking cars*. He wanted to get even. Mouthed off about tagging Kiro's fleet."

Blood roared through Toro's head. Hanger wouldn't be so stupid. If Shark Man got him—it didn't bear thinking.

"He told you that?"

Pharaoh fiddled with Bella's Greek eyeball paperweight. The cracks running through it were a visible reminder of Kiro's bombing of the old Siren. He set it aside and looked up. "Hanger still talks to me— sometimes."

Toro rolled her shoulders back. "You using him to spy on T-Crew? Find out what we're doing?"

"No. He helped me home a couple times when I was—"

"*Blotto.* How dare you have anything to do with my brother? Get him involved in your degraded life?" She pulled away from Bella and stomped over to the counter. "You freaking piece of dog turd. You knew Hanger was after that bastard's cars, and you didn't check to see if he'd gone inside the garage?"

She slammed the countertop with her fist. "I don't understand you. You—you used to be such a great guy."

Bella dropped her clipboard on the counter. "Stop it, you guys. We have to focus on Hanger. If Vernon's brother has got him, no telling what he'll do. Kiro—he's—" Bella gasped and leaned forward. Her face whitened. Her lips trembled. She cupped her hands atop her belly.

Toro rushed over. "*Cielos.* Sit down. Is it the baby?" Steading her, she guided Bella to the sofa.

Between gasps, Bella gave a little shake of her head,

Pharaoh came around the counter with a paper bag. "She's hyperventilating. Here, hold this to her mouth."

Toro held the opening to Bella's lips.

Pharaoh knelt down and rubbed the tattoo artist's back. "It's okay. Hanger's probably fine. Playing one of his games."

Bella gave the bag a feeble shove. "You—have—no idea what Vernon's rotten brother is capable of. If Hanger damaged Kiro's cars, he'll—he'll kill him."

Toro's heartrate skyrocketed. "He wouldn't. He couldn't."

"Sure he could," Bella wheezed. "He's a cold-hearted murderer."

"Who's a murderer?" Vernon came into the studio swinging his tool box. One glance at Bella, and his smile died. He dropped the box to the floor and draped his arm around her. "Bella, you okay? The baby?"

She lowered the paper bag and palmed him away. "Panic attack."

"Thought you were over those." He looked up and

scowled at Pharaoh. "What did you do to her now?"

Toro frowned. If Pharaoh had looked miserable when she'd entered, he looked ten times worse now. She might be furious at him for abandoning her brother, but she couldn't let him be falsely accused.

She held up her hand. "Not Pharaoh. We think Hanger might have been messing with Kiro's cars and got caught."

Vernon punched the sofa seat. "The idiot kid. I told him in no uncertain terms to stay away from my brother."

Bella tugged on his sleeve. "Call your brother and find out."

"Worst thing I could do." Vernon snugged Bella closer and kissed her neck. "Didn't want to say 'cause I knew it would upset you, but Kiro's been pressuring me to help him. Can't handle wheeling and dealing at that level. Everyone's taking him to the cleaners. His Middle East gun deal fell through."

Bella jerked back, her face pale as death. "You promised not to have anything to do with him."

Vernon traced the seal tattoo on Bella's arm. "And I intend to keep that promise. But if he has Hanger? That gives him a bargaining chip." He glanced over at Toro. "For what it's worth, I don't think he'll hurt him."

Toro stood up and took a step back. She never meant to drag these two good-hearted people into her messy life. "Look. This isn't your problem. He's my brother. I'll find him."

"No, Toro. You have no idea how vicious Kiro is." Bella captured Vernon's hand in hers and squeezed so hard her knuckles turned bone white. "Hanger will try to escape. The kid thinks he's indestructible. And your brother will hurt him. *Bad*."

Vernon let out a puff of air. "Then I'll have to get in touch."

"No. He'll dig his claws into you and never let go. I can't lose you. Not now. Not with the baby." Bella laid his hand on her belly. "This child needs a father. There has to be another way."

"Wait." Pharaoh slapped his fist into his other hand. "We don't know Kiro has the kid. Maybe something else held him up? Like an accident? Or he's sick?"

Toro latched on to the "something else." Anything would be better than Hanger being in Shark Man's clutches.

She gave a nod. "Right. I'll check the hospitals and clinics."

Pharaoh came up behind her and put a hand on her lower arm. She could feel the heat radiating off him, smell his unique scent.

Once upon a time, when he'd first joined T-Crew, reeling from the death of his mom, she believed he was her Prince Charming come to rescue her. A ragged, suffering one, for sure. But one day he'd heal, realize all on his own she was a girl, take her in his arms, and tell her he loved her. But he never had.

And then he'd betrayed Bella. Turned against T-Crew. And acted like an iceman when he was around her. Ever since she'd healed, he'd avoided touching her. Not one slap on the back, not one hand clasp, not one tousle of hair. Not one touch guys did to each other without thinking.

She glared down at his hand with its intricate

tattoos. Now he touched her.

Now. When he'd chosen drink and anger over asking her for the forgiveness she would have given freely.

Ignoring the spirals of heat swirling through her, she elbowed him in the ribs and jerked her arm away.

He drew back behind her. "Got some contacts. I'll check around and see what's happening on the street."

Vernon nodded. "I can call some police buddies and see if they picked him up and sent him to juvie."

Bella let out a breath and hefted herself up from the couch with a groan. "Sounds like a plan. Now back to work everyone. And you"—she turned to Toro—"don't go skipping out on me and Ari now. No matter what's going on with your brother, you show up tonight at that art awards ceremony at seven p.m. sharp so you don't miss the important bits. Take your cell to the museum, and we'll let you know the minute we find Hanger."

Toro slowly blew a breath out between her teeth. The last thing she wanted to do was dress up in some make-believe concoction and attend the awards ceremony while her brother might be lying dead or dying in some alley. Or worse, trapped in hell with Vernon's brother.

But Bella was right. Mixing with the New York art scene for a half an hour or so wouldn't make a difference in finding Hanger. But what it would do was put her in a financial position so once she found her brother the two of them could flee to somewhere safe.

Somewhere far away from underhanded bastards like Shark Man and—she peeked over at the tattoo artist avoiding her gaze—cold-hearted princes named Pharaoh.

Chapter 6

Pharaoh wedged himself into his stalking niche opposite T-Crew's apartment building. It had rained in the afternoon, and the damp pavement and rushing sewers accentuated the overwhelming stink of urine emanating from the bricks behind him. He wasn't the only down-and-out inhabitant who used this shadowy jog in the wall.

Not daring to lean back against the reeking bricks, he stamped his feet to keep the blood circulating. It wasn't cold. A bit chill and damp for a late April evening, but with a level of humidity that made his tee shirt stick to his skin and perspiration gather under his arms.

He stared at the graffiti-covered door. Toro had to come out soon. Bella had said something about an event or something at seven. He checked his cell. Six-thirty.

This time he was going to talk to him. Apologize and ask forgiveness. He couldn't live with the burning in his gut and overwhelming guilt any longer.

Minutes later, an empty taxi pulled up in front of the apartment. What the hell? Toro never used cabs. No one at T-Crew did. Waste of money, what with buses and subways and roofs all around.

He stalked closer, keeping a parked car between him and the door. It was risky, but he had to see who the cab was picking up.

Even though he was totally focused on the door, he jumped when it actually opened, and a woman stepped out onto the steps. An absolutely gorgeous woman.

Her face was hidden under a hooded cape, but that didn't matter. Strands of wavy black hair peeked out from under the hood, and the woman's form-fitting dress moved with her body, revealing perfect breasts and a narrow waist that flared into full hips. A man's dream. His dream.

All the blood whooshed from his head to his lower regions. He imagined that body under his hands, his tongue licking her nipples, her shapely legs wrapped around him.

He gave himself a vigorous shake and concentrated on getting himself back under control. He'd never felt such an instant and powerful attraction to a woman. A woman he didn't even know.

Well, that could be remedied. He moved around the car and gave a smile and a wave and a shout. But it was a no go. She never looked up.

Head down, his mystery woman dashed down the steps and slid into the back seat of the taxi.

The last thing he glimpsed as the door closed was her well-toned legs and a pair of pale-colored ballet slippers on her feet.

Ballet slippers?

Stilettos turned him on. Not childish flats. But those scuffed leather dance shoes made the woman seem more approachable, more human. More loveable. The kind of woman who valued herself enough to flaunt the rules and didn't care what others thought of her.

His kind of woman.

He wanted to slip those little shoes off and kiss her toes, kiss her lovely legs, kiss those high, round breasts.

The cab took off, taking the vision of loveliness with it. *Cielos.* He whacked the hood of the car parked alongside him. What kind of an idiot was he? He wasn't going to be kissing anything.

The woman was gone, the taxi's taillights a disappearing blur as it turned the corner and headed in the direction of the Williamsburg Bridge and Manhattan.

He peered back at the three-story building that housed T-Crew's living quarters. What had she been doing there? As far as he knew only Toro and Hanger and Solo and Neto were resident there now. He knew from Hanger that his old apartment hadn't been rented out yet.

Through the poster-covered window of the ground-level store front, he watched the twins tidy up the shop. Big Bad, the Brooklyn street art tour company, had been Bella's brother's idea. He'd thought Ari crazy when he proposed setting up the operation. After all, who ever heard of homeless street kids running a business?

But surprisingly, the almost-former graffiti artists were doing well. Solo and Neto worked like crazy bees guiding groups of tourists to the major street art sites in Williamsburg and Bushwick.

He'd done it himself for a few weeks, but couldn't stand the dopey sightseers who gaped at a professionally hired-out billboard painted from stencils like it was some Holy Grail, and who snickered at the real graffiti throw-ups done freehand by street artists dodging the cops.

Toro might be content to paint new pieces for the tourists to sneer at for free for the rest of his life.

Pharaoh shoved his hands in his pockets and strode down the street. He had bigger dreams.

Wait. He stopped dead and turned and stared at Big Bad. The shop lights winked out, and then Solo and Neto tumbled out into the street, slapping each other with their hats, duffels swinging off their shoulders, ready for a night of tagging.

Pharaoh hid himself behind a parked van. It didn't add up. If Solo and Neto were in the storefront, who had that woman been visiting up in the T-Crew apartments over Big Bad—Toro?

T-Crew's King's appreciation of the other sex had always seemed lukewarm to him. In fact, he'd often wondered if the King was gay. Whatever he was, Toro was too young for a woman like that. Wasn't he?

He leaned back against the van and squeezed the back of his neck. How old was Toro anyway? The kid had always seemed like a high schooler to him, a teen with very old eyes. But then he wasn't old either, and he had the same look. Came with the territory. Bad parents. Cold streets. Bone-deep distrust.

Toro had been fifteen when they'd met. He did the math. They'd been crewmates for six years. That made him at least twenty. A very young looking twenty, but hot potatoes, plenty old enough for sexy ladies.

A hard knot formed in his stomach. That woman had to be Toro's girl. He took a deep breath, but it only made the knot tighten. He rubbed his belly. The gut-wrenching ache swirling through him was not jealousy. No way.

Fernando Pharaoh didn't need Ballet Slippers.

Plenty of other women were willing to warm his bed. All he had to do was ask.

He twisted his torso in a futile attempt to relieve the cramp in his stomach. He was hungry, that was all. How could he be jealous of Toro, who'd talked him down off the bridge when all he'd wanted to do was jump to his death?

Toro deserved all the pleasure he could find in this stinking, miserable world. He owed him that much. Kid saved his life. If the King had found a gorgeous woman to bed, good for him.

Still, he gave a glance over his shoulder. That woman had sure been hot. He wouldn't mind seeing her again. He grew hard at the thought, and he shook himself in disgust.

No way should he be lusting after Toro's new girl. He might be a bastard of a friend, but he'd never betray Toro that way.

He checked the time. Right now, he needed to head off to his first night at his new off-the-books tattoo job. G-Man's wasn't in the best section of Brooklyn, but the studio had been clean enough and the heavily tattooed and pierced owner welcoming.

Yet something niggled at the back of his mind. There had to be a reason the shop stayed open till two in the morning. All the studios in Williamsburg closed by ten at the latest. And the pay seemed way too high for the type of Marvel comic book tats he'd been hired to do.

He rubbed his rib where Toro had elbowed him—the kid packed a wallop—and set off at a lope for G-Man's Tat Parlor. On the way, he'd ask a few homeless he knew if they'd seen Hanger.

****

Four hours later, Pharaoh had no better idea where Hanger might be, but he knew why he was getting paid so much. The leather-jacketed guy pressing him into the edge of the counter and holding a knife at his throat wouldn't take no for an answer.

From the back, the tatting machine buzzed. G-Man had made it clear he wasn't to be interrupted when he had a customer. "You have a problem, you handle it," he'd said.

Pharaoh peered out of the corner of his eye at the sketch lying on the countertop and gritted his teeth. He didn't like the knife at his throat. He liked the requested tattoo even less. And he certainly didn't like the condition of the girl standing next to Leather Jacket.

He could see her story written all over her face. A slight bruise on her cheek, eyes slightly unfocused, a missing tooth. Drugged and beaten and probably pimped. A maiden in need of rescue—the kind who belonged in Mercy House—not a tat parlor.

He'd deal with the knife first. "Don't tat boyfriend's names on pretty ladies. So kill me." Tightening his shoulders, he seized the hand holding the knife and twisted it down and away at the same time he threw his head forward, whipping it into the guy's nose.

The knife fell to the floor, and Leather Jacket made the low-pitched huffing sound of someone with a broken nose. Good.

Pharaoh leaped up and over the counter. He was out of here. G-Man could find another tat boy.

The girl who'd come in with the guy jumped out of his way like a startled pigeon. Damn. Bella would hate him if he left her behind.

He stopped in mid-flight and held out his hand. "You coming with me?'

She glanced at the guy he'd bloodied and slowly shook her head. He eyeballed the man and wished he hadn't.

One hand gripping his bleeding nose, Leather Jacket pulled out a handgun and waved it at him. "Like her?"

Pharaoh's heart rate sped up. The mind-sharpening heat of released adrenaline flooded his body. The door was only a few feet behind him. Alone, he could probably make it. He knew how to disappear. There weren't many walls he couldn't climb.

But the girl was so young and so scared. His chances of grabbing her and getting her to safety were less than nil. Still, he'd never live with himself knowing he'd saved his own neck at her expense.

He eyed the gun, thinking fast. Maybe the guy would hand her over for cash?

"Five hundred dollars." Pharaoh tipped up his chin and forced his lips into a smile, trying to give the girl a bit of hope, praying five hundred was enough. It was all he had on him—the pay from the last tattoo job he'd done. "It's in my pocket." He reached toward it.

"Stop." The guy wiped away the blood dripping from his nose. "You misunderstand. Like her *alive*, idiot."

Pharaoh's hand froze.

"Because right now you have a decision to make."

The girl went white and took a step back.

"Stand still, Yola. You know how easily this gun goes off." He brought the muzzle to her head. The girl closed her eyes. Her lips quivered.

"Now G-Man hates bloody messes in his shop. So let's start this transaction again." He cocked the gun and shouted, "G-Man. Get up here and explain who I am to your new assistant."

The buzz of the tatting machine stopped. His boss snorted. "Middle of a job. This better be important, Jax."

"Bring my buddy with you."

G-Man, potbelly swaying, came around the corner and halted. His lips twisted up. The piercings surrounding his mouth created little pleats in the skin. Behind him stood his client, apparently Jax's buddy—a bruiser of a man as wide as he was tall. Neither of them seemed surprised by the gun.

G-Man slowly stripped off his plastic gloves finger by finger. "Problem, boss?"

"My girlfriend, Yola, here wants my name tatted on her." Jax wrapped his free hand over her shoulders, leaned in next to the gun, and kissed her on the neck. "Right here. Don't you sweetheart?"

The girl's head moved.

"Say it. Tell Mr. Death Wish guy here, you will love having him tat my name wherever I want it. J A X—Jax. Short. Simple. Clear as a bell."

The girl mouthed something. "Louder." Jax pressed the muzzle against her head, the tip gun-metal dark against the pink shell of her ear. She gazed at Pharaoh, her eyes so wide her brown irises were ringed in white. "P—please."

Pharaoh looked at the two men, looked back at the girl who was slumping against Jax's leather jacket, her whole body trembling. Was she asking for the tattoo or asking him to let the guy kill her? If he turned and ran, would the bastard still shoot her?

He opened his mouth to say he'd do the tat.

"Took too long." Jax pulled the trigger.

The gun went off.

Pharaoh slapped his hands to his ears as the shot ripped through the air and blasted his ear drums.

The girl's brains sprayed across the room. Blood and gore splattered his shirt and skin. He fell back, turned to flee, and hit smack into G-Man's weighty body.

G-Man's fist came up and caught him under the sternum. All the breath flew out of him, and he landed on the floor sucking desperately for air. Pain radiated through his torso and rattled through his head.

Pharaoh could see the men moving around him, hear the men's voices above him, but he couldn't twitch a muscle, couldn't draw in enough oxygen to make sense of anything.

He tried to push himself up and fell back, choking, feeling like he was going to die and knowing he wouldn't. That would be too good an ending to this nightmare.

Toro should have let him jump off the bridge all those years ago.

G-Man kicked him in the side. "Now this is how it's going to be, Mr. Pharaoh—Mr. Jax here is the boss. Runs this place and everything else around here.

"From now on, you do exactly what he wants. If he wants you to tattoo his name on his girlfriend's wrist or on her butt or across her forehead, you're gonna do it with a smile. You want to know why?" He wrestled on a new pair of plastic gloves and then held out his hand.

"Give me the gun, Jax."

He clicked out the magazine and wiped the gun thoroughly on his apron. Then he put a foot on Pharaoh's wrist, bent down.

"No." Pharaoh struck out with his legs and struggled to rise.

The bruiser grabbed his ankles.

Jax caught him under the chin and yanked his head back. "Listen to the man."

G-Man pressed Pharaoh's fingers around the grip. Then he picked up the gun with a clean part of his apron. "Because if you don't, poor Miss Yola's *unsolved* murder will suddenly be *solved*." He kicked him in the ribs. "Now get your ass moving and mop up this mess."

Chapter 7

Toro shifted on the seat as she peered out the cab window at the brightly lit New Museum. The taxi pulled to a stop directly in front. She'd visited the off-kilter stack of white rectangles that gave the building its distinctive layout many times, soaking in the quiet and reverence given the artworks.

This time was different. To think that her canvases of layered walls and buildings covered in graffiti were hanging here, sent mind-numbing twitches fluttering through her. In just minutes, she'd be stepping up on the platform before hundreds of eyes and accepting the first-place prize.

"Getting out, lady?" The cabby's cigarette-hoarse voice made her jump.

"Yes." She fumbled in the unfamiliar purse and drew out the fare and tip. Then she opened the door and extended first one ballet-shoe-clad foot and then the other.

Bella had wanted her to buy heels. But a visit to the shoe store had settled that argument. Not only could she not find a pair that fit her long narrow feet with toes malformed by years in the wrong size sneakers, but she refused to wear shoes she couldn't run in. The idea of being hampered by the dress disturbed her enough.

She wiggled her toes. Besides, who would be looking at her feet?

She slid out of the cab and tucked the small black suede purse Bella had lent her under her arm. She hated to carry money in such an exposed way.

T-Crew laughed at the women dangling their worldly goods over their arms like lures for street thieves. Hell, she couldn't count the number of times she'd rescued a snatched handbag.

She'd only agreed to the mini-bag thing because the dress had no pockets. She wasn't carrying much, just the bare essentials. Some cash for the cab home, a Metrocard, her crappy old cellphone, the knife she was never without, the emergency cherry bomb all T-Crew members carried, and the ridiculous pink lipstick for the touch up after she ate that Bella insisted was what ladies did.

Oh, and her invitation. She needed that.

She hurried to the door while fumbling in the idiotic purse. She extracted the gold-bordered engraved card with her name on it, and ran her finger across the raised letters—Alba Vargas—an apparition from another time, another world.

Alba Vargas had been a timid, frightened child who'd spent her nights huddled at the bottom of a closet with her hand over her baby brother's mouth, hoping that whoever was beating her mom didn't start on her next.

She was no longer that girl. Tonight she would be the new Alba Vargas, reborn and rebaptized as a woman with power. Tonight she would be one of the movers and shakers in the art world. Tonight she was a winner.

The glass door loomed in front of her. She drew to a halt and peered into the museum lobby. It was like watching a ball scene in one of those boring chick flicks. Overly skinny women in glittering gowns gathered in small groups, their manicured hands moving like flighty little birds.

Men stuffed into black tuxes hovered over them, claiming ownership with carelessly placed hands on an upper arm or on the curve of a waist. Others stood in animated pairs conversing about whatever denizens of the art world talked about.

A slight breeze ruffled the edges of her cape and a chill swept across her exposed skin. She didn't belong here all alone, wearing these too-revealing clothes and flaunting false femininity.

Toro gripped her purse tighter. Didn't matter. She had to do this. For herself. For Hanger.

Taking a deep breath and praying that her brother would be home safe and sound when she got back, she wrapped her hand around the cold metal of the door handle and tugged.

The door, lighter than expected, flew open, and she, who could balance on a cornice five stories up, tripped over the doorsill. Her arms flailed. Her invitation went flying. Her purse slid across the gleaming floor.

Heads turned. Eyes blinked. Voices hushed. Mouths gaped.

She recovered her footing, turned to escape, and found herself trapped against a warm body smelling strongly of expensive cologne.

She jerked away and looked up. A dark-haired man, in a black tuxedo that emphasized his narrow waist and trim hips, stared back at her. His model-perfect face was fit for the cover of *Esquire* and his ultramarine blue eyes gleamed violet under the lights.

"Are you all right?" He cupped her fingers in his and gathered them against a palm, smooth and uncallused, tender and warm.

Hoping she'd gotten all the spray paint off her fingernails, Toro tipped back the hood of her black velvet cape, and nodded. "Fine, thank you."

For a moment, they stood, peering into each other's eyes, and for the first time in her life, she melted a little bit—the way the heroines in storybooks did when they met their prince.

He lifted her hand and kissed her knuckles. Cool lips brushed her skin, followed by a whisper of heated breath. The combination raised goosebumps up and down her arm.

He let go, and she pulled her hand back, surprised to find she was trembling. She tucked her hand behind her and glanced around. The lobby was empty. The onlookers gone. "Oh, I must be terribly late."

His face softened into a smile. "No, you're right on time." He swooped down and picked up her purse and invitation.

He held the card out in front of him. "Alba Vargas," he read, his voice rich and mellow like the golden honey on the Greek island of Eudokia. He placed the invitation on her palm with a flourish. "Please to meet you. I'm Claude Rendell, art connoisseur and admirer of fine wine and women."

She opened her mouth and a sound came out of her throat she'd never heard before. Was that a giggle? El Toro King of T-Crew giggling? Damn. The first handsome man she crashes into flirts with her, and she turns to mush.

Nerves. She was nervous. That was all. She shifted away.

He reached toward her. "Your cape? May I check it for you?"

"Oh." She toyed with the tie at the neck. Bella had made her promise she'd take it off. "No hiding allowed," she warned. "Flaunt your stuff, lady."

Toro tugged the end of the bow, and the cape slipped down.

Claude swirled it off and gave her an appreciative smile that sent warning signals up and down her spine.

He handed it to the coat check girl, and then offered Toro his arm. "Shall we?"

She hesitated and then slid her arm around his and rested her palm on his sleeve, the way she'd seen actresses do in old-time movies.

With practiced grace, he guided her into the elevator. The door closed with a gentle swoosh, and the cab whirred up, carrying her ever closer to the reception, ever closer to standing up in front of all those people.

Bing.

Bing.

The floor numbers flashed by. With each floor, the pressure in her lungs increased. The lime green walls, a shade lighter than her dress, closed in around her. Perspiration gathered along the hairline at the nape of her neck.

Fool. She had no idea how to behave like a woman in a formal gathering. She'd nearly fallen on her face in front of them. What if she forgot and used a curse word? What if someone asked her about her nonexistent art training?

Toro bit her lip, and the pasty taste of the lipstick filled her mouth. What if they saw through her cosmetic bag disguise?

Despite the heat pouring off the man next to her, a chill ran through her. Coming here was a big mistake, but it was too late to change her mind. Too much rode on the sale of her artworks.

Claude shifted position next to her. Poor man. If he knew he was escorting a grubby street kid who'd been living as a boy for years, he'd stop the elevator and toss her out.

She drew in a slow inhalation and peeked up at his handsome face. Well, at least she didn't have to enter alone. She just hoped she didn't embarrass the man. He was being kind.

At the seventh floor, the elevator slowed. She curled her hand over his sleeve, the expensive suit warm and silky beneath her palm. This is what women did, right? Leaned on a man. She clasped his arm tighter, steadying herself against rising waves of panic.

She was going to carry off this masquerade no matter what and leave with her money and enough patrons so that she would never have to go through this again. For the next hour or so, she'd hold her head up and pretend she was a princess entering court with her prince by her side. In less time than it took to read a book of fairy tales, it would be over, and Alba Vargas would disappear.

The elevator door opened, she looped her hand more securely around Claude's arm, and stepped into the Sky Room.

City lights shone through the glass walls that ran along two sides of the room. Hundreds of candles lit the tables. The high-ceiling space hummed with a symphony of voices. Hands fluttered. Chairs squeaked. In the background, music played. But all she could hear were the occasional high notes.

Toro slowed, having no idea where to go or where to sit. All the seats appeared occupied. Waiters bobbed around the circular tables, passing out plates of salad, the leaves brilliant green under the lights.

Fortunately, her partner knew what he was doing. Cupping a firm hand over hers, he steered her down the center aisle to a table way up front near the dais.

There were two empty seats. Claude nodded to the other occupants. "I bring you our grand prize winner."

Toro's head jerked up. "You knew?"

"The minute I saw your name." He gave her an open-mouthed smile and pulled out the chair for her. He gave a small palm up wave. "This is the board of the Emerging Artists Foundation. They are very excited to meet the artist who created those intricately detailed paintings."

She looked around the table. Elegantly coiffed women tipped their heads at her. Gray-haired men, bowties cinching their necks, smiled. No one sneered. No one rose in outrage. No one asked a digging question or gave her a second look. They murmured a greeting, mouthed a welcome and then returned to eating and talking among themselves.

The disguise was working—so far. She slipped into the offered seat and after finding what she hoped was the right fork, concentrated on downing a plate of vinegary greens that stung her tongue and turned bitter in her throat.

****

By the time she had picked at a puff pastry full of some unidentifiable meat, enjoyed a flute of sliced fruit, and relished a soft, airy roll that tasted more like cake than bread, Toro knew she was in trouble. She had never sat still or listened to people mumble about silly nothings for so long in her life and been afraid to say a single word.

She glanced around the table. These were the people she needed to woo and win if she and Hanger were ever to have a better life. They liked her art. Had chosen her as winner. These were buyers for her paintings.

And she, who'd fought off rapists and gang members, was scared to death of them. Scared of middle aged men with enough gray to look distinguished. Scared of skeletal women with bare, knobby shoulders and beringed fingers. So frightened, her throat had turned to sandpaper.

She shifted the glaringly white napkin on her lap and tried to think of something to say. They'd all been introduced to her. A CEO of a nonprofit, two gallery owners, a theater producer, and a hospital director and his wife. Nice normal people with interesting jobs, not a graffiti artist or homeless person in the bunch.

She picked up a fork and gave it a twirl. It wasn't that they were wealthy that frightened her. She knew rich people. Her mentor, Ari, had been a billionaire once. Until two years ago, he'd owned a thirty-room villa with a full staff of servants and even a helicopter.

And Vernon had been a mega-billionaire, too—before Kiro stole everything. But Ari and Vernon hadn't cared that she was an uncouth street kid, more handy with a spray can than a place setting, more likely to curse than not.

These people would.

She placed the fork carefully down next to her plate. Her fingers trembled. Every nerve ending tingled. She glanced up at the dais. In minutes, she'd have to do more than make small talk. She'd have to get up in front of the entire crowd and make a speech. The idea made her stomach turn over.

She reached for her wine glass and miscalculated. The thin-stemmed goblet tipped precariously. Half-rising, she whipped it up before it could spill. Two or three heads turned in her direction. She let out a low whistle of air between her teeth and gripped the stem in her fingers. That had been close.

Claude turned from the narrow-faced gallery owner he'd been deep in discussion with and gave her a boyish grin. "Doing okay, Miss Vargas? Enjoying the conversation?"

Was he kidding? He had to know she hadn't said a word. She gave him an off-sided smile and then took a bite of her roll.

Claude steepled his hands beneath his chin and tipped his head toward the dais. "Won't be long now. Here comes dessert. Then we'll drape you with garlands and hang you out to the winds of fame and fortune." He shifted to within a whisper's breath of her ear and murmured, "There's a lineup of collectors anxious to meet you and acquire your work." He wagged his finger at her. "I'm hoping that I will be first in line. I must have the long painting with the sunset view with the Williamsburg Bridge in the background."

She couldn't help but correct him. "Sunrise."

Claude's eyes narrowed. "Ah—sunrise. So you're

an early riser, Miss Vargas?"

"Uh—" Toro clutched the wine glass. Not really. Normal people slept at night. Night was when she created her art. Sunrise was when she went to bed. But he didn't need to know that. He'd think her a weirdo. "Uh—yes."

The lie lay bitter on her tongue, and it was just the first of many she'd be spilling. Bad enough she was pretending to be comfortable in a barely-there dress and showy makeup.

She surveyed the room. She still had to woo the collectors and potential patrons. Still had to wow the reporters. She glanced up at the dais. Still had to give an acceptance speech.

Hell. She gulped down a mouthful of the wine. The sour liquid trickled down her throat. She scraped her tongue with her teeth.

Phew, it tasted awful. How did Pharaoh down gallons of this stuff every night? He must be more of an idiot than she thought.

Toro gave the burgundy red liquid a swirl. Bubbles gathered around the rim of the goblet. She really shouldn't drink another drop.

Beside her, Claude raised his glass and gave her a quizzical look. "A toast?"

"What?" She peered up. Everyone had their glasses lifted, their eyes focused directly on her.

"Oh." She raised the glass, willing her trembling fingers not to spill her wine.

Claude grinned at her. Then he tapped his glass to hers with a clink. "Cheers, Alba. Here's to a successful evening for the best young artist we're seen in years."

All around the table, the board members seconded

his statement.

She clasped the stem of the glass, afraid to drink, afraid not to. Over the rim, she could see everyone waiting for her.

Oh, what the hell. The whole point of being here was to fit in, get her paintings sold, Drinking a glass of wine, no matter how bad it tasted, wasn't the end of the world. Not for someone who had subsided on leftovers swiped from garbage bins.

She brought the rim of the glass to her lips and swallowed it all. The wine burned all the way down to her stomach.

For a moment, she thought the sour stuff wouldn't stay down. But it did.

Tiny bubbles of warmth swirled through her. The lights brightened, the noise around her clarified, heat built between her legs and spread through her like fizz. Her cheeks flamed.

She might be a virgin, but she'd touched herself enough to know what this feeling was—arousal. She hadn't realized wine had that effect. But then she was a virgin alcohol drinker, too.

She pressed her thighs together and working her hand under the tablecloth, yanked the hem of the ever-rising, thigh-revealing skirt back down. Heavens, did it affect everyone this way? She glanced around. Was that why people drank?

"Excuse me, Madame." A waiter placed a clear glass bowl with what looked to be vanilla ice cream in front of her. A sliver of an overcooked cookie and a green weed thing stuck out of the top.

Toro jerked her hand up from her skirt, her heart pattering. Had the server seen her fussing with the dress? She glanced at Claude. Had he?

She fumbled for her spoon and sliced off a semi-circle of the ice cream, slipped it into her mouth, and swooned. It was sweet and spicy and a tiny bit fiery on her tongue. "Oh. What is this?"

Claude rested a hand on her arm. *Cielos*, she'd said that aloud. Toro lowered her eyes and studied his hands. She'd never seen a man with fingernails so perfectly clean.

"A local specialty—Naga Indian curry and coconut. Like it?" he asked.

She couldn't resist grinning. "Best part of the meal."

He pushed his dish over to her. "Enjoy."

"But—"

"No buts. I want to see that look on your face again. I wish it had been my lips that put it there."

Her eyes focused on his mouth. She'd read about kisses. Seen kisses in the movies and in the park, but she'd never been kissed.

She bit hard on her lower lip. Fool. Claude Rendell was flirting with a masquerade character. If he knew who she really was, he'd turn away in disgust.

A noise on the dais gave her an excuse to look away. An official-looking dignitary stood at the microphone. The ice cream turned tasteless in her mouth. The awards ceremony had begun.

****

As the first-place winner, Alba Vargas was last. By the time it was her turn to mount the dais, Toro had seen enough other young artists stride up to the platform and accept their awards, each giving bountiful thanks to their art teachers and parents, to have a good idea what was expected.

She picked at the puckers in her dress. She had no art teacher, no parent to thank. Not that it mattered. Her throat felt like it was stuffed with tissue wads. She doubted she could get a word out.

When her name was called, she tugged the stupid dress down again, rose, and forced her rubbery legs to carry her up the steps to the platform.

In a blur of motion and swirl of heavy cologne and deodorant, the exhibit sponsors handed her the certificate, the check envelope, and then presented the first-place award—a five-sided slab of frosted glass with her name engraved on it. The palm-size trophy was much heavier than she expected.

For a moment, everything threatened to slip from her hands. With reflexes borne of years of catching Rustos and tossing duffle bags up on roofs, she juggled the items, caught them neatly and turned to face the crowd.

She gazed out at the upturned faces. All through dinner, this was what she'd feared the most.

Heart hammering, she leaned in still not knowing what she would say. She opened her mouth and taking a deep breath forced out a soundless, "Thank you—uh—"

Somewhere in the back, a suited figure stood and began clapping. Then another and another. The applause spread. The slow crescendo rose around her and slithered down her back. She peered out at the mass of pale pink faces, suddenly aware of the darkness of her own skin, the improbability of her being here. Was this what she really wanted? The adoration of these rich dilettantes?

She gripped the envelope with the check in her

white-knuckled hand. Yes, she'd do whatever it took to get Hanger to a safe place so he could become something more than a ragged street kid.

Money was everything. It gifted the owner with power and choice. Men like Kiro and Vernon killed for it. Ari sold his paintings. That was what she'd do, too. She'd sell anything. Do anything. And she had just gotten started.

Claude Rendell would be her prime target tonight. Ari had told her not to let anything go for less than five thousand dollars. She'd make Mr. Rendell pay much more for her "Sunset" as he called it.

She raised her chin and smiled.

At the bottom of the dais, Claude, his answering smile perfect on his perfect face, held out his hand. "This way, my dear. Time to unveil your masterpieces."

Clutching her bounty, Toro threw back her shoulders and descended the steps like she imagined a princess would. "Lead on, Sir Knight."

Claude tossed back his head and laughed, a deep strong sound that made her heart beat a little faster.

She rested her hand on Claude's arm and joined the turtle-speed procession of potential patrons and buyers heading down the stairs to the floor below where the works of the winners hung.

Yes, Claude would do fine as her first art patron, and then she'd find the man whose applause saved her from having to speak.

Chapter 8

Toro stepped into the soaring gallery space, her ballet slippers slipping slightly on the highly-polished floor. The exhibition area was large and white and smelled of fresh paint and wax.

Behind her, voices rose, punctuated by little gasps and ohs as people gazed at her work for the first time. Even she was captivated by her own artworks prominently displayed on the opposing wall as people entered. She'd never seen them brilliantly lit before.

Her three paintings of Brooklyn, looking across the rooftops, the angle off-kilter so you felt like you were flying on the back of a swooping bird, were designed to draw the viewer in and lose them in the details. The walls of each building, every brick and shingle, were festooned with graffiti—neon colored tags, and throw-ups that carried messages if you knew how to read them.

She glanced around at the other works on display. Her canvases were huge compared to the others. Next to her paintings, the competing entries faded to nothingness.

She let out a breath of satisfaction. She'd had a good teacher. The best. If anyone knew how to make millions as an artist, it was Bella's brother. During her stay on Eudokia, he'd taught her his three golden rules.

Rule One: Work large. People would shell out

more for wall-sized works, and they were harder to hide away. The new owners would hang their expensive purchase in a prominent place in their home or office, and the artwork would be seen and remembered.

She glanced at her center painting, which was well over ten feet long and seven feet high. She would have worked huge anyway. Any size canvas felt constraining when you'd honed your talents spraying graffiti on the sides of buildings and the cross-spans of bridges.

Claude patted her arm. "They've done a wonderful job mounting your works."

He led her closer to the bridge painting he'd already put dibs on and stopped in front of it. "I can't imagine how you painted these views. It's like you were flying in a plane or something." He turned to her. "Is that what you do? The committee discussed it extensively. At first, it was thought you used Google Maps, but the angle is impossible from any vantage point on the ground." He shifted closer. "Can you share your secret?"

Toro held in a snort. There was no secret. She knew every building, every wall in the two hundred-some-odd square block area she'd haunted for seven years.

Ari's Rule Two: Never tell your secrets. She plucked at her dress. Not that she'd needed to learn that one. Her whole life was a secret. She shrugged. "I closed my eyes and pictured it."

"But the buildings are real. The graffiti, while exaggerated, is real—I checked before I cast my vote."

Toro tipped her head. "You were a judge?"

"Yes."

There was a movement behind her. "So was I."

63

Toro turned and stared into two very familiar steel gray eyes.

Kiro.

The crooked murdering bastard was standing right here in this fine gallery. Looking for all the world like he belonged here. The last time she'd seen him, he'd been wearing a motorcycle jacket, his mouth had sported filed teeth, and she'd been tied up in that foul cellar half-unconscious from the beating he and his brother Theo had given her.

She took a step closer to Claude.

Shark Man gazed at her as if he wanted to eat her up. She didn't think he could recognize her—not with the hair and the makeup and the dress. Besides, the cellar had been dark, and he'd been too busy smashing her face to get a good look at it.

Still, she put her hand on the clasp of her purse. If she had to, she'd draw her knife and escape any way she could.

At the same time, if she could hold her ground, this could be just the chance she needed to weasel out if he held her brother.

Kiro moved to stand in front of her. "Introduce me, Claude."

"Yes, of course. Alba Vargas, this is Cole Tuccio, law partner at Williams, Cowell, and Tuccio Associates."

Curling her toes to keep her feet from breaking into a run, she dropped her eyes, and offered her hand, praying he'd not notice it was trembling.

Kiro's hand slipped into hers, his palm fleshy and cold like a worm's. He squeezed gently and held on. "How lovely. I couldn't help noticing the way you moved so gracefully up on the dais. Where did you study dance, Miss Vargas?"

Dance? He thought her a dancer? Her pulse speeded up. He couldn't know she'd once trained in ballet.

He looked down at her feet. "The ballet slippers?"

She relaxed back on her heels. "Oh, no. I don't dance. Just like to be comfortable."

"Do you?" He gave her a broad smile. She was shocked to see a row of perfect teeth instead of the pointy ones she remembered all too well. He actually looked human, and for some reason, that scared her more than anything.

He moved closer and wrapped both his hands around hers. "May I relieve you of your companion for a moment, Claude?"

"Of course." He backed away, leaving Shark Man in possession of her hand—in possession of her.

Toro glanced toward Claude, praying he'd stay, but the traitor was already heading to the other end of the gallery.

She called after him. "But we didn't negotiate the price."

Claude stopped and peered over his shoulder. "We'll discuss the artwork later." With a wave, he disappeared into the crowd, leaving her alone with her nemesis.

Toro turned back to face Kiro and caught the look in his eyes. It was all male and all lust, and it sent a shiver right down to the tips of her toes. Vernon's brother might be tall and blond with a movie star face and a warrior's body, but he was no hero. Not at all.

She had the scars to prove it.

Kiro's thumb caressed her palm.

Her heart thudded against her ribs. Every one of her muscles tensed. Every part of her screamed *run*.

She scanned the brilliant white exhibition hall. Art buyers, news reporters, gallery owners mingled in the crowd, all waiting to meet her as soon as she dumped Kiro. He might deserve a knee in the groin and a knife in his belly, but acting like the street kid she was wouldn't get the fame and fortune a budding artist needed. It wouldn't save Hanger.

She slipped her hand free. "People are expecting to talk to me."

She tipped her head to take her leave. But before she could do so, Kiro looped his arm around hers and trapped her hand on his sleeve with his own.

He tilted up his head with an arrogance only power and money could buy. "They'll wait, Miss Vargas. Come. Tell me about your work. I find it fascinating." Arm locked in hers, he dragged her closer to her paintings.

"I really have to meet with the reporters." She tugged as politely as she could, but her arm stayed trapped under his.

"Oh no, my dear. We've hardly gotten to know each other." He flicked a finger at the largest painting. "So this is what you paint—Williamsburg?"

"Yes. They're all Williamsburg views." She looked around for some distraction. Any excuse she could use to escape. But no one was paying attention to them.

The so-called art connoisseurs circled around them, consumed in their conversations, barely glancing at the artworks. And if the press were waiting to talk to her, they were lying low or had been warned off by this bastard.

And where was her supposed friend?

She took a quick peek over her shoulder. Claude was in a corner whispering something in the second place winner's ear. The blonde gave him a tiny smile with her pouty little mouth.

Toro swallowed hard. Dark prince, golden princess, they looked perfect together—like they'd walked out of a story book. She didn't belong in that fairy tale.

Toro turned back. She peered down at her hand trapped beneath Kiro's, her olive brown skin a sharp contrast to his. It looked like she was stuck with the villain. She'd just have to play the witch and cast a spell on him if she wanted to find out if he had her brother.

She glanced at him. Well—she could let him think she was interested in him. That's what a woman would do.

But how? She ran through all the movie seductresses she knew. A sexy secret agent or a singer on the make would touch him. Snug up against him. Thrust out her chest. Speak in a sexy, low voice.

But how could she? His tuxedo might fit perfectly, gliding over his broad shoulders and snugging in at his waist. His bowtie might sit straight under his neck. He might be expertly groomed with not a bit of stubble showing on his jaw. His professionally styled white blond hair might glow with health.

For a vicious underworld criminal, Cole Tuccio could do a good imitation of a corporate lawyer.

But she knew who he was inside. Shark Man might look the part, but he was not bound by it. At this moment, he could be having her brother tortured somewhere.

Toro swallowed hard and focused on calming herself the way she had done every day for the last seven years, using the body relaxing techniques she'd learned in dance class. Panicked people didn't survive long on the streets.

Vernon might say she knew nothing about being a woman, but she did know how to survive—and if that meant pretending to be dazzled by a vicious lawyer, then that's what she'd do.

Praying she found Hanger before the masquerade went too far, she gave Kiro her sweetest smile and a tiny roll of hip that was her closest approximation of a movie star's come hither. She let her arm relax, her face soften, and forced her breathing to slow. She shifted closer until she felt the heat pouring off his body. Until his musky cologne filled her nose.

"Ah. That's better. I don't bite, you know." He gave her a smile so wide she could see his fake tooth covers. He turned and studied her artwork. "So which of these three paintings is my young Claude interested in?"

Her throat was so tight with fear, she had to force the words out. "The center one. The bridge."

Shark Man made a show of studying the work, tipping his head one way and then the other as if he knew what he was looking at. "He has excellent taste. I'll buy it."

Her heart was thumping so loudly she wasn't sure she'd heard him right. "What? You want to—but Claude—"

"Whatever Rendell said he'd pay, I'll double. I have a lot of blank walls in my new place, thanks to my brother." He trailed his fingers over the back of her hand. "I'll buy them all, darling. And every time I look at them, I will think of you. Name your price."

She shifted her weight from one foot to the other. On the one hand, she'd have enough in one fell swoop to pick up and leave. Reinvent herself. Get Hanger to a safe place once she found him.

On the other hand—she glanced at Kiro's profile as he examined the painting with eyes narrowed to reptilian slits—she was pretty sure it wasn't just her paintings he wanted to buy.

"You have that much money?"

His breath brushed her cheek. "Oh, my sweet, I have so many things."

Toro forced herself to stand still as he let go of her arm and slid his hand around her waist. The hair on the nape of her neck rose. She'd never let anyone hold her that intimately before. Never.

But she'd risk her life to save Hanger. Surely, she could bear the bastard's touch for a few minutes. Still, she eased away from his creeping hand as much as she could.

Besides, she knew what he was doing. He was more than flirting; he was claiming her in front of all these high-brow people.

There was a swish of movement behind her, and Claude joined them, his arm firmly locked in the blonde Cinderella's. "Kathy Schneiderfelder wanted to meet you, Alba."

Kathy Whoever waved her hand at the artworks. "I have to say, I've never seen paintings like these. The scale is so grand. The detail so intricate. So *perfect.* They must take you a gazillion hours to do." She looked over her shoulder at her own painting—four matching red squares divided by pastel blue bars. "Make my pieces look tiny in comparison. Do you use a ladder to paint them?"

Toro let out a small breath, Kiro's hand on her waist a reminder not to say too much. "No, I have an adjustable scaffold. Kind of like what Michelangelo used to paint the Sistine Chapel. But metal. You can buy them at lumber yards." Not that she had. She'd stolen hers from a construction site.

The girl moved to stand in front of the largest canvas. "Your studio must be huge."

"A whole floor of an old factory." She clamped her lips closed. *An abandoned one.*

The girl clapped her hands and turned around. "I'd love to see it. Do you allow visitors?"

Visitors? Damn, why couldn't Kathy Whoever ask how she achieved the textures or the colors or what inspired her. Toro thought fast. "Uh, no. The landlord was quite specific about it. Insurance reasons. The building's in bad shape."

"But he lets you work there?"

Toro ran the toe of her slipper up and down her ankle. Oh, this was not going well. If Kiro discovered her makeshift, illegal studio, she'd be exposed for what she was—a lying, thieving street kid.

She spouted the first lie that came to mind. "I have special insurance—only covers me." Hell. That sounded lame even to her.

Kiro rubbed his chin. "Who's the landlord, Miss Vargas? I own a lot of properties in Brooklyn and handle the dealings of many more. I probably know the owner—I'm sure I could make an arrangement so all of us could come see the rest of your work. It must be something to behold."

There it was again—that lustful look in his eyes, the little squeeze at her waist.

Her brain spun. *Cielos,* if they actually did intend to come, she could claim she'd been evicted or something. If there was one thing she knew how to do, it was how to disappear.

But wait—she peeked up at Kiro. If she could get him to pay her for her paintings tonight, then she could abandon the factory and rent a real studio somewhere for these busy bodies to visit. That would give her time to find out if Kiro knew what happened to Hanger.

Toro pasted on a big smile and turned to Kathy and Claude. "Mr. Tuccio wants to buy my paintings. All of them."

Claude's eyes narrowed. "I spoke for the bridge scene first."

Toro bit her lip. She hated doing this. She moved closer to Shark Man. She could feel the brush of his suit against the bare skin of her arm. "What are you willing to pay, Mr. Rendell?"

Claude ran a hand through his hair, mussing it. Parts stood up giving him a boyish appearance. "Five thousand dollars."

It was an overly generous amount. Exactly what Ari said should be the most to expect. She was a beginner, after all. Surely Shark Man would drop his offer. She swiped her hair out of her eyes and looked up at Kiro. "That's more than fair, don't you think?"

"Then I offer ten, Miss Vargas."

Toro blinked. Ten thousand? He'd meant it then. He'd said he wanted to buy them all. She looked at the other two. Ten each? She'd have thirty thousand dollars. Her mind whirled. After living on pennies, she couldn't imagine having that much money.

The hand on her hip pressed down like a brand. Clearly for that price Kiro expected more than just paintings. She clamped her purse under her arm, comforted by the knife she knew it held.

Claude's lips thinned. "That's way out of line, Mr. Tuccio. She's new on the scene. Her work might not take."

"But you assured me she would."

Toro looked back and forth between them. They arranged this? "I don't understand?"

"Claude is a close associate of mine, Miss Vargas." Kiro said. "And I am not pleased he was going behind my back to buy this artwork after he particularly suggested it as an investment *for me.*"

There was a brittle look around Claude's eyes. "As an art appraiser, I strongly suggest you lower your offer."

"Do you? Well, it's of no matter. I like throwing around my money. Easy come, easy go, as they say." His hand drew her against him. "I am sure Miss Vargas will accept my offer."

Toro bit the inside of her lip. Easy come? Easy go? It wasn't his money. He'd stolen it from his brother Vernon. Of course, she'd take back a smidgeon of it. This would be her revenge for the beating he'd given her.

With a quick conciliatory glance at Claude, she widened her eyes like those actresses in the movies, and focused on Kiro, hoping she looked as star-struck as possible. "You're offering ten thousand for each of the paintings? Thirty thousand dollars?"

Beside her, Claude coughed. The blonde—what was her name—Kathy—put a hand over her mouth. Kiro just smiled and tightened his fingers on her waist.

Toro wrinkled her nose and tried to look naive. "Oops. Did I say something wrong?"

"No, my dear. I will buy all three and anything else you produce. Consider me your one and only patron of the arts for the foreseeable future." Each finger pressed deeper into her flesh. "I expect it to be a very close relationship. In fact, you must visit my home and paint the view from my window."

Fear shot through her right down to the soles of her feet. No way was he getting her alone in that Fort Knox of a penthouse that used to be Vernon's. "Oh, I don't work that way."

Kiro turned those hard, silver eyes on her. It was like looking into a reflectionless mirror. "No? How do you work?"

She needed a lie fast. Oh yes. She glanced over at Claude and shrugged. "I shouldn't say. It's a bit illegal."

Kathy studied the painting again and frowned. "Illegal?"

"Yeah. I use"—she lowered her voice—"a drone." It wasn't that much of a falsehood, more an alternative truth. T-Crew had talked about getting one to take photos of their street art. They just hadn't done it yet.

Claude moved nearer to her painting. "So that's your trick. The detail is amazing. The closer you get the more there is to see. Like here." He pointed to a window showing a man and a woman kissing. "You use the drone to peep in people's windows?"

"Uh, no. I use a lot of imagination, too. Things I read in books and that I see at the movies. That couple are supposed to be Romeo and Juliet, Williamsburg style." She made a move forward and found herself trapped by Kiro's grip on her.

She put her hand on Kiro's arm and tried to push it off her waist. He tightened his hold. She pushed harder. He gave her an oily smile and let go—but not for long, his eyes said.

Chills ran up and down her body. She needed to get away from this man. But her money first. She smoothed down her dress and pointed her toes together little-girl style. "I'm going to have to leave. And I don't know how this works. Do you pay me for the paintings now?"

Kiro's mouth tipped up. "Why—on delivery to my penthouse. That's the way it's usually done. Right, Claude?"

The art collector rubbed his fingers together. "Yes."

Damn. Why had she thought the buyer would handle that? She'd have to arrange crating and transport somehow. Solo and Neto had rented a van and helped her get them here. She'd never ask them to take them to Kiro's. They'd kill him for what he'd done to her and Bella. She'd have to do it on her own. "As soon as the exhibition is over, I'll have them shipped."

"No. For what I am paying I expect personal delivery. You must come with them and select the proper place to hang each of them. The long one over the sofa, for sure. But the other two?" He ran a finger down her arm. "Perhaps my bedroom. You'll have to help me decide, Miss Vargas." He reached in his suit pocket and took out a card. "My address. Phone me with the delivery date."

Then he whirled around and disappeared into the crowd. With Kiro gone, it was like a bubble burst around her. Sound hurtled in. The swirl and stink of people's bodies assaulted her nose. Her heart rate slowed.

"Are you all right?" It was Claude, a frown creasing his brow and creating fine lines under his eyes, giving a hint of what he'd look like when he was an old man.

"Yes, uh—that man—he's overwhelming." She bit her lip—and scary as hell.

Claude straightened his already straight tie. "That he is."

"And you work for him?"

"As an art investment advisor. Art is not his thing. So he asked for my assistance."

She rubbed the hand Kiro had held. "I'm sorry he bought the painting you wanted. But the money will help pay for my brother's education—I couldn't say no. I hope you understand?"

Claude shrugged. "Don't worry about the painting. I'm an art collector and appraiser, and Mr. Tuccio just made you the hottest thing this side of the Atlantic." He looked over at her paintings. "People think art is all about creativity. It's not. It's about making money. When word gets out what he paid, you won't be able to keep up with the demand. Do you have any other works?"

Toro scuffed her foot. Ari's Rule Number Three: Make it seem like there are only a few pieces to drive the value up. Besides, she'd like to see Claude again. He was the first man to treat her like a person worth respect even if he had abandoned her to Shark Man. And she had to admit, she was a little bit attracted. "I only have one more canvas. It's not as big, and it's not finished."

"I'd be interested in seeing it and so would a friend of mine who blogs at *Hot New York Art*. Could I bring him with me?"

"When it's done." That would give her time to get a legal studio space somewhere. "Do you have a business card? I'll ring you."

"Of course."

The card he placed on her hand was thinner but more elegant than Kiro's. She tucked it into her purse.

"Now come." His hand was back on her upper arm. "Let me introduce you to the important people here. There's the *New York Times* art critic. She's asked for an interview. And our winning emergent artist usually appears on *Good Morning America*. The producer is waiting over there."

After an interminable time of being smiled at, hand shaken, and talked about, Toro was ready to scream. There was so little she could tell these people about herself. Bella had coached her for hours on the fake biography they'd made up, starting with her struggling single mother dying—the only true part. Years in foster care. A kind high school art teacher, now deceased, who'd taken a liking to her and encouraged her. Finally, workshops at the Brooklyn Museum and the Art Students League. But mostly self-taught.

All things that sounded possible, but were too general to check up on—she hoped. She looked toward the exit from the gallery and curled her toes inside her slippers. She wanted to run and leap and climb. Her body wasn't made for all this standing around, and her head wasn't capable of lying for hours straight.

It must have shown.

Claude moved closer. "Are you getting tired?"

"Yes. Would it be rude to leave so soon?"

"No, of course not. I think you've met most of the more important people."

Toro patted her purse. "I have a ton of cards from people who want to see my work."

He made a sad face. "Some big collectors are disappointed Mr. Tuccio snapped up all three of your paintings before they had a chance to make an offer. But you did the right thing. No one else would have paid that much. You really impressed him. Cole doesn't understand art at all. Sold a whole lot of Ari Stavros' landscapes for almost nothing. Complains all the time to me about how he was taken to the cleaners on them. That's why he's hired me."

Yeah, right. Toro knew exactly what Kiro had done with those paintings. Vernon had made him give them back to Bella and her brother. She swallowed a small smile. "Ari who?"

"Oh, a big-name Greek artist. Heard he's stopped painting." Claude rubbed his palms together. "What I wouldn't give to have one of his landscapes. But here, I'm gabbling on and you're asleep on your feet. Come. Let me get your wrap." He took her arm, escorted her down to the lobby, and then retrieved her cape from the check-in.

She swiveled to allow him to drape the black velvet thrift-store find over her shoulders, praying he didn't notice the frayed and torn lining. "It's been a pleasure meeting you."

He gave a nod. "Now don't forget to buzz me when that next painting is finished."

"I won't."

"Then I will look forward to your call. Shall I flag down a cab for you?"

"No. Not necessary. I know my way around the city." She stepped out the glass door and halted on the pavement. She glanced back. Claude had taken out his phone and was talking to someone. But catching sight of her, he stopped, and raised his hand in a quick wave.

Toro smiled. He was making sure she was okay. Warmth filled her. Nobody had ever looked out for her before. She'd been the one watching out for everyone else.

Toro turned and flagged down a passing cab. The driver cut across the traffic and got held up behind a bus. Time enough for her to call Bella and see if there was any word of Hanger. Maybe she wouldn't need to cultivate Kiro beyond delivering the paintings. Oh, wouldn't that be a relief.

With a click, she snapped open the purse thing she'd been holding all evening and took out her cellphone. But along with her phone came Claude's business card. The small white rectangle fluttered down into the gutter.

Oh, no. She didn't want to lose that. She bent down and retrieved it as a car pulled up next to her. She rose, expecting the cab. Instead, it was a long black limousine. She looked over her shoulder, figuring the limo belonged to one of the bigwigs leaving the gallery. But all she saw was Claude pocketing his phone and heading back toward the exhibit hall.

The rear door opened. "Get in, Miss Vargas."

Kiro.

Toro looked directly into Shark Man's metallic eyes. No way was she getting into his car. No way would she let him find out where she lived.

She rolled a shoulder. "Don't need a ride."

"You signaled for a cab."

"Changed my mind. My place isn't far."

Kiro slid over as if to get out. "Let me accompany you. The streets aren't safe for a young woman alone at night."

If she could have, she would have thrown back her head and laughed. The streets were a heck of a lot safer than being anywhere near Kiro Tuccio.

She stepped back onto the sidewalk and gave a finger wave. "That is most kind, but I know my way"—she made a show of shaking her purse—"and I have my pepper spray." Then she took off, not running, but at a good pace, heading in the opposing direction. Thank heavens Kiro was too lazy to get out of his fancy car, and Bowery had a divider down the center.

Kiro might think he'd catch up, but by the time Kiro's driver got the car turned around—*pouf*—she'd be gone.

She swung the purse, keeping one eye on the limo as it fought across the lanes of traffic and then got caught at the stop light.

Perfect. She yanked the hood of the cape over her head, stepped beside an overflowing waste bin and, holding her breath against the stench, huddled down, doing a well-practiced imitation of a discarded garbage bag—one more invisible piece of trash in the night.

She opened her purse and withdrew the knife. Safe for the moment—at least from Shark Man. She hoped.

Chapter 9

Idiota. He was a fool. Pharaoh stumbled blindly up the street, not caring where he headed. His only thought to get away—far away from G-Man and Jax and the blood and gore that had once been a young girl.

They'd let him go. Let him stand up and barge out the door. As if he were free. But he wasn't. He was a murderer. He may not have pulled the trigger, but the girl had died because of him.

Another human life snuffed out in a flash-bang of gunfire. His life turned to hell in a gory instant so like his mother being gunned down that he could barely breathe or think or lift his feet.

At the corner, his toe caught on the raised lip of a paving stone, and he hurtled downward, landing face first in the gutter. The rancid stink of the sewer filled his nose and reminded him where he was headed. He wrenched himself up and stumbled onward. He knew where he had to go.

The bridge. He needed to get to the Williamsburg Bridge and finish what Toro had stopped all those years ago. It was the only answer.

****

By the time he reached the middle of the bridge, Pharaoh was cold-sober for the first time in days. He was also a mess—unshaved, reeking of sweat, his shirt stained with the girl's blood. He tore off his tee and tossed it over the railing. Then desperate to wipe away the foul taste of that girl's death, he pulled a stick of gum from his jeans pocket and jammed it into his mouth. Not that it mattered.

He'd never feel clean again.

He looked up at the massive bridge tower rising two hundred feet into the night sky, the huge steel beams a crazy quilt of dark angles silhouetted against the light of the Manhattan skyline.

This was where he had restarted his life, and where he would end it for once and for all. Stairs led all the way to the observation deck at top of the tower, but he had no interest in going there. That was too safe.

He wrapped his hands over the damp, cold metal of the lowest strut and hauled himself up. He'd climbed high up on the bridge many times. Some of the tags on the topmost girders were his.

But tonight wasn't for tagging. This time he took no duffle of Rustos. No crew member's friendly hand helped hoist him from one beam to the next. No one kept watch below in case the cops showed.

This time he was alone. Hand over hand, he climbed higher and higher, hands gripping the girder, sneakered feet pushing up, using the bolts for traction.

With practiced ease, he worked his way along the thick steel beams that crisscrossed the tower forming large X's. Sixty feet up, he moved to the outside and crouched down in the notch where the girders met in the middle.

He'd wait until there was no traffic passing, and then all he had to do was edge forward and let go and hopefully hit the water and not the roadway below. He stopped and stared down. Cars whizzed by, the drivers and passengers unaware he clung to the steel above. Subway cars rumbled past, the beam beneath his feet vibrating in rhythm with the clacking wheels. A gusty breeze buffeted him and stole his baseball cap. He watched it flutter down and land on the roadway, only to be crushed under the wheels of a semi.

The rising wind off the river blasted his bare torso. Every breath drew the chill deep inside him. But that was nothing like the hell waiting for him below.

One last look—he owed himself that much. Pharaoh crouched down and peered out at the city. The view from up here was glorious.

Downriver, the lights on the Brooklyn Bridge twinkled like multicolored stars. Along the bank on the Williamsburg side, old factories and new high rises were stacked like children's blocks. Upriver, more of the same.

The trees of East River Park formed a dark blot on the Manhattan side. And on both sides of the river, lit windows spoke of families settling in for the evening, eating a meal, watching TV, bundling a child into bed.

Happy people. People with everything to live for. People whose very existence brought happiness to those around them. Not someone like him. He brought death and destruction to those he loved.

He was a Jonah. It's what his sister had called him after their mom was shot. No one would miss him. He took a last chew of his gum, the cinnamon taste a sad reminder of his distant childhood, and then stood.

Slowly he edged his feet closer to the edge until only the life-grip of his hands on the beam above kept him from falling. Below, the ink black water reflected the lights of the city. Finger by finger, he loosened his hold and prepared to fly.

Pharaoh tracked the cars passing beneath him. It was past midnight, the traffic thin. A huge gap opened up. No headlights shone in the distance. Now. Now was the time.

He rose on his toes and leaned forward until there was no part of him in contact with the bridge except the balls of his feet. He closed his eyes. One gust of wind, one twitch of muscle, and it would be over.

He sucked in his last breath and stilled. Had he heard a whistle?

He opened his eyes and peered down.

A lone figure jogged along the pedestrian walkway. A girl wearing ballet slippers. Her cape billowing around her. Her dress swaying with each kick of her legs.

He teetered for a second and then whipped out his arms and caught himself before he tumbled over the edge. He pressed himself against the beam, his heart pounding.

Who was she?

He gripped the rough steel tighter and scrutinized the woman. She moved like a dancer, her strides long and graceful. Her arms, tucked tight to her body, cradled something as if it were the most precious thing in the world.

If she had kept on running, he would have stayed his course. He would have let go and fallen, happy that the last image he'd take to his grave was a thing of beauty—an angel in a green dress.

He blinked. Hard. *Green dress?* No it couldn't be.

Not Toro's woman. The woman he didn't deserve. Couldn't have.

He waited for her to continue down the pathway and disappear. But she didn't.

Instead, she slowed, stopped, and turned until she was facing in his direction. Her head tipped back, the hood shading her face, the wire safety fence blurring her features. The distance was far, but there was no question that she was looking at him.

A long moment passed. Cars zipped by. Another train rattled below. The wind whistled in his ears. Pharaoh edged farther back. Only an angel or someone with eagle eyes, someone who knew the bridge structure well, could see him up here in the dark.

She cupped her hands to her mouth. "Hey you." Her voice, high-pitched, fluttered up to him on the breeze. "Come down."

He held his breath, listening.

The girl moved slightly to the left and called up again, "Cops heading this way."

It wasn't the police coming that gave him the impetus to move. It was the voice—strange but familiar.

It was always faster heading down than going up. Gripping the beams, he swung over and under until he was directly above where he'd seen the girl. Then, with knees flexed, he dropped down on to the walkway, sure the girl would be gone or would take off running at the sight of him. But she wasn't, and she didn't.

Ballet Slippers stood there in front of him as if she had known exactly where he'd land. Only the tip of her nose and a full-lipped mouth showed beneath her hood. She held out a hand.

"The cops are right behind me. Kiss me."

Kiss her? He peered over her shoulder. She was

right. Two cops on the beat were hurrying in their direction. Had they seen him come down off the girder? If he kissed her, would they believe them lovers on the bridge?

He closed his eyes and lowered his mouth to hers, intending to barely touch her, to pretend. But she smelled so sweet, like some heavenly flower garden, and the tip of her tongue showed just enough that he couldn't help himself. His lips met hers and settled like they belonged there.

His hands found her shoulders and drew her closer. Her luscious breasts pressed against his bare chest, causing his pulse to speed up. The heat of her body drove away the chill on his skin. All the blood rushed from his head to his groin.

He wanted to eat her up. Possess her. Drive into her and make her his own. Holding on to his fragile control, he ran his tongue along her lower lip, tugged gently with his teeth until her mouth opened slightly.

Her lips relaxed, and he slipped inside. She tasted like heaven—fizzy as champagne, sweet as vanilla.

One of his hands slid down and cupped her perfect rear end, drew her tight against his erection. She was an angel—his angel—and he never wanted to stop kissing her.

A police baton rapped against the metal railing. "Step away." Pharaoh jumped back, not because of the hulking policemen in their black uniforms and shiny beaked caps, but because he was aghast at what he'd been doing to a woman he had no right to.

The bigger officer pointed up at the tower. "You climb down from there, young man?"

The girl held up an envelope. Her voice trembled

slightly. "My paycheck blew up against the top of the fence, and my boyfriend jumped up and got it for me. Got to pay the rent."

Pharaoh put a hand on her shoulder and wiped his mouth. "Yeah, she was just thanking me."

The other cop gave his partner an elbow in the ribs. "Ah, leave the young lovers alone, Mitch. There's a lot worse going on around here."

The first officer adjusted his duty belt and then nodded. "You two get a move on. Find a more private spot for your thank you."

Pharaoh bowed his head. "Yes, sir."

The two officers moved off toward Brooklyn. Pharaoh took the girl by the hand and headed in the opposite direction, back toward Manhattan.

He had no idea where he was going. All he knew was he had to hold on to her, had to finish that kiss.

She'd saved him. Not just from the police, but from killing himself. Because after one kiss, he knew he had to go on living. If only to kiss her again.

Chapter 10

Reeling from the kiss, Toro let Pharaoh drag her back the way she'd come. She couldn't believe he'd been about to commit suicide again. Couldn't believe she was passing underneath that bridge span and happened to look up to check out T-Crew's tag—the one Ari put there three years ago—and seen Pharaoh standing on that beam.

At first, she'd thought he was touching up T-Crew's crown or doing his own tag. But when he'd swung forward, she'd known better. She'd seen him do it before.

The first time they'd met, Fernando Pharaoh has been preparing to jump off the bridge, punishing himself for causing his mother's death. She'd talked him down, then handed him a can of spray paint and showed him how to make a mark on the steel in his mother's memory instead.

She'd thought him saved. But the desperation was back again. She could see it in his eyes. Something had driven him up there tonight. Was he blaming himself for Hanger going missing? He *had* been the last one to see her brother. Had he learned something terrible? She had to know.

Heart racing, she gripped Pharaoh's hand tighter as he drew her off the pathway and pulled her into a corner by one of the old restrooms. The low rectangular building, long closed, was surrounded by an iron fence and wire netting. Even so the cracked walls sported a messy canvas of competing graffiti tags, sloppily painted throw-ups, and peeling go-overs.

He pressed her back against the bars and leaned in. "I don't know who you are, but thank you for saving me back there." He pushed back her hood and stared at her face.

Toro blinked up at him. It was dark and shadowy. But surely, he'd recognize her.

His eyes swept over her. She waited for him to say her name, shove her away in disgust for her deceit. Then she'd attack him and find out what he knew about Hanger.

But he didn't draw away. Didn't gasp in recognition.

Instead, he let out a long slow breath. "Angel, my angel, you are so beautiful. I can't believe I'm doing this." He cupped her face in his hands and kissed her, really kissed her. This time, his tongue swept in and claimed her mouth. His fingers stroked her cheeks, his touch tender as if she were glass and might break.

Toro sank into the kiss. Warm fizzing bubbles filled every part of her body, reminding her of the effect of the wine at the gala. Her purse and trophy tumbled to the ground as she looped her arms around his neck and touched her tongue to his.

Pharaoh tasted the way she always dreamed he would, spicy like cinnamon and cloves. She ran her hands down his bare back, reveling in the smoothness of his skin, the rippling of his muscles, the slight tremble wherever her fingers touched.

She'd loved him from afar for years. This close, he

was irresistible.

She tossed off her cape, lifted her leg up, and wrapped it around his hip in invitation. She'd seem plenty of couplings in the parks, and in the dark corners of the city. She knew what men and women did. That's what she wanted to happen to her, right now, with this man.

It had to. Her whole body ached with need. She throbbed everywhere, but especially at the core of her sex. Her silly panties were wet. She rubbed her leg up and down the worn denim of his jeans and pressed against his erection. He hardened even more.

Vernon was right. Women had a power all their own. She was the one doing this to him. Causing his breathing to speed up. Setting his body afire. Driving him mad with want.

Her hands slid down his neck and moved over his bare shoulders. She hugged him closer. Surely, he knew what she was offering.

Beneath her palms, Pharaoh's muscles tensed, and for a brief moment, she feared he'd stop. But he didn't. Instead, he skimmed his fingers down the sides of her breasts and cupped them, brushing his thumbs across her nipples. His touch, light as it was through the cloth of the dress, electrified her to the core. She moaned, and his hand dropped lower, sliding over her buttocks, and at last, pushing up the hem of her dress.

Ahh. The pads of his fingers caressed the tender skin on the inside of her leg, traveling higher and higher. Flaming heat coursed through her and settled between her thighs. She rocked against his hard cock, willing him to take her, thrilled when he groaned.

She wiggled her fingers down between them and

popped open his jeans button. She had to hurry. Sooner or later, he'd realize who she was and pull away in shock.

She might have been tempted by Claude, but this was the man she wanted to be her first and, most likely, her last lover. She found the zipper tab and tugged. "Take me, please."

"No." He shoved her hand to the side, set her on her feet, and then reeled away to stand by the pathway fence. Head down, he stood staring out at the river, gasping in noisy breaths of air. He did up his jeans and straightened up.

He spoke with his back to her. "Sorry. I can't."

Toro tugged down her dress and struggled to get her own breathing under control. Curse the man. Pharaoh was a dissolute who, according to Solo and Neto, slept with anyone in a skirt.

Here she was offering herself, and he was going all uptight on her. She came up to him and seized his hand. "I want you."

He stepped back, his eyes wild. "You crazy, two-timing bitch. You'd like that, wouldn't you. You should have let me jump."

His mouth twisted into a sneer, and then he was gone, racing down the walkway like a man fleeing a demon.

Toro's knees buckled, and she slid down, her dress catching on the rough concrete, the damp, cold pavement sending shockwaves along her bare legs.

All the wondrous heat of his kisses and caresses fled into the night. All her hopes and wishes popped like an overinflated balloon.

He must have recognized her and been disgusted.

Tears welled, and she swiped them away. She hadn't cried since her mother died, and she didn't intend to start now.

Calling forth all her willpower, she rose to her feet, grabbed her cape, and threw it over her.

Then she picked up her purse and trophy. This was it. Next time she'd let him jump.

Chapter 11

By the time he stopped running, Pharaoh was at the Manhattan end of the pedestrian walk. He knew the area well. It was one of the few places he could go where he could get away from Solo and Neto's constant pursuit.

Crossing Delancy Street, he headed for his current refuge. The building under construction was little more than steel girders and plastic sheeting snapping in the wind. But at night, it was quiet and peaceful and all his. Not even the angel-turned-temptress, with her amazing vision, could find him here.

With a glance around, he swung over the board fence and snuck in under a loose bit of the plastic. Inside, it was like a whole other world—a cement and steel jungle gym enshrouded in a filmy bubble. Scuffing his sneakers on every step, he climbed the concrete staircase to one of the upper story beams and curled up in a tight ball.

Qué diablo! He'd kissed Toro's girl, and she'd wanted—no, demanded—more. He licked his lips and spat, trying to rid his mouth of her taste. But he couldn't.

Kissing her had been heaven. Feeling her body pressed against him and responding to him had been earthshaking. Knowing she had wanted him made him want to live, but whatever life he had from now on

92

would be hell.

He tucked his chin against his chest and huddled tighter. Damn. Toro needed to know the girl was no good. But his once-upon-a-time friend would never believe him. He ran his tongue over his lips again. Not unless he proved to Toro he still cared.

Pharaoh banged his fist against the concrete, then sucked his bleeding knuckles. Finding Hanger was the key. It was his fault the kid was missing. If he showed up with Hanger beside him, Toro would forgive him for coming on to his girl—he hoped.

He must have finally slept, because when Pharaoh opened his eyes, the sun glimmered off the plastic sheeting as it billowed in and out. Outside, the morning traffic whizzed by, and the aroma of coffee and fried eggs wafted through the air from the nearby eateries.

The workmen would arrive shortly. With a groan, he stood up and stretched, brushed the cement dust off his jeans and skin, and rubbed his aching head. Then he headed down to street level and set a course for the nearest bus stop.

First thing on the agenda, get to Bella's on time, take care of his appointments and then quit. Second thing—go check out Kiro's place. He knew Kiro's garage door had been open. He'd known something was wrong. If he'd been thinking straight, instead of being hung over, he'd have gone around the corner and checked on the kid.

Third thing—he rolled his shoulders—go to G-Man's and see what hellish tattoos he would have to do to stay out of jail long enough to find Hanger. Maybe search out where that bastard had hidden the incriminating gun.

After that, who cared what happened to him?

****

Toro sucked in a breath of early morning air not yet contaminated by the commuter rush hour and joined the handful of up-before-dawn exercise nuts jogging up the ramp to the Williamsburg Bridge walkway.

Dressed in jeans and sweatshirt, she was ready to set about searching for Hanger. Today was Sunday. The perfect day to visit every one of his classmates and find out what they knew.

But first—she was going to mark the spot of that incredible kiss.

In minutes, she was standing in front of the old, abandoned public restroom. In the slanted rays of dawn, it looked unspectacular—dirty gray, covered in peeling tags—a block of cement encaged in weathered red fencing. She'd ignored it for years.

Yet now, the ugly structure was unforgettable. She wrapped her hand around one of the bars and rested her cheek against the cold metal. Any anger she'd nursed against Pharaoh had long since chilled.

He might be a bastard, but he'd given her a gift to treasure—the most wondrous first kiss in the world.

She took the Rusto cannon out of her sweatshirt's kangaroo pocket and glanced around. Good. No one within viewing distance. With a running jump, she leaped onto the top rail of the fence, then scurried like a spider up the wire netting. Where the cornice started, she had free access to the long flat surface of the lower part of the cement roof. Taking aim, she spray painted the first line.

Yes. It felt good to have her finger on the nozzle again—to be El Toro, the Graffiti King, instead of masquerading as some naïve girl. With a sweep of her arm, she outlined the cupid's bow of an upper lip, then a curved lower one. Five feet wide, two feet high, it covered over the other tags there, but she didn't care. Going over another crew's throw-ups might cause a turf war if they knew who did it.

Only one person would be able to figure out who'd bombed this tag. She pulled out the other can and filled the outline in with a coral pink that mirrored the lipstick she'd worn the night before.

She stilled as a bicycle sped by, but didn't try to hide. She was safe enough. This early on a Sunday morning, foot traffic was meager, the cops busy buying their morning Joe.

Now for one more finishing touch. Toro flicked her supersize marker out of the back pocket of her jeans and signed her work with her real initials A. V.

A puzzle for Pharaoh to figure out.

Voices rose from the pathway below. Kids on a lark probably. She could hear them kicking the fence. She finished her tag and tucked away the tell-tale cannons and marker.

Then she jumped down, shocking the two young hoodlums enjoying an early morning joint. She gave them a Cheshire Cat grin, then stepped back to survey her work. Huge and vibrant, it was surely an eye catcher. No way Pharaoh could miss it.

Wiping her hands on her jeans, she took one last look at the site of her first kiss, and then set off running—this time at full speed. Time to resume searching for Hanger. Time to arrange to have her paintings delivered to Kiro.

****

By the dusk, Toro had covered one end of Brooklyn to the other, ending up where she started—outside T-Crew's storefront.

Hope of finding Hanger had dwindled to a thin slice of wistful thinking. She'd checked the apartment a hundred times, but no testy teen raided the fridge. No grubby kid curled up on the bed.

She'd talked to all Hanger's schoolmates, every tattoo artist, street artist, and store owner she knew and had come to the only conclusion possible. Somehow, Kiro had caught Hanger that day in the garage and was holding him somewhere—if he hadn't outright killed him by now.

A shiver ran down her back as if a cold hand touched her. No. She wouldn't even think of Hanger being dead. Kiro might be cruel and nasty, but he wouldn't murder a young boy for defacing his cars, would he? That seemed extreme even for a bastard like Kiro.

Well, there was only one way to find out. She was going to have to deliver those paintings and suck up to Shark Man.

With a calmness she didn't feel, she opened the door to Big Bad and stepped inside.

Solo looked up from the computer, a half-eaten doughnut in his hand. In the last month, he'd grown a moustache and chin beard. His long, wavy hair was pinned up in the back. With his well-muscled body and trim hips, he looked hot, but she'd never tell him that.

She pasted on a grin. "What's up with the man bun, Solo?"

He touched the knot of hair. "My girlfriend did it. Thinks it's cool."

"Cool, huh? Which girlfriend?"

"The one who works in the coffee shop down the way."

"Oh, the free-caffeine-and-doughnut lady."

"We send all our customers her way." He took a bite of his doughnut. "Says it's my commission."

Toro came around the counter and swiped one of the doughnuts from the plate. Someday, she'd get handy on a computer, but right now Solo was her go-to guy. "I need a favor. But I can't offer any perks."

"No prob, King. Your wish is my command. What's going on with your search for Hanger? You must be going crazy with worry. Neto's been on the phone calling everyone, even the police. We gave them his photo and vitals. But they don't get excited until a dead body turns up. Think he's a runaway."

She hated to lie. But there was no way she'd let the twins get involved in her mess with Kiro. She shrugged. "Seems unlikely, though kids do crazy things. I've checked everywhere too." And she had only one hope left.

She leaned back and nibbled on the doughnut and, despite the growing panic twisting her stomach into knots, kept her voice calm. "I hate to ask but can you look up artists' lofts for rent? I have to find a legit studio."

He pushed a lock of hair off his forehead and swiveled around in his chair. "They cost a fortune."

"I'll only need it for a month so collectors can look over my other paintings. I've got some money saved. Maybe a sublet?" With luck, she and Hanger would be out of here in two weeks.

And if something bad had happened to Hanger?

She patted the knife at the small of her back. Then it wouldn't matter. She'd be locked up in prison. Because if Kiro or anyone else had hurt her brother in any way, she would gut them.

Solo scrolled down the screen. "Hey, look. Ari's place is available. The old machine shop on River Street."

"Really? They didn't tear it down yet?" She leaned over his shoulder. Ari's old studio was right next door to Kiro's building. Perfect for keeping an eye on him. "Who's the realty company?"

"Banker Hudson." He tapped the keyboard. "Should I call?"

Heart thumping, she said the words, knowing there'd be no going back. "Yeah. Do it."

****

An hour later, she was the proud subtenant of The Factory. Well, Bella's brother's untraceable shell company was. That subterfuge was even better. Using the fake business identity Ari had created for them had been Solo's idea. With the help of Ari's lawyer, she hadn't even needed to give her name. The key would be delivered by courier to the tour office before closing hours.

Now for the rest of the plan.

Down the block from Big Bad, she hitched herself up the nearest fire escape, climbed up the five stories, and scrambled onto the roof. She settled herself on the street side, legs folded under her, and peered out over Brooklyn.

Up here she truly was King. All around her, rooftops lay like black tar rectangles, punctuated with the occasional chimney or vent. Up here no one could touch her. No one could see her. It didn't matter what she looked like or who refused to make love to her.

But none of that was helping her save her brother. She surveyed the cityscape around her. Kiro owned a tremendous amount of Brooklyn real estate. He could be holding Hanger anywhere.

She took out her cellphone and the business cards. If finding out exactly where Hanger was meant getting close to Shark Man, then so be it.

She tapped in Kiro's number.

A sharp-voiced secretary answered. "Williams, Cowell, and Tuccio Associates."

"Alba Vargas here. I am calling to set up a delivery date for the paintings Mr. Tuccio bought last night."

"Of course, I'll put you right through."

Moments later, she was talking to the man she hated, setting up a time and date, pretending to be the naive girl she'd been last night, only this time, dressed in her loose baggy clothes, sitting on top of her real world, there was a rod of steel up her spine and a plan formulated in her head.

If Kiro Cole Tuccio had her brother, she'd know very shortly. First, she'd get paid. Next, she'd check for graffiti on his cars, and then she would get him to confess.

But to do that, she needed Claude. No way was she going anywhere near Shark Man's place without a witness. And as Kiro's personal art appraiser, he would surely be allowed to park in the garage.

She rubbed her hand down her thigh. Would Claude have turned her away like Pharaoh did last night, if she'd come on to him? She'd like to think not. She'd seen the male appreciation in his eyes, and she was relying on that interest still being there.

She pulled out Claude's card and entered his number. The phone rang.

Click. "Claude Rendell, art appraisals."

Toro smoothed stray hairs back into her ponytail. "Hello Claude. This is Alba. Alba Vargas."

There was a brief silence. "Of course, Alba. How can I help you?"

"I need you to come with me when I deliver my artwork to Mr. Tuccio. I really know nothing about hanging paintings."

He cleared his voice. "Eh—my schedule is quite full."

Right. Claude Rendell wanted to see Kiro as little as she did. Not that she blamed him. She shaped her mouth into a pinched bow and imitated the wheedling voice of that Kathy girl. "I can't wait to see you again. In fact, would you like to visit my studio before we go to Kiro's? I have that other large canvas and several in progress."

"Oh." His voice brightened. "That would be fantastic. When were you thinking?"

"Tomorrow?" That would give her all night to move her stuff in.

"What time?"

"Any time in the afternoon works for me. That's when I do most of my painting."

There was a clatter of computer keys. "Just cleared my whole afternoon. Can I bring my friend, the art news blogger?"

Toro scratched the back of her neck. The publicity would be great for her career, but for what she planned, she needed to be alone with him. "No. Just yourself.

This is a private showing—for you alone."

There was an audible inhalation on the other end of the phone. Grinning, she gave him the address and hung up. Claude Rendell had gotten the message.

Now she had to perform a miracle and move her stuff from her illegal warehouse by tomorrow. She peered over the edge of the building. Neto was shaking hands and patting backs as he dispersed his tour group. Great timing. Between Solo and Neto and her heave ho, they'd manage just fine.

She started for the fire escape and halted. Claude Rendell had liked her in the pickle dress, but she couldn't wear the same thing again. She'd need something really girly to deepen his interest. None of Bella's loaner things would work.

She patted the pocket where she'd stowed the cash she'd gotten from cashing her prize money check. Time to hit the vintage stores.

El Toro, King of the Street Artists, was going to masquerade again. She pressed a hand against her bound breasts. Only this time, it wasn't going to be pretend. Claude might not know it yet, but he was going to be her boyfriend. The thought excited her and made her cringe at the same time.

She pictured Claude's handsome face, his unusual violet-blue eyes. Claude Rendell would be the perfect first lover. He was kind and gentle and smelled clean. He'd gain her entrance into the art scene. Sell her work. Get her into Kiro's garage. What not to like about that?

She jumped down onto the top rail of the fire escape, then hurried down the rattling metal ladders. At the bottom, she slowed.

Sure, Claude was attractive. The problem was he

wasn't Pharaoh.

Chapter 12

This time he would make it all the way out.

Hanger moved slowly down the dark corridor of the old hotel turned brothel. At this hour of the afternoon, the place was silent as a graveyard. The johns gone. The girls worn out. The guards snoozing.

If it weren't for the bad ankle, the concussed skull, and the strange throbbing in his upper thigh, he'd have escaped two days ago. The locks on the doors were a joke. But tonight, he'd do it. He was only a little bit dizzy.

The sloppy footsteps of the guard he called Lout came up the stairs. Hanger crushed himself against the wall and waited. The man was coming to visit his "girl," the teenage runaway they had locked in the room at the far end. The one who cried day and night.

Hanger shrank back. This was the tipping point. If the hallway was dark enough, and the man filled with enough lust, Mr. Lout would pass him by.

Once the hall was clear, he'd fly out of this place and come back with help for these poor girls locked away up here.

Lout Man came abreast. Hanger held his breath. Just let him go by, please. But the man slowed.

Not good.

Hanger pressed farther back into the doorway. Prickles ran up and down his arms. Surely, he was invisible. His skin was dark, his clothes colorless. Still, something caught the bruiser's attention. Lout Man halted and turned.

Rats. Hanger closed his eyes and pretended he was a tree, a cement pillar, a bird. *Cielos*, he wished he were a bird. If he had a beak, he'd peck the bastard's eyes out.

"You." The thug's hand clamped around his neck. "Feeling better, huh? Boss man will be happy to hear it. He has plans for you."

In seconds, Hanger's hands were zip tied behind his back, and he was being forced marched down the stairs, his bad ankle screaming every time his foot hit a step.

At the bottom of the staircase, they turned right. Lout opened a heavy wood door and shoved him into what appeared to be an office. File cabinets lined three walls. A large, battered oak desk occupied the middle of the room.

Lout nudged him forward. "Our baggage woke up and was on his way out. Tell the boss."

The man behind the desk looked up and pushed back his glasses. "Take our little escape artist to the bunker. Jax will be in soon."

Hanger winced as he was hauled up again and half-pushed, half-carried down another flight of stairs, through a set of double doors, and into a hallway lit with one bare light bulb.

Gray paint sloughed off the walls. Water dripped. A dank smell rose from the wet cement under his feet. The basement.

Hanger grimaced as he was dragged forward. It would be a lot harder to escape from here.

"Wake up, Tapper. Got a customer for you," Lout said. He gave the guard a kick in the shins.

The beer-bellied man lumbered up from the folding chair he'd been sprawled on and took out a set of keys. "Which one?"

"The old storeroom. Sec's order. Kid's an escape artist. Somehow got out of his nice locked room upstairs. Needs some cooling off."

"Well, that can be arranged." The Tapper character unlocked one of the metal doors. Lout Man shoved Hanger forward into a room that stank of something rotten.

He landed on his ankle. Pain shot up his leg and radiated through his body.

The guard stepped back. "There's a piss bucket in the corner." The man laughed. "If'n you can find it."

Then the door slammed closed behind him, leaving him alone in total darkness. Hanger pushed up onto his knees, swaying slightly as the dizziness returned. Creeping on all fours, he worked his way to the wall and leaned back. Cold damp soaked through his sweatshirt and sent chills skittering down his spine.

For the first time in his life, he was afraid. No escape artist could get out of this hole, not even his hero Houdini. He needed help. But who would ever find him here?

He sank down to the hard cement floor and closed his eyes. But he couldn't sleep. His ankle still ached, but that was nothing compared to the other pain.

In the dark, he couldn't see his thigh. But the skin was hot and swollen, especially where he'd tatted his mark. When he touched it, tears filled his eyes—it hurt so much. Not a good sign.

Neither were the chills and fever raking through his body. He should have listened to Pharaoh.

Tattooing yourself was a stupid idea.

****

Lost in a fevered dream in which he was leaping from rooftop to rooftop just steps ahead of the demons pursing him, his mother waving encouragement from heaven, Hanger barely heard the door clang open.

Light flooded the cell. White pain shot through his throbbing head. Through slitted eyes, he glimpsed a fireplug-shaped man wearing a slimy leather jacket.

He gave a slight wave of his hand and croaked out. "Go away, whoever you are. I'm done for. Dying."

He inhaled a breath of the semi-fresh air wafting in the door and let his head fall to the side. Being dead wouldn't be so bad. At least, the pain would go away. Not that he'd expected to fly to heaven. But hell couldn't be any worse than this rat hole.

The man loomed over him. "Don't think so. The boss wouldn't like that. He's got plans for you."

Hanger sank lower as the man bent down and grasped him under his arms. "Can't stop me dying."

"We'll see about that."

Fiery pain shot up his leg as he was hoisted to his feet and then slung over someone's shoulder.

One last thought zipped through his head before he passed out. He couldn't die yet. Not until he told Toro what he knew.

Chapter 13

Toro twirled around in the Foundry's mirrored bathroom, enjoying the slight flair of the skirt and the way the deep burgundy cloth swung about her thighs. This dress fit much better than the green pickle one. The vintage A-line velvet floated over her body like it had been made for her.

Its high neck and long sleeves were her armor. She planned to use all the feminine wiles she could think of to win his agreement, but Claude Rendell wasn't going to touch any more of her bare skin than necessary.

Still, if she needed to be more persuasive, underneath the dress, she wore the frilly lace bra and the panties from the awards ceremony. She ran her hands over her breasts and down her stomach. She still felt way too naked, but she was getting use to the airiness of girly underwear.

With a last glance to make sure her lipstick was on straight, she stepped out of the bathroom and surveyed the apartment. Hopefully, she could accomplish everything in the studio below. But if not, the bed was made and ready.

Bang. From downstairs came the loud clank of the door knocker.

He was here.

She glanced at the necklace lying on the table top. The gold medallion with the engraved fleur-de-lis had once belonged to a princess. At least, that's what her long gone father said.

She'd kept it hidden all these years, buried under a paving stone behind the first abandoned factory she and Hanger squatted in. She'd retrieved it just the other day.

If she was going to flee to Greece with Hanger, she didn't want to abandon it. The pendant was all she had left of the father she barely remembered.

She hated to put it on, but she didn't want to leave it sitting out. Who knew what would happen tonight. Besides, it dressed up the high neck of the dress.

The door knocker banged again.

What the hell. It was a just piece of cheap jewelry. Toro fastened on the medallion and then, gathering her skirt, she padded down the Foundry's unique suspended staircase. Beneath her ballet slippers, the metal treads vibrated slightly with each step.

She glanced up at the huge chains that supported the staircase. Hanger had loved to climb those chains and hang upside down, making monkey sounds. Ari had nearly killed him the first time he'd done it. "What if he fell and landed on that metal crap below?" he'd said.

Toro looked around. Ari had been right about that. The first floor was one bloody accident waiting to happen.

The Factory belonged to a well-known metal sculptor currently finding inspiration in Iceland. Scrap iron and pipes littered the floor. Towering, sharp-edged, unfinished sculptures stood at odd angles, giving the place the feel of an alien landscape.

She loved the wild danger of it. It had been easy to make it her own.

Large steel tables were now covered with her

paints and brushes. Her huge canvas rested against the far wall. It would be the first thing Claude saw when he entered.

On the side walls, she'd tacked up her sketches. Thanks to a friend of Neto's, she had a loaner drone hanging from a wire rack. The best thing so, she hadn't even needed to bring over the stolen scaffold. There'd already been one here.

She tugged down her sleeves. She was ready. A little kissing. A little touching. Perhaps something more. Whatever it took to convert Claude into her avid lover and defender and make him an ally against Shark Man.

She put on her best imitation of a temptress's sexy smile and pulled the battered metal entry door open. "Claude."

The art appraiser grinned, revealing a dimple in his right cheek. He held out a bottle of wine, a jaunty red bow on its neck.

She opened the door wider. Seducing this guy wouldn't be too bad. He was cute in a business suit kind of way and came bearing gifts. She touched the medallion. She'd been given very few gifts in her life.

Smiling, she took the bottle from him. "You found the place okay?"

He glanced back over his shoulder. "Uh—yes. Looks like graffiti heaven outside. Wasn't sure it was safe to park. Those rotten kids won't mark up my car, will they?"

Toro tried not to laugh. "I can guarantee no one will spray paint your car."

"Have an in with those guys, do you?"

She shrugged. "I feed them. They inspire my art."

"Ah, yes." Claude was no longer looking at her. Instead, he beelined toward the painting on the wall. He stopped five feet away and stared. "It's better than the ones at the show."

The compliment sent warm ripples through her. She moved to stand next to him. "Really? It wasn't done in time to enter. Still needs a few more touches. The large building at the bottom—I planned to put—"

But he had stopped listening to her. He paced from one end of the painting to the other. "Yes, indeed. Maybe Tuccio was right to pay you that exorbitant sum."

Cradling the wine bottle against her chest, Toro trailed after him. "So you like it?"

"It's magnificent. A modern masterpiece."

She latched on to his sleeve. "You can have this one for the five thousand."

He spun around and stared at her. "But Tuccio will want this, too. He wants all your work."

"No. I want you to have it. I felt terrible when he bought the bridge one out from under you."

"But—"

"I can paint more for Mr. Tuccio. I love painting." There was a funny expression on Claude's face. Oh, dear she'd embarrassed him. She'd assumed he was rich. "If you don't have the money, that's okay. You can make payments or whatever."

"I can't."

"Oh, well—then consider it a gift." She held out the bottle. "Let me fetch some cups, and we'll drink on it. Get to know each other better." She brushed against him in a friendly cat sort of way and wiggled her hips.

Claude's face turned a bright pink. His shoulders

tightened. "Look, Alba—"

Damn. She chewed the inside of her lip. She was doing something wrong. He wasn't reacting like a man ready to seduce her. If anything, he looked ready to run.

She stepped away, creating a space between them. Of course he did. She was hopeless at being a woman. Why would any man want her? Pharaoh certainly hadn't. And now it seemed neither did this guy.

Her teeth dug deeper into her lip. She was uneducated and gypsy dark. She didn't know how to walk like a woman. Or talk like a woman. She was nothing like that blonde Kathy doll Claude had hung all over at the gallery.

All she had going for her was a woman's body. And the dress probably didn't show enough of it. She should have worn the pickle dress.

Too late to change now. She was going to have to work harder.

She hefted the bottle. Alcohol would help. Drunks didn't care what the women they took to bed looked like. Right?

She headed for the table in the corner where she'd put out some crackers and cheese and chips and popped open the bag of plastic cups. She twisted off the cap and filled both cups to the top.

She peered down at the burgundy red liquid, remembering how a few sips had dizzied her at the museum. If she drank a whole cup of this wine tonight, she'd end up flat on her back.

Yeah, well that was the plan, right? And Claude could handle that amount. He'd drunk much more at the dinner. She picked up the cups and turned around.

Claude was leaning in, examining one of her

sketches. She approached him and held out the cup. He checked his watch and then peered into her eyes. "Have you signed the contract with Mr. Tuccio yet?"

"No, he won't pay me until I deliver the paintings personally. I assume, if he still wants to buy the rest of my work, we'll complete the contract then." A chill trickled across her shoulders. It wasn't her artwork Kiro wanted.

Claude took the offered wine and swallowed down a good fourth of it. "I can't take the painting, but if you would let me have the sketches, rolled up in a tube, I'll see if I can sell them before he knows they exist."

Sneaking on Kiro. How nice, a fellow conspirator.

Toro gulped down her wine. The bubbly feeling tickled her tummy and sent a wave of pleasant warmth through her. She moved closer. She could see the fine pores of Claude's skin, the pale blue flecks in his eyes. She liked that he wasn't as tall or as broad as Pharaoh or even Solo or Neto. It made her feel more powerful. More in control.

She put a hand on his arm. "But I want you to have the painting. It's mine, and I get to say who can have it."

"It's—it's—too—"

"Too what—?"

"Memorable." He reached out and caught a lock of her hair, then twisted the curl around his finger "I wanted to do that since I met you. The color is like a raven's wing." His lips tightened as if he was having trouble deciding whether to kiss her or not.

Toro arched her back and turned her head in what she hoped was a seductive pose. His reticence was beginning to bother her. As far as she was concerned there was nothing to decide.

She could smell his clean citrusy scent, feel the heat of his body through the thin velour of her dress. In the movies, the femme fatale would undo his tie. Unbutton his shirt.

Toro hesitated. This was no film performance. Unfastening a man's clothing seemed a lot more intimate in real life.

She settled instead for brushing her fingers along his jawbone, the skin soft and smooth as the velvet of her dress, unlike Pharaoh's rough stubble. Damn. She forced Pharaoh from her mind and pushed up on her toes. "Kiss me."

He jumped back. "Ah. That would not be a good idea, Miss Vargas. Not a good idea at all."

"What would not be a good idea?"

Toro whirled around. Shark Man stood in the doorway, a key dangling from his hand, his fake plastic-toothed smile radiating satisfaction. All the warm fizz from the wine evaporated, leaving her stomach leaden.

He stepped inside. "Imagine my surprise to learn you're one of my tenants."

He swished his way across the studio. "Is this the painting you mentioned, Claude?" He stared at it for a moment, and then faced her, still wearing that hungry smile. "I was disappointed, Miss Vargas, when you called *Claude*—and not me." He stalked towards her. "I believe we had an arrangement?"

Claude moved behind her. "She asked me to appraise it. That's all, boss." His voice came out high-pitched and tinny like all the air had been sucked from his lungs.

Toro glanced at Claude from the corner of her eye. Traitorous coward. She'd been tricked by a handsome face and a few kind words. A knight who was no more than Tuccio's pawn—a well-played one. She wondered what hold Tuccio had on him and then pushed the thought aside. It held no relevance to finding Hanger.

She looked down at the cup of wine in her hand. She'd been a fool to think Claude Rendell would help protect her from the two-footed predator standing a few feet away. She lifted the cup to her lips and took a swallow.

But she played chess, too. It had been one of the few sources of cash she'd had in her years on the streets—acting the fool, challenging the old men in the park, and winning enough for dinner. She could beat anybody at chess. Except Pharaoh.

Her move. "Can I get you a glass of wine, Mr. Tuccio?"

Shark Man wrinkled his nose. "Cheap wine in a plastic cup. I think not." He pulled out his cell and tapped in a text message. "Now, Claude. Show her the contract."

Underhanded bastard. Toro fisted her hands in her skirt to keep from smacking the appraiser's handsome face.

Claude mouthed "sorry" and took out a tri-folded paper from his breast pocket. He handed it to her.

Toro unfolded it slowly, trying not to breathe in the aroma of the man's scent still clinging to it. She moved into a patch of light and peered down at the formal words that would bind her to Kiro Tuccio forever.

Not in body. That wasn't on the paper, although it would surely come to that.

There was no hiding the intent in Kiro Tuccio's eyes.

If she signed this—her art—her spirit—would belong to him. Her joy would be his. The bastard would own everything she drew, everything she painted.

In return, she would be rich—a millionaire—for the rest of her life. He would be her patron. She would be his slave.

She folded the paper back up, running the folds between her fingernails and bringing the creases to a razor's edge. "I'll have my lawyer look at it."

"You'll find it all in order, Alba. I am a lawyer."

She put the contract down and set the plastic cup on top. She hoped it left a stain. "As you probably know, since you apparently own it, I rented this studio only yesterday. Used some of my prize money." She puckered her mouth into a hint of a smile and glanced at Claude. "I wanted someplace better to showcase my work. Invite *friends.*"

Kiro gave a tiny nod of his head. "I am pleased you chose the Foundry. We'll be neighbors." He moved closer, picked up her medallion, gazed at it a moment, and then laid it down again on her breast. "Perhaps more. I find you quite—interesting."

Toro swallowed and stepped back as far as she could. The hard edge of the table stopped her. She caught a glimpse of Claude's white face and wringing hands. The wimp would be no help if Kiro decided to rape her in front of him. He'd basically given her to him.

She wondered if Mr. Traitor would have been as giving if she'd managed to seduce him. She shook her head to clear it. Totally irrelevant thought. She shoved it away with all her other failures and turned her attention back to the real danger.

She had to keep Shark Man talking, play cozy, but stay hard-to-get. She bit the inside of her cheek. In a way, it would be no different than staying ahead of the graffiti cop patrol while tagging.

She smoothed her voice. "I find you interesting, too. Claude said you are not really into art. Why are you so interested in mine?"

"Because *you* painted them." He seized her hand. "You are the most beautiful woman I have ever seen. I saw you standing in the gallery, and it was like a song sprang into my ears—she's the one."

She stared at her darker hand in his. "The one what?"

"The one I'm going to marry."

Her head snapped up. Marry? Any woman married to Vernon's nasty little brother would end up dead or wishing she was. And why her?

Still this was a twist she could work with. "Is that a proposal?"

He caressed her hand. "Not yet."

Someone banged on the door. He signaled Claude, who trotted off like a sadly obedient puppy and returned with two white-clad caterers rolling in a food cart.

Using the side of his arm, Kiro swept her paints and brushes off the nearest work table to the floor. "Arrange it here."

One-handed, the shorter caterer whipped a white linen cloth over the rusty, stained table top. The other waiter set two place settings of china plates, silverware, and crystal goblets across from each other. Then, like

116

the well-oiled servants they were, they stepped back, one to either side of the food cart, hands tucked neatly at their sides.

Kiro came behind her with a folded chair. "Sit, my princess."

Toro hesitated, and then, drawing the soft velour skirt of the dress under her, she sat, keeping her back straight, her legs tightly together, and her hands folded in her lap.

Things might not be going to plan, but she was safe enough for the moment. Two men to serve, and Claude to watch. Shark Man obviously didn't plan to attack her right off.

"Champagne?" Kiro asked.

She glanced around at the three men standing at attention like footmen in a PBS drama. The situation couldn't get more absurd. She lifted a shoulder like actresses did in seduction scenes. "Why not? Never tasted it."

"Delightful." Kiro signaled, and the white-aproned man behind her poured a clear fizzy liquid into a long-stemmed glass and set it down in front of her.

She brought it to her mouth. Tiny bubbles landed on her lips and tickled. She took a sip. It burned slightly, but was sweeter than the wine. More like the beer she sometimes drank with the crew. But much lighter. She peered up at her enemy. "I like it."

The shark across from her grinned. "I thought you would." Kiro reached into his coat pocket. "You will like this, too." He flicked it open and took out a ring.

Toro was no jewelry expert, but even she knew the flashing diamond was worth a gazillion dollars.

He held it out to her. "Will you marry me?"

Her breath whooshed out as if she'd been punched in the stomach. "Huh?" Behind her Claude shuffled his feet. The caterers didn't move a stitch. Fancy food guys probably saw this happen all the time. "But we only met last night. We talked for less than twenty minutes."

Kiro leaned back in his chair, laughing. "Look. I know I've shocked you. Put my craziness down to love at first sight. I have to have you. As my wife."

He reached across the table, lifted her hand and slipped the ring on her finger. "Now that *is* a proposal."

The ring was cold and heavy and fit perfectly. She folded her fingers down, and the hard metal band cut into the flesh of her palm. "I haven't said yes."

Kiro took a sip of his champagne. "But you will. I'm going to make it very worth your while."

He signaled the caterers. Plates bearing flesh-colored patties topped with slimy black pearly things were set in front of them.

He took a bite. "Delicious. Salmon with caviar sauce. I want you to know you will never go hungry as my wife."

Toro glared down at the unappetizing food on the plate. "Really?"

"Taste it."

She put a small forkful in her mouth. A bit fishy and a lot salty. She could probably swallow it down. But did she want to? Toro laid down the fork. She had to show him she was no pushover.

Kiro smiled. "You will come to love it." At his signal, the caterers whisked the plates away and replaced them with bowls of soup. He waved his spoon. "Asparagus."

Asparagus? Something else she'd never eaten. She

hesitantly scooped up a smidgeon of the green goop. She slipped it into her mouth.

Yuck. Not only was it salty, but also grainy on her tongue. She pressed her lips together and forced herself to swallow. She put down her spoon. "So tell me another reason why I should marry you."

"I'm a billionaire. I have a castle in the Catskills, a villa in the Caymans, and a yacht in the Mediterranean. I understand you have never been much beyond Brooklyn. Marry me and see the world."

"I like Brooklyn." Toro glanced over her shoulder where her painting hung. "The inspiration for my artwork is here."

"Is it? That's terrific because I have a penthouse right here in Williamsburg, too."

He snapped his fingers. Her barely touched soup disappeared, replaced by a slice of meat and whipped potatoes decorated with red stuff.

Meat and potatoes. At last, something recognizable. Toro worked her way through the plateful, then set it aside. Then the dish was gone and a crystal bowl of very familiar-looking ice cream appeared in front of her.

Kiro twirled his spoon. "I know you are going to like this."

Toro raised an eyebrow at Claude. "You told him everything?"

The man had sense enough to back away. "I should leave now. May I, boss?"

Kiro nodded. "Yes. Yes. All of you. Go. My future bride and I need to talk."

In seconds, the caterers had loaded their cart and disappeared out the door, followed by a grim-faced

Claude.

The Foundry's door banged shut, leaving her alone with her personal demon.

Toro clamped her thighs together, wishing she had her knife. But she'd taken it off when she changed into the dress. It was in her knapsack, and stupid her, she'd left it on the other side of the studio.

Still, there were plenty of other weapons lying around. Sharp-edged sheet metal. Heavy iron bars. She was safe enough for the moment.

Kiro loosened his tie. "Now, where were we, Alba dear? Oh yes, the marriage proposal. Do you have an answer for me?"

Toro slipped the ring off her finger and trapped it in her fist. "Not yet. This is all too whirl-windy for me. I barely know you."

"I have billions and billions of dollars. That should be enough to convince any woman."

She stood and held out the ring. She wanted to throw it at him, but that wouldn't help her save her brother, if Kiro had him. "I'm not every woman."

She debated asking outright if he had Hanger. But she couldn't. Not with those cold, pale eyes glaring at her and with nowhere to run. Better to keep him on the hook. Make him think he had her interested. "I think you should leave. I will consider your proposal."

"Of course." Kiro rose from his chair, retrieved the ring and tucked it away. "There's something else I can offer to convince you to marry me."

"Is there?" She forced herself to laugh. "A new wardrobe? Dance lessons? All your prisoners freed?"

Something flickered across his face, and then he was pushing her back against the wall. "No, this."

Before she could step aside, he was on her, his hands clamping her head, his body trapping her, his musky smell washing over her, his mouth descending on hers. She mashed her lips tightly together.

The kiss when it came was anticlimactic, closed-mouthed, dry-lipped, only a hint of tongue touching the seam of her lips.

He drew back, a slight line marring his brow. "I can see you have a lot to learn." His hands fell away, freeing her. "It will be a pleasure teaching you."

Chapter 14

Finally, the bastard was gone. Toro scrubbed even harder at the table top where they'd eaten. She wanted to wipe away every trace of the man. But it was impossible.

Kiro's expensive cologne still tainted the air. The taste of his lips still poisoned hers. She swiped her mouth with the back of her hand and considered taking a shower upstairs, shivered, and rejected the idea.

Shark Man could come back at any moment. She had enough trouble getting him to leave without stealing more than that chaste kiss. She threw the sponge in the bucket. Water splashed up and wet the front of her dress. It would be ruined, but she didn't care. She'd never wear it again.

She needed to get back to her apartment, back to where she felt safe and normal. Back to figuring out how to discover if Kiro was holding Hanger captive somewhere—without marrying him—or doing anything else obnoxious with him.

She slung her knapsack over her shoulder. Enough of that. She needed to think of another way to find out where her brother was.

She bent down and picked up the brushes and pencils Kiro had swept to the floor. Assuming Kiro had Hanger, he wouldn't be stupid enough to keep him at the penthouse. He'd hold him at one of his off-the-books businesses. All she had to do was figure out which one.

Maybe she could go out to dinner with Shark Man, pickpocket the bastard's cellphone, and check out the places he called.

Risky if she were caught. But it might work.

She hitched her knapsack higher on her shoulder. She'd call Kiro tomorrow and set up a date. For now, she'd get some needed sleep, and then come morning, do another round of the neighborhood.

Not that she had much hope. With Hanger missing for a day and half, the possibility he was fooling around or hiding was highly unlikely. Kiro had him. She knew it in her bones.

After one last glance at the painting, she turned off the light switches, yanked the door closed with a bang, and headed out into the night.

****

At three in the morning, the street was empty and silent. Cars, sprinkled with fine mist, sat parked along the curb. Soft tendrils of fog enveloped the buildings. Only a few windows were lit in the tall condos towering over her. Toro glanced up at the top floor of the nearest one.

Kiro's penthouse.

No light shone from the windows. Did that mean he was asleep, or was he out here waiting for her?

She rubbed her hands up and down her arms. There was no way to know. She'd have to chance it.

Staying inside the plywood fence that encircled The Foundry and the neighboring construction site, Toro slunk around the side of the building. She knew how to be invisible, how to disappear into the shadows.

The trouble was, so did her enemy.

Kiro could be anywhere, ready to seize her and finish what she'd managed to avoid. The idea of letting his slimy hands touch her made it hard to breathe.

She slithered along the building, speeding up as she came to the end of the construction fence. She'd take to the roofs as soon as she crossed the street at the corner.

"You." A hand came out from the dark and seized her by the shoulder.

Toro whirled and kicked for the balls. But whoever had her was fast and limber. Her foot met air. She flailed and tugged and twisted. But her assailant was bigger, stronger, and seemed to know all her moves.

This couldn't be happening. No one could hold El Toro. She punched upwards and got him under the chin. There was a grunt, and then she was being dragged behind the building and gathered against a very familiar body. An even more familiar scent filled her nose— *Pharaoh.*

All the fight went out of her. After being on razor-edge all night, adrenaline pounding her body, it was like coming home. Her breath evened. Her racing pulse slowed.

She nestled against his chest and waited for the trembling to stop. His heart beat resounded in her ear. His body heat warmed her bare legs and arms.

His chin came down and rested on her head. His hand rubbed up and down her spine. His other hand drew her against the heat of him. "It's okay, angel. Sorry to have scared you." His voice was a soft rumble. "But what are you doing walking the streets at this hour?"

"I'm going home." Home. She curled up tighter

against him. This was home. Here in his arms. But she couldn't tell him that. The minute he realized she was Toro, he'd flee.

"You don't live in The Foundry?"

"Staying with friends." The lie came easily enough. She'd been lying all her life, after all.

"Why are you down here then? It's not safe for someone like you."

She stiffened slightly. "Someone like me?"

He cupped her chin and turned her face up to his. "Oh, angel, don't you know? Any man seeing you— he'd be unable to control himself." He brushed his lips across hers. "Any man. Even me."

Did he mean that? Before he could change his mind again, she reached up and pulled his head down to hers, pressed her lips to his.

He resisted for a moment. And then he was kissing her, claiming, licking, nipping at the tender flesh of her lips until she opened and let him in.

Yes. His tongue swept inside. She could taste his breath, sweet and minty as if he'd been sucking on a candy.

For a second, she wondered what she tasted like to him. The wine she'd drunk at dinner, the MarieBelle chocolate ganache Kiro fed her after the ice cream? Or did she taste like Kiro?

Damn, she was acting a fool again. She pushed against Pharaoh's chest and broke the kiss. "Stop."

He let go instantly. "Sorry."

Deep in the shadows, she couldn't see his expression, but she could feel the vibes coming off him. Could sense how he was holding himself back, wanting to leave her, yet unable to flee.

She should be the one to leave. He'd never catch her. She'd always been faster, able to fit through spaces his broad shoulders couldn't.

But she couldn't pull away. Couldn't hurt him.

He wanted her. She wanted him. It was like a fairy tale come true.

But not like Cinderella and her prince. More like a doomed Juliet with her doomed Romeo. Because any love they shared would only lead to tragedy.

But hell. Who knew what the future held. It was only a matter of time before Kiro took what he wanted—took her.

So why not take what she wanted now?

Toro reached up and ran her fingers along Pharaoh's jaw. He was no pretty-faced Claude Rendell. She loved the jutting shape of the chin bone, the hardness of it, the way the late-night stubble pricked her fingertips.

She loved the rich brown of his skin—a painterly mix of sienna and umber. She loved the strong planes of his face, the flaring nose, the midnight black eyes that drew you in.

She loved him for what he was on the outside—a perfect man—broad-chested, hard-muscled, narrow-hipped.

But even more, she loved him for what he was on the inside—a loyal friend with a tender heart—an easily-bruised heart he kept buried deep inside him.

Her hand found his ear and traced the curves and whirls. How many times had she drawn his portrait, painted him on her canvases? His image was in every one of her works.

She moved her hand down his neck and across his

chest, reveling in his rough intake of breath when she touched his nipples through the thin cotton of his tee.

She hadn't known men were sensitive there. "Promise me—" She circled his nipple with her finger. His whole body vibrated. She did it again. "Promise me you won't—"

"Won't what?" The words whipped out of him.

She ran her hands down his chest. "Run."

He rested his forehead against hers, gasping like a defeated athlete. "I—won't—run."

The promise wasn't enough. She didn't want him hurt.

She swept her hand lower and found his hardness. She stroked down. "You won't regret."

"Never." His breath blew warm on her skin.

"Good." She threw her arms around his neck and crushed herself against the length of him. "One night. One night for you and me under the stars."

He made a slight groan. "It's cloudy."

"No. It's whatever we imagine it to be. For us, there will be stars."

****

Stars in heaven. Pharaoh struggled to control the response of his body to her touch, but it was too late. His angel was taking him where he didn't want to go. He'd intended to protect her. Keep her safe from the two goons Jax had hovering outside The Foundry—the ones he'd been following for the last hour. Instead, he was putting her in more danger. Danger from him.

He snugged her soft, rounded body against his. As much as he resisted the idea, he had to have this woman. Had to make her his even if it destroyed everything.

There was some kind of cataclysmic pull between them. Like they'd known each other in some other life, and joining their bodies was the only way to find completion.

He'd had women before. Bar hookups. The girl in the apartment below his. But he'd never felt this powerful attraction. This unbearable need to possess, to protect, to become one.

She felt it, too. He was sure of it. This woman wanted him. Desperately. And he wanted her back. She smelled right. Felt right. Fit right.

But making love to her would be so very wrong.

Hell. Toro would never forgive him for taking his girl. But it was too late to stop.

He ran his hands over the delicious curves of her rear end and stifled a moan. Why should he hold back? He was a Jonah. He'd hurt everyone who'd ever cared for him. His mother. Ari. Bella. Why not Toro, too?

He had weeks, maybe days to live. Jax considered him expendable. He had a murder charge hanging over his head.

Once Hanger was found, he'd jump off the bridge or walk in front of a train and put an end to it. Toro could join all the others who hated him.

It wouldn't matter when he was dead.

The one thing he wouldn't do was hurt this girl. Tonight, he was going to take her to heaven and make her see those stars.

He clutched her against him and drew her back into the shadows. "Not here. There are men following you."

She went rigid in his arms. "What?"

"I tracked them here from—where I work." He slipped his hand into hers. "Come, it will be a little rough, but I'll get you away from them."

She squeezed his fingers like a trusting child. "Lead on."

Warmth exploded up his arm and filled the hollowness inside him, driving away the last remnants of remorse.

"Come." Gravel and broken glass crunching under foot, he led her around the back of the Foundry, and nudged her into a bend in the fence. "Stay in the shadows. And don't move. There's a pit about seven feet in front of you. I'll go distract them." He put a finger on her lips. They were soft and wet from his kiss. "Please don't leave. I'll be back in a second."

He dashed back the way he came, hoisted himself up to the top of the fence and peered at Jax's two goons smoking cigarettes under the streetlight. From his jeans pocket, he whipped out a cherry bomb, one-handedly lit the fuse with his lighter, and tossed it at the two men.

The firecracker exploded in midair. The sound ricocheted off the walls of the buildings sounding all the world like a gun shot. He left the men crouched in the gutter, hands over their heads, and hurried back to his angel, sure she'd be gone.

But she wasn't.

The girl poked her head out of the shadows, eyes wide. "You shot them?"

Pharaoh laughed. "No way. Get caught with a gun in this neighborhood, and I'd be tossed in jail." The image of Jax's girl lying in a pool of blood and brains washed over him. Get caught period, and he'd be shut away for life. He grabbed her hand. "Got to move while they're still ducking."

There was something about her hand being in his

that made his whole being sing. Sure there was lust. But there was something more, much more, between them.

He didn't know her name. Didn't know where she'd come from. But he knew this woman. She knew him.

They were like a team. She had no trouble tagging after him, hopping from concrete slab to sand pile, and leaping across barely visible ditches in her ballet flats like some prima donna ballerina.

At the far corner of the lot, he stopped, slipped out his utility knife, and used it to pry up one of the plywood panels.

Sticking his head through the hole, he checked that the street was empty. Then he pulled back in and drew her down. "You'll have to duck through here. And watch the dress. Edge of the board is rough. Then as soon as you're on the other side, make a dash across the street, and stand way back in that doorway."

The girl nodded and crouched down. He yanked the board up with all his strength to make the biggest opening he could, and she whizzed through without a hair or hem touching the jagged edge.

Letting the plywood drop back down, Pharaoh hefted himself over the fence. The girl waved. He crossed over to her, amazed she'd waited, and then they were off again, flying down the street and around the corner, her hand grasped tightly in his.

Five blocks later, he slowed and glanced over his shoulder. Surely, she'd be tired or out of breath, perhaps frightened. But she wasn't. The girl's face looking back at him was suffused with joy. Her breathing came easy, like she could run forever. Laughter bubbled up and out of her. She was enjoying this.

Incredible. Few people could keep up with him. Only T-Crew and a few of the other local graffiti boys. The woman had to be an athlete or a dancer. Or could she be another street artist? He glanced back again and took in her glorious head of raven black hair, the gold medallion round her neck, and the expensive velvet dress. No. No one this elegant, this beautiful, could be a street kid.

The girl halted next to him and rested a hand on his arm. "We're far enough away, don't you think? Slow down already and kiss me."

Pharaoh stared down at her delicious mouth. How could he resist that invitation? He spun her around and clutched her against him. He was going to hell, but first he was going to taste heaven.

Their lips met, and heat exploded through him. He rubbed against her, warning her of his intent, glorying in the feel of her softness against his hardness.

She pressed back. One leg lifted and hooked around his hip, then the other. It was the sexiest thing any woman had ever done to him. Blood fled his brain, pooled in his groin.

He'd resisted her before. Not this time. He needed to be inside her. Hell, he just needed her.

But not here on the street like a hooker. She deserved to be taken with care and gentleness.

"Wait." The word hissed out as if he were being strangled. If he didn't stop her now, he wouldn't be able to. He'd drive into her right here against the wall of the all-night drug store.

He'd give her one more chance. "Are you absolutely sure you want to do this? Be with me?"

Large eyes, the irises black in the dark, peered up at him. "Yes."

It was all he needed to hear. His good intentions dissipated into the river mist, leaving behind a mere whisper of worry.

He lowered her to the pavement and seized her hand. "All right. But not here. Come. We'll go to my place. It's three more blocks."

One night, she'd said. But would one night be enough? He tightened his grip on her hand. Could he let her go come morning?

Chapter 15

By the time they reached Pharaoh's five-story walk up, Toro was having second thoughts. The adrenaline that had filled her with panic and the need to get Kiro out of her system had calmed. All that was left, beneath skin that burned from Pharaoh's touch, was a cold awareness.

There could be no good ending to this. Sooner or later Pharaoh would recognize her. Sooner or later Kiro would make his move. Sooner or later she'd be gone. One way or another.

She shouldn't be leading Pharaoh on. She would break his heart, and only she, in all the world, knew how fragile that organ was.

She watched the muscles of his biceps tense as he unlocked the apartment house door. He was so calm, so strong. Since the moment she'd pulled him off the bridge so many years ago, Pharaoh had been her one point of safety.

He was not a tame man. He was rough and jagged, cut from some primitive mold. He claimed, and he defended. He'd bonded to the street kid Toro, and he would give his life for him. She had no idea what he would do for the reincarnated Alba Vargas.

When the team was tagging, he was their backup, always watchful, always ready to stand up to the gangs that harassed them and the night watchmen with their clubs and the police with their batons. Only Pharaoh had ever been caught and arrested.

He'd taken the fall so that she and the others could get away. And he'd still be rotting in jail, if Bella's brother Ari hadn't gotten him out.

She stared at his face. Like her, his features bore the stamp of many mixes of people. His smooth brown skin spoke of African ancestry. But his slightly slanted eyes, tapered chin, and high cheekbones gave hint to Hispanic and Asian and Native American roots.

Somewhere in his past, one of his ancestors had gifted him with the body of a warrior. Not with the thick muscles of a football player, but with the broad chest of a runner who could race forever, the powerful thighs of an athlete who could climb to the tops of mountains, and the strength of a weightlifter who could heave obstacles out of his way with a single hand.

Whatever he was, there was a feral quality in the way his skin flowed over his muscles and bones and formed the whole of him. She could never get enough of looking at him. She'd sketched and painted his face many times, trying to uncover that essential part of him. Never to capture it.

Yet, she was going to capture him now. Tame him. Make him hers. She placed a hand on his back and felt the muscles clench. Heat from his skin spread through her, warming her fingers and toes, driving away the last of her reservations.

As a guy, she'd had to hide her appreciation, but as a woman she could show him. Her body thrummed with anticipation.

At the same time, fear swam around her belly like a bloodthirsty piranha ready to eat her from the inside out. She had no idea what making love would feel like. Would it feel as good as she imagined? Or would it be the way it had been for her mother, the man thrusting and groaning, her mother whimpering beneath him?

It didn't have to be that way. She'd seen movie love scenes. She'd read romance books. Joining with a man could be fun, exciting.

She touched her lips where Pharaoh had kissed her. It could be more.

She wanted to know that ecstasy once in her life. She rolled her shoulders and followed Pharaoh into the battered entryway with its dirty gray tiles and chipped paint.

He bent over and kissed her on her neck. "Scared?"

She gave him what she hoped was the right kind of smile. The kind a woman looking forward to a one-night-stand would give. "Never of you."

He wrapped an arm around her and led her through the hallway. "Close your eyes and hold your breath. This building is a dump. Ugly and dirty as all get out. Absentee landlord does nothing to keep the place up. But at least the plumbing works." He swiped at her nose. "You can take a shower later. Get the grime off from the construction site."

Toro rubbed her nose where he'd touched it. The image of Pharaoh's wet body pressed to hers started up the heat again. "Sounds good, as long as you join me."

He grinned at her. "I can't wait."

They bounded up the last flight of stairs and burst into his cramped apartment. Toro came to an abrupt halt. In contrast to the decaying building, Pharaoh's rooms, although small, were clean and elegant. Wooden pallets and spools, sanded and varnished to a high gleam, served as coffee and end tables. An old sofa covered with a bright red India print cloth sat to one side. The walls displayed his boldly colored tattoo designs.

But it was the view directly in front of her that took her breath away. Instead of looking out to the river, the window overlooked street art heaven. Down below, building after building sported glorious pieces—mermaids, cats, faces, hands—all done with Pharaoh's characteristic flair.

She spun around. "You painted the graffiti?"

"Huh?" He gave her a strange look. "I'm a tattoo artist."

Damn, she'd slipped up. Toro bit her lip. "Ah, a tattoo artist." She extended a finger and traced the twin snakes twining up his lower arm. "These your designs?"

He drew in a ragged breath at her touch. "Yes. I drew the artwork, but my mentor tatted them for me."

She rested her hand on his arm. "I'd love you to ink me."

Pharaoh closed the door and leaned back against it. "Maybe someday. When I have my own place. So I could do my best work." He lifted her hand and turned it over, exposing the wrist. "I'd put a heart right here." He kissed the spot. "And here." He kissed the inside of her elbow. "And—"

She pulled away. She had a tattoo. One she didn't want him to see. She spun around and walked over to examine one of the designs on the wall. It was a masterful rendition of a rising phoenix. "You're going to strike out on your own?"

He came up behind her. "It's just a dream. But

136

someday, if I ever get enough money, I plan on leaving New York and heading somewhere south. Somewhere warm. Somewhere near the ocean. Somewhere I can kick my feet in the sand and breathe."

Toro pretended to study the design. She'd never heard Pharaoh talk of a future. Of having plans. It gave her hope. "You ever been down south?"

"Yeah, when I was a little kid. My mom and my aunts took the family to Florida. We crowded into some cheap-rate hotel. But it was near the ocean. There was something about swimming in the sea—like you became a part of it."

She understood what he meant. She felt the same way about diving into the turquoise blue water of the Mediterranean Sea surrounding Eudokia.

"So you like that tattoo?"

Toro tossed her head back. She'd been staring at the design too long. "You've got a real eye for beauty."

Pharaoh put his hands on her shoulders and turned her around. He tipped his head, his gaze running over her. "I think I do. You are the most beautiful woman I've ever seen."

Her? Beautiful? The idea was so preposterous she almost stuck out her tongue, the way Toro would have. But in this moment, she wasn't a street kid, she was a seductress.

She didn't put much stock in outer beauty. Claude was handsome; so was Kiro. But inside they were ugly and rotten as the rubbish in a garbage bin. But seeing Pharaoh's appreciation made her pulse speed up. She gave what she hoped was a sexy shake and moved toward him.

"Angel," he whispered in a voice rich with hunger.

Suddenly he lifted her up and carried her through a short, narrow hallway and into what had to be his bedroom. It smelled rich and dark like him.

She barely had a minute to take in the bold black and red geometric shapes painted on the walls and the huge mattress on the floor, before she was laid in a soft nest of pure white sheets and comforters.

She stared up. Above her, an amazing map of Williamsburg as seen from the rooftops spread out in a circle from the bare light bulb in the middle of the ceiling. She felt dizzy, as if she'd been flipped upside-down, and the world she knew was suspended from the heavens, and she was floating on a cloud.

"Do you like it?" The mattress tipped as Pharaoh knelt next to her. Her eyes met his, and the ceiling didn't matter anymore. Only him.

She smacked her lips. "Yeah."

He feathered his fingers along the hem of her dress. "You are so beautiful." He slipped the velvety cloth higher. Cool air brushed her thighs.

She pinched her legs together. "What are you doing?"

"Getting ready to make you beg for mercy."

The tone of his voice was so like his taunts when they arm wrestled or when he challenged her Toro-self to a race that she let her legs fall open as he lifted her skirt higher.

He nodded his approval. "That's my angel. Relax, and let me take you to heaven."

With his other hand, he ran his fingertips up her calf, and then along the inside of her thigh, coming so close to where she throbbed with need, she had to bite down on her tongue to keep from begging.

138

His fingers found her silly lace panties, worked under the leg band, and brushed the curls between her legs. For a moment, embarrassment swept over her, and then he touched her again. The blood pounding through her slowed. All sense of time and self-consciousness fled.

Everything centered on that spot, his slow-moving fingers stirring up currents of desire that zipped through her like an electrical current and settled in that place between her legs that throbbed and ached—the place she'd kept hidden for years, always pretending, always making sure the other guys didn't see her pee, didn't know when she had her period.

The part of her that made her like her mother—vulnerable.

The thought made her want to snap her legs closed and wiggle out from under him. But it was too late. His finger was already there swirling, pressing, and circling. Against that slow, steady rhythm, she could no more move than she could stop painting.

All she could do was focus on the sensation of gentle invasion as his questing finger slipped inside the place that made her a woman and touched her there.

He leaned over until his lips were a breath from hers. "You are so wet for me. So ready. I am going to eat you up, my angel, my wild, passionate angel. My mouth is going to devour you until nothing is left, but the bright shining essence of you."

And she believed him.

He was no longer Pharaoh, untrustworthy tattoo artist. She was no longer Toro, girl masquerading as boy. They were starry-eyed lovers in some fairy tale kingdom.

Whatever happened was meant to be.

"But first, I need to see you, all of you." With an acrobat's controlled agility, he straddled her, balancing his weight on his knees, and slowly rucked up her dress.

His clever fingers followed the slinky velvet as it tugged over her hips and bottom and skimmed across her tummy. Then he was lifting her shoulders and sliding the fabric up and off, tossing it away.

Eyes darkened with masculine hunger, he peered down at her. He slid his hands under her breasts. His thumbs brushed across the thin lace of the bra. Her mouth fell open. Her head tipped back, and she moaned as he slipped his fingers inside the lace and swept his callused thumbs across her nipples. Over and over, his fingers flicked and teased until she could barely draw breath. Then he pinched each one.

It was like he'd lit a fuse inside her. Her body arched off the bed. Blood pounded in her ears and heat flamed between her legs.

Before she could draw breath, he unhooked her bra and tossed it over his shoulder.

Pharaoh leaned down and took her nipple in his mouth. She let out a little squeak.

He whispered in her ear. "Perfect. Do you know how perfect you are, angel? You are everything a man could want."

He lowered his head and licked her bare nipples as his hands moved lower. Every lick sent a tremble through her body. Every almost-nip of his teeth sent waves of heat radiating outward to every part of her. Every brush of his clothing against her naked skin sent white hot heat racing along her skin.

She strained up against his firm muscular torso,

frustrated he was still clothed. She wanted more. Needed more.

She peered into his eyes, so dark and black and bottomless it was like looking right into the core of him.

This wasn't the haunted man who'd followed her lead in T-Crew. This man was commanding and strong, an expert on women's bodies, but also warm and alive, gentle and loving, and oh how she was going to hurt him when he found out who she really was.

But she couldn't help herself. She twisted her hands into his hair and let the pleasure he was giving her carry her worries away.

He licked her nipples again. Blew on one and then the other. Then licked again. She let out a soft breath of air. "I love your mouth on me."

He pushed up on an elbow and grinned at her. "Do you now?" He sat back and hooked his thumbs in the waistband of her panties and rolled them down and off. He nudged her thighs farther apart. "I bet you'll like this even more." He looked down.

She was suddenly aware he could see every inch of her. The intimate feminine places she had never seen herself lay open to him.

Could he tell she was a virgin? She brought her legs back together.

He lifted his head and eyed her. "Uh-uh. Come now. Let me see you, angel."

Toro forced herself to keep her arms still at her sides as his hands slid between her thighs. Chill air swept in. She squeezed her eyes shut. Now he would do what men did to women. In out, in out, and it would be over.

Instead, the mattress shifted under her and suddenly the warmth of his mouth was there—licking and sucking her most private places, doing the same amazing things he'd done to her breasts.

"Wait, no." She put a hand on his shoulder and tried to wiggle away.

"Oh no, you don't." He tightened the grip on her thighs and smiled at her. "You said you liked my mouth on you."

"But—"

He raised an eyebrow and gave her a curious look like a puzzle he didn't quite understand. "Has no one ever kissed you here?"

"No." Women took men into their mouths. She'd come upon a hooker doing it to a john in an alley once. A blow job. The guys talked about it like it was the Holy Grail of sex. But she never imagined any man wanting to do that to a woman.

He scrounged around the bedcovers and found her underwear. He gathered the flimsy piece of lace in his hand and held it to his nose.

"What the hell are you doing?" She grabbed for the panties. "That's—that's—disgusting."

He batted her hand away. "It's wonderful. Learning the smell of you. The taste of you. Storing it away. Imprinting it on my brain. It's what smart men do who care about their lovers."

Her mind scrambled to make sense of what he'd said. Lovers? It was the second time he'd used that word.

He mustn't think this meant more than a quick bedding—a night of good sex with a stranger. "We're not lovers." It hurt to say the words. He'd been her fantasy lover too long.

"Not yet." Still laughing, Pharaoh lowered his mouth to her tender folds and licked lightly. It was the barest of touches, but so warm and soft and wet, she melted into a puddle of want.

He made a noise of male satisfaction and licked again, this time deeper with a twist at the end, and then he did it again and again in an increasingly fast rhythm that mirrored the speeding up of her heart. With each lick, ripples of pleasure spread up and outward until even the tips of her fingers tingled.

Suddenly, he reached up and pinched her nipple. She shattered.

Sparks exploded behind her eyes and waves of pleasure rippled through her body over and over until she floated limp and weightless, her head a whirl of lights and colors. Her breath coming in short gasps.

It was the most exhilarating feeling in the world. A feeling of lightness. Of floating. Of ultimate release from the bounds of everyday existence.

The only thing holding her in place was the strong, lithe body of the man who'd given her this heavenly gift.

She let the last waves of pleasure roll over her. If this was sex, she wanted it all the time. She opened her eyes to thank him.

But Pharaoh was busy stripping off his tee and shucking his jeans. His hard cock sprang free. She'd seen him naked when he'd lived at the apartment with T-Crew. The guys had little sense of modesty. But she'd never seen any man fully erect. He was huge. Magnificent. And he would never fit.

He tore open a condom packet with his teeth and

then slipped the rubber on with practiced skill. At least, he knew what to do. She hadn't even thought of the consequences.

She couldn't have a baby. Not now. Not when she was failing her brother at this very moment.

Hanger—he'd been far from her thoughts again. Here she was having a good time while he could be in torment or dead. The thought drove the last of the pleasure from her veins.

She gazed into Pharaoh's eyes and saw the need and want and hesitation and knew she could never deny him her body. Not after he'd taken her to heaven.

How hard could it be? Men and women had sex all the time. They had to fit.

He'd be done in minutes, and she could get on with her search. She let out the breath she'd been holding and held out her arms. "Come."

Pharaoh climbed over her and straddled her, the sharp planes of his face soft in the dawn light streaming through the window. He must have picked up on her chill because he curled over and kissed her belly button. Then he ran his tongue up her abdomen and around one nipple, then across and up and around the other.

It was like he had switched on a heater. Fire followed his tongue. By the time he reached her neck and whispered in her ear, "You sure you want *me*?" she could only nod in answer.

He drew back and stared down at her. "I want you to be very sure. Because once I start, I won't be able to stop. And I won't be able to give you up. I want you that much." His erection rested hard and long against her stomach. "Say it."

"Yes. I want you."

"No regrets?"

"No. Never." Toro rested her palm against the hawk tattoo that covered his broad chest. Her hand rose and fell in time with the beat of his heart.

Pharaoh was thought cold and hard—Cooler Man.

Well, he was hard all right, but there wasn't anything cold about him. He was heat. He was fire. He was lightning.

He was hers.

He nudged her legs open with his knees, positioned himself at her opening and drove in. It was like being impaled by a burning rod of steel. She bit her lip to keep from crying out, but a small gasp escaped.

Pharaoh stilled and tipped his head forward, the strain visible on his face. He peered into her eyes. "Shit, angel. Am I your first?"

She nodded.

He licked his lips, the muscle along his jaw trembling. "I am most honored. But you might have said. I would have—ah, hell—I would have taken more care."

"If you can't—"

"Hush. I'll do my best to make it good for you. Just never had a virgin before."

He pulled back, almost all the way out and then slid back in again more slowly. It still burned, but then he did it again, and little by little, the wonderful heat came back, building at the spot where he rubbed against her.

It went on and on until she was lost in the rhythm, until her gasps matched his, until her hips rocked in concert, until her whole body hummed.

"That's my girl." He leaned his weight on one arm

and found her nub with the fingers of his other hand.

She peered up at him through her eyelashes. Sweat glistened on his shoulders. The muscles in his arms flexed with the strain. He was the most enchanting thing in the world. He was her prince. And she loved him. Always had and always would.

And then she was convulsing again, her inner muscles quivering around him, sparks flickering on the edges of her vision. He pulled in a breath, moved faster, and then with a groan, fell limp on top of her.

For a minute, she feared he was dead. Then he rolled to his side, draped his arm across her stomach, whispered, "Mine" and collapsed into sleep.

Toro sat up and peered down at this amazing man. She loved him. But the feeling growing inside her chest was more. So much more.

She wanted to be with this man forever, licking him, tasting him, doing the things to him he had done to her. Sleeping the night with him by her side. Laughing together. Dancing across the rooftops. Being their real selves. Becoming true lovers.

But it could never be. She slipped off the mattress, then leaned down and pulled the sheets up and over him. She regretted she would not get that shower with him, another chance to hold and touch. But it was better to leave now. Disappear from his life.

She would go back to being good old buddy Toro until she had to flee the country or until Kiro did her in.

"I love you, Pharaoh." She bent down and kissed him on the cheek. If she were lucky, he'd never know who his mysterious angel was.

She pushed up off the mattress and set about retrieving her clothes. She'd had her fun. Now it was time to focus on finding her brother.

Chapter 16

Hanger opened one eye, caught sight of Shark Tooth in the doorway and closed it again. He so didn't want to be in this place. He wanted to be home. He wanted Toro.

He squinted through his lashes. But what he wanted didn't matter. One wrist was handcuffed to a metal bedframe, and his leg was throbbing with pain. He was trapped but good.

"Our little guy waking up?" Kiro's voice had that wheedling tone Hanger knew too well. It meant something bad was going to happen—to him.

A soft feminine hand pressed against his brow. "Still feverish."

"Step back, Cami."

Cold water splashed over Hanger's face, and he came up choking. "Hey." The sudden movement made the room spin. His head rattled, and his stomach verged on the threshold of upchucking. If he hadn't known he was in Kiro's dump, and his leg wasn't as hot as a burning balloon ready to pop, he'd have sworn he was on the Soaring Eagle rollercoaster over at Luna Park.

Shark Tooth approached the bed and loomed over him. "I've been trying to decide what to do with you, Mr. Escape Artist. But maybe the decision will be taken out of my hands." He rested his palm on Hanger's infected thigh and slowly pressed down.

A ball of fire shot through him. Hanger couldn't hold back his groan. "Stop. Please."

Kiro lifted his hand. "A please from the Deco Boy. Will wonders never end?" He raised an eyebrow. "I should let you die for all the trouble you've caused me, and the damage you've done to my cars."

"Not *your* cars," Hanger hissed. "You stole them."

Kiro slapped his thigh.

Pain shot through him. His whole body shook.

"Now as I was saying before I was interrupted, I should let you die of that infection. I would enjoy watching your flesh rot away. However, I think it might stink the place up. So I have a deal for you. Do what I say, and I'll give you antibiotics." He laughed. "I think it's a neat twist, don't you? Usually, people I deal with want other kinds of drugs—the kind that kill. You're going to work for the kind that saves lives. So what do you say, Deco Boy? Like the idea? Or do you prefer to die?"

Hanger peered up at the man through teary eyes. He had to say yes as much as he hated the man. Hated being trapped.

He remembered the stupid quote he'd seen in one of the homeless shelters he'd stayed in when his mother was alive. The poster showed a garden of brilliantly colored flowers looking out of place on the dingy wall and proclaimed in curlicue letters: Where there's life, there's hope.

He'd thought it the stupidest thing he'd ever heard. Standing in line with stinky drunks, spaced-out addicts, and twitchy bag ladies, he hadn't had much hope in his life at the time.

But he'd hold on to the idea of hope now. It would

take about five days for the antibiotics to fix his leg, and then—he'd escape again.

He might even be able to swipe the bottle of pills and take off sooner when he felt a little better. He swallowed the bile in the back of his throat. He hoped Kiro didn't ask him to do something he'd regret the rest of his life before he could get out of this hellhole.

He croaked out his answer with all the sarcastic politeness he could muster from his shaking body. "Yes, Mr. Kiro, sir."

Shark Tooth gave him a wide smile revealing the four filed-to-a-point top teeth he only revealed when he was slumming. "Good boy." He turned to the tiny Asian woman hovering in the background. "Cami, yank down his pants and give him his shot."

"Shot?" Hanger shifted back on the bed.

"That's what we deal in down here. Nice sharp needles. And rarely do they deliver antibiotics." Kiro bared his teeth. "Do you well to remember *that.*"

The woman padded over and grabbed the back of Hanger's sweats. He tugged them back and glared at Kiro. "You watching?"

"Worried a skinny boy's butt excites me?" He signaled the woman to proceed. "Relax, Deco Boy. I'm into girls. In fact, I think I've found the woman I'm going to marry. Yes indeed, proposed yesterday. I'm waiting for her answer, and I'm pretty sure she's going to say yes."

"Proposed?" Hanger said, looking over his shoulder just as Cami jabbed the needle in. He winced and bit his tongue to keep from yelling.

"Such bravery, Deco Boy."

Hanger yanked up his sweats and glared at Shark

Tooth. "Who'd marry you—the Fanged Bat from Hell?"

"Gonna have to do something about that nasty mouth of yours." Kiro sat down on the edge of the bed and placed his hand on Hanger's swollen thigh. He rubbed it up and down. Hanger hissed through his teeth.

"So sore. Too bad penicillin takes a while to work, isn't it? But so handy for me to get your complete attention." He nodded to the woman who was packing up what appeared to be a briefcase full of medicine bottles and syringes. "Leave, Cami. Come back and give him another shot in four hours. Bring a guard with you."

The woman gathered her case up and scurried from the room. Kiro rose and closed the door. "Nice and private. Now let me tell you about my soon-to-be-bride. I think you might know her."

****

Pharaoh scowled at the back of the goon leading him down the hallway of the old hotel. He should be out searching for Hanger, not here in this dump answering Jax's summons.

He glanced down the corridor with its line of doors. It was a brothel. It had to be. He could smell old cooking oil and the stink garbage got when it was kept too long. But underneath was the sickly sweetness of cheap cologne and men's sweat.

He caught up to the hulking man striding ahead of him. "I still don't know why the tat couldn't be done at G-Man's. This is totally unsanitary."

"Shut up." The goon turned a corner into an even darker hallway, only one overhead lightbulb working. He kicked open the first door to the right, grabbed

Pharaoh's arm, and shoved him forward. "In you go. Jax will explain everything."

Pharaoh peeled the man's hand off him and stepped inside.

Jax lay sprawled on a worn sofa, clasping a naked girl against his bare chest. The room smelled of sex and drugs. The murdering bastard waved his hand. "Sit."

Pharaoh surveyed the dingy room, found a partially broken folding chair, spun it around, and sat.

He stared at the girl. She was small-boned and dark-haired. For a moment, he thought it was his savior from the bridge, and his heart jumped. Then she raised her head.

The girl was beautiful, but she wasn't his angel. The nose was longer, the lips thinner, and the eyes those of a scared doe. She was the color of milky chai, long-legged with perfect little toes. She wore nothing more than panties and a skin-tight halter top that clung to her high full breasts.

She was everything a man might lust for. Any other man. Not him. He dreamed of his no longer virgin angel, disappeared into the dawn.

Jax ran a finger down the girl's cheek. "Like what you see." It wasn't a question.

Pharaoh's stomach clenched into a ball of agony. Not another girl he'd have to watch die. He pressed his ankle against the chair leg, the hidden knife in his sock a hard lump, and weighed his chances. He might take out Jax with the tiny blade, but he'd never get past the bodyguard outside the door or all the other ones they'd passed on their way up. Still, he'd save her if he could.

Jax tipped his chin and grinned. "You won't need the toy knife. All you have to do is put that tattoo over there on her butt." He bent his head at the sketch on the side table. G-Man's work. Ugly as hell.

Pharaoh gripped the chair back tighter. "Could have done it at the shop."

"Too public. No one gets to see this butt." He chucked the girl under the chin. "Right, sweetheart?"

"Yes, Jaxy baby," she simpered.

Jax stood up. "In the next room you will find a complete tattoo studio. All nice and sanitary. G-Man set it up to your *high* standards. Even brought your kit over. From now on, you will be working here, not at G-Man's. Full time."

"G-Man's was a part-time thing. My full-time gig is at The Siren."

"Quit."

"But—"

"Oh, my dear boy, don't be a fool. Maybe your own life doesn't matter much to you. Maybe a murder charge doesn't worry you. But you wouldn't want anything happening to The Siren and—what's her name—the pregnant tattoo artist? That's right—Bella Bell. And there's her husband—poor man's got a big target on him. Vernon Newell left a lot of people high and dry when he dropped out of the game.

"You want them to stay a happy couple, enjoy their upcoming stork delivery—you follow my orders." He pulled the girl up off the coach. "Because if you don't, I'll kill you first, and then I will kill thcm. Now, strip down to the undies and get to work. You have a customer waiting."

****

Several hours later, Pharaoh threw down his tat machine and pulled off his plastic gloves. Jax and the girl might be gone, but the horror of what he'd done would never leave.

He slammed one fist into the wall and then the other. Over and over, until his knuckles were bloody and plaster dust filled the room.

The damage he'd wreaked on that girl's body would rot his soul forever. It hadn't just been her butt Jax wanted tatted. He'd tatted the man's name on her wrist and her neck and the sensitive spot on her pubic bone.

After one hour, the girl had been writhing in pain which had only excited the bastard who sat in the side chair watching every run of the needle with an eagle eye.

Every time he'd asked to stop and have her come back for another session, Jax had added another tattoo. Dark, heavy, ugly tattoos that would be hell to cover over.

Pharaoh pressed his bleeding hands flat on the tatting stand. Never in all the months he'd been tattooing had they shaken like this. His ability to create incredible skin art had been his only source of pride.

Now he knew his skill could be warped into ugliness, his hands capable of cruelty. Now he understood why Bella's brother had cut off his fingers when he'd accidently killed that athlete.

He held his hands up in front of him. If he still had his knife, he might do the same. But he'd been stripped down to his underwear, his clothes and shoes and cellphone carried away before he was allowed to touch the girl.

He stood up and checked the door to the hall. Still locked. He wandered into the bathroom and washed his face and hands, used the toilet, and then returned to the room to wait.

Jax would be back, and then he'd be turned free again. Only he would never be free.

The creepy bastard had threatened the people he cared about—Bella and Vernon. He went over to the window and peered through the blind slats. There were no bars on the window, but he was as trapped as if there were.

He'd betrayed Bella once. He'd never do it again. If that meant he followed Jax's orders and tattooed these women, then that's what he'd do.

He turned away from the window. If he could lull Jax into thinking he was settled in, he might get away doing the tats with cheap ink so they'd fade eventually.

And no matter what, he would keep looking for Hanger. In fact, being one of Jax's thugs probably gave him an advantage. People would be more likely to talk to someone who had friends like the two goons who'd escorted him here.

Then somehow, after he'd found Hanger and delivered him safely to Toro, he'd put an end to it all, even if he had to commit murder to do so.

The doorknob turned, and the door slammed opened. A hulking goon tossed his clothes at him. "Jax said you can leave so you can dump your tattoo job. But he expects you back by midnight with all your gear. Must like you. He's given you your own private room. Right next to mine." He clamped a hand on Pharaoh's shoulder and squeezed hard. "Name's Bear. We're going to be best buddies, you and I. Heard you like to drink."

****

155

By the time Pharaoh cancelled all his appointments, left his resignation and key to The Siren on Bella's counter, and lastly gathered up his belongings, he definitely needed a drink.

He climbed to the second floor of the Sunset Palace Hotel where Jax's men were lodged and hefted his stuff into the bedroom he'd been assigned.

He glanced around. This set of interconnected rooms must have once been the honeymoon suite. The pink sunken tub in the bathroom was a dead giveaway.

No self-respecting newlyweds would stay in the place now. The once red and white heart-and-flower wallpaper was stained, the plasterwork on the ceiling cracked, and the bed sway-backed.

And if that didn't turn potential lovebirds off, the clientele would. He'd gotten a good glimpse of the people checking in. The place served the dregs. Johns and hookers looking for a private quickie, an occasional lost foreign tourist fooled by the word Palace in the name. Then there were the thugs working for Jax, and now him—the resident tattoo torturer.

He rubbed his hands down his face. Time to pretend to settle into his new life. Pharaoh tucked his pack under the bed and kicked his suitcase into the closet. He'd brought nothing of value.

He'd been in many flop houses after he left home and took up residence on the streets. This hotel was no different. It had the same stink of despair and violence. The kind of place where nothing was sacred. The kind of place where your best friend would kill you in your sleep for a half-drunk bottle of rotgut.

He glanced through the open door. His new roommates, Goon One and Goon Two—better known

156

as Bear and Pitstop—sat in a haze of cigarette smoke, watching a football game on a TV that had to be from the 80s.

So far the two men had been friendly enough, slapping him on the back as if he were actually one of them. Pharaoh punched his fist into the mattress. Hell, he *was* one of them.

The vision of the bullet blasting the girl's head open at G-Man's ripped through him. He may not have pulled the trigger, but he'd killed her just the same.

Everything he touched turned to ruin. The angel he'd kissed on the bridge. Innocent. Lovely. She'd been Toro's—a virgin, for heaven's sake—and he drove his cock into her anyway. Didn't matter she'd said yes. Didn't matter he'd taught her pleasure. That had been Toro's role to play.

He should never have touched her with his traitorous, filthy hands. And now the lives of Bella and Vernon and their unborn child were at risk because of him.

Damn it. He was a bastard as vile and immoral as these hired thugs. He belonged here.

He shut the door, noticing with unease the deadbolt was on the outside, and lay down on the bed. But he couldn't sleep. Every time he closed his eyes he saw his angel. He relived their kisses, the curves of her body, the pure bliss of being inside her as she gasped in pleasure.

The door flew open. Bear yelled in, "There's a card game going on in the next room. Plenty to drink. Big Boss sent over a case of whiskey to celebrate his impending marriage. You coming?"

Pharaoh stood up and rubbed his hands down his

157

jeans. Getting blotto sounded about right. Maybe if he drank himself into oblivion until he couldn't see straight, Jax wouldn't trust him tattooing anyone.

Wait a minute. The pimp was getting married? He caught up with the guy. "Did you say Jax is tying the knot?"

Bear's shoulder butted into him. "Jax? No way, man. Big Boss is. Calls himself Kiro, but he's some bastard lawyer. Owns everything around here."

Every part of Pharaoh's body went on alert. "Kiro? Kiro Tuccio?"

"Yeah. That's him." His new buddy opened the door to the next room. "This place is his. Jax says he'll be checking you out later. You being a new hire and all." He turned back and gave him a wink. "But don't you worry. Kind of a wimp. Nothing like his brother. Vernon Newell was one of us. Grew up bad. All that lawyer education turned this Kiro's brain to mush. Needs us guys around to handle the dirty stuff.

"Heard you did a great ink job by the way. If you have Jax's approval, you'll do okay. And the pay's better than anything out on the street. In fact, if I win a bundle here, maybe you can do me a tat or two. A big snarling bear. My buddies will want one, too. Having our own resident tattoo artist, how smooth is that?" Bear poked his elbow into Pharaoh's arm. "You'll make out like a bandit here, bro. Just mind the bosses."

Pharaoh followed the bruiser from one smoked-fogged room into another. He headed straight to the coffee table, where mostly empty whiskey bottles were lined up like soldiers. He poured himself a glass and swallowed it down. It was cheap stuff and burned from his tongue to his stomach.

He filled the tumbler again. But this time he didn't drink it. Thoughts bombarded his head. Thoughts didn't want to be having. Kiro Tuccio ran this operation?

He didn't think Kiro knew who he was. If he did know him, then all bets were off. But if he didn't? This could be his chance to find out what happened to Hanger.

In fact—he glanced over at the men huddled around the rickety card table—this might be the perfect time to do a little detective work of his own.

Chapter 17

The gray light coming through the high windows of The Foundry was perfect for close work. Toro stepped back and examined the area she had repainted. There. All identifying tag marks that would lead to T-Crew were removed. All the images of Pharaoh erased.

She glanced over her shoulder. The shipping crew was due to arrive any second to take her paintings to Kiro's. They would meet there, she'd oversee the uncrating and the hanging of the artworks, and then Kiro was taking her to dinner. "To celebrate," he'd said. But what he really wanted was her answer to his proposal.

Her stomach clenched so tight she struggled to breathe. Weaseling her way close to Shark Man was probably a stupid idea, but Hanger had been missing three days now, and she was getting desperate.

The police were still considering it a runaway case—one among thousands. Vernon could find out nothing, and Pharaoh, despite his promises to help, had quit The Siren and disappeared.

She'd finally gone to Ari's lawyer, Walter Hanlin, and asked him to hire a PI. But the detective was tracking down leads they'd already followed, and she dared not mention Kiro to him.

The crime lord would eat the poor man alive.

No. Kiro was hers to deal with. He had her

brother—she was sure of it—and she was going to dig it out of him even if she had to marry him in order to get close enough to put a knife to his neck. But first, she'd try picking his pockets and snitching his cellphone. With access to his contacts and e-mail, she'd have people to question and places to search.

She looked down at her dress. She'd used some of the prize money and splurged on this one. It was cream chiffon and floated around her like butterfly wings. It even matched her new ballet slippers.

She hiked up the off-the-shoulder top. She almost liked it—from the front.

But she hadn't chosen it for the front. Rather for the back, which plunged so low it made wearing even the stupid, skimpy underwear impossible.

Kiro might be a bastard, but he was also a man. She gave another twirl. Yep, no question about it. This dress would draw the Shark in very close. Very close indeed.

There was a knock on the door, and she shook off the shiver inching down her spine and hurried to answer it.

The shipping company crew stood waiting. She let them in and moved back to let the packers do their job. They'd already picked up the three works from the museum. All they had left to do was crate up the one on the wall.

The men were professionals. In minutes, the rooftop scene was lowered into its packing crate, hammers banged in the nails, and her last painting was moving out of The Foundry and into the panel truck.

She trailed along after them. Today, she was going to let herself be courted in this farce of a whirlwind romance. And she was going to let Shark Man propose again and she was going to say yes and see what happened next.

She stopped to pull the door closed, then turned and ran directly into a hard body.

"There you are, my darling." It was Kiro. He bowed and handed her a single red rose.

No one had ever given her a flower before. She had no idea what to do with it.

He picked up her hand and rubbed the smudge of paint on her thumb. "You've been painting? In that dress?" His face broke into a straight-lipped smile so predatory her insides clenched again.

But she couldn't show fear—not if she wanted to save her brother.

She extracted her hand. "You like it?" She gave a whirl like she'd seen models do on TV. The chiffon floated down around her.

"Love it. Now let's go." He took the rose from her, tucked it behind her ear, and then looped his arm in hers and guided her to the curb.

Toro slowed. "Wait. My purse."

"Don't need it. You're under my total care this evening."

"But I thought we were going to your place. I'll have to have my tape measure to hang the paintings straight." And her emergency escape kit. Her cell. Her cherry bomb. Her knife.

"Claude's there. He'll take care of it. We are going to be eating on the terrace at Jean-Georges. Very French. Have you been there?"

Toro shook her head. Her idea of a fancy meal was getting a slice of pizza at Forinino's and actually sitting in one of their booths to eat it instead of gobbling it down out on the sidewalk.

"Good. I am so going to love showing you the finer side of life."

The red convertible outside the graffiti-covered fence was low and sporty-looking. Toro narrowed her eyes, looking for a splatter of spray paint. But the highly-polished finish was as pristine as if it had just rolled off the showroom floor.

Kiro helped her into the passenger seat and went around to the other side. "It's a lovely spring evening. I thought you'd like the top down." He started the engine and zipped out into the traffic headed toward the bridge. "So tell me a little about yourself. Have you always lived here in Brooklyn?"

The Williamsburg Bridge loomed in front of them. "Yes."

Actually, according to her birth certificate, she'd been born in Seattle, Washington. But she didn't believe it. No matter how hard she tried, she couldn't imagine her frail, half-crazed mother finding her way across the country with a baby in her arms.

Kiro merged onto the bridge and stepped on the gas.

Toro looked up as they whizzed under the crown tag Hanger had put on the crosspiece and felt her stomach twitch. She was doing this for him.

Then they were beneath the place where Pharaoh had almost jumped and racing past the abandoned cement restroom where he'd kissed her. She swallowed down a sigh. If only the two of them had been born in a different world—one where she had been a princess, and he'd been a prince. One where wishes came true.

And then they were in Manhattan, coming off the bridge and heading uptown. Kiro spun the wheel to the left and yelled at a biker he'd nearly hit. He zoomed through a red light, swerving in and out of the stop-and-go city traffic like an Indy racer.

She'd ridden in buses. She'd ridden on subways. She'd ridden in taxis. But sitting low to the ground, the wind whistling past her, and a crazy man driving, terrified her.

Toro grasped the seat edge as the car careened around a corner. What had she been thinking, getting in a vehicle with him? The man drove like a demon possessed. She'd be lucky to arrive at the restaurant in one piece.

****

By the time they arrived at Trump Tower, her heart was beating wildly, her knuckles bone-white. Kiro tossed the keys to the doorman and came around to open her car door. "Sorry, I couldn't show what the Spyder can really do. Someday I'll take you out to the race track and we'll press it up to its top speed." He took her hand. "Why, you're trembling. Come here, darling. Let me warm you up."

Toro didn't want to be near him or anyone. She wanted to run away from him as far and as fast as she could. But this was what she'd needed—to have him close enough so she could slip her hand inside his jacket and lift his phone. She steeled her back and moved closer, praying he didn't hear her heart thumping or feel her fingers searching.

She brushed up against him, her hand trailing down his lapel, her thumb slipping beneath the silky fabric.

"Oooh, my sweet. There will be plenty of time to

164

explore each other later." He yanked her against him, trapping her hand against the heat of his body, and then kissed her brow. "No frowns, my dear. Now come. I have a treat planned for you. Have you ever had Yellowfin Tuna Tartare? It's one of my favorites."

****

By the time the meal was finished, Toro had a good idea why the yellow fish thing was Shark Man's favorite—the fish was raw.

She glanced around. The elegantly dressed diners were a reprise from the art exhibit. Same stiff-necked men. Same simpering women. Same turtle slowness.

Two couples had actually come up to talk to her about her artwork. If Kiro hadn't demanded all her paintings, she could have sold them ten times over. Her dream of a successful career as a fine artist could have come true.

Now, once she found Hanger, she'd have to run and hide. She'd never be able to sell her work in New York City—probably not anywhere.

She put down her fork. No use pretending she was eating.

"You don't like it?" Kiro's slick voice cut into her.

She lifted a shoulder and gave him a small truth. "I'm not used to all this."

He reached across and covered her hand with his. "But you will be. Just give it time. Here—let me order you dessert. You like chocolate?"

"Sure." Chocolate she should be able to handle.

Kiro crooked a finger, and a waiter appeared. He whispered something, then turned back to her. He tilted his head to one side and then the other. "You fascinate me, Miss Vargas."

"Why?"

"Such amazing talent to spring from nowhere."

"I had lessons."

"Did you? There's no record of you studying at the Brooklyn Museum or the League. No record anywhere of an art student named Alba Vargas. I had my law clerk check. You're a little liar, sweetheart."

Toro's stomach cramped. The mouthful of food she'd eaten turned to a hard, indigestible ball.

She ran her fingers over the white cotton tablecloth. "I'm self-taught. But I couldn't say that on the Young Artists application. I wouldn't have won without some kind of art background."

"And you like winning?"

"Yeah. Who doesn't?"

His mouth spread into a wide grin, so wide she could see the edges of the tooth cover he wore. "You are perfect."

"Huh?"

"I was stunned when I first saw you standing there next to Claude. So petite, so nervous, so totally innocent. Those little ballet slippers and the graceful way you moved, like an escapee from the New York City Ballet Company. But when I discovered you are a living, breathing, talking lie, I was smitten. You and I are a perfect match. I'm not what I seem either." He reached into his coat pocket and drew out the ring he'd tried to give her before. The huge diamond flashed in the light streaming in the window from Central Park. "Marry me, Miss Nobody."

Toro blinked. She'd resolved to do this. But what if he didn't have Hanger? What if she couldn't escape him? She was looking at one of the most powerful crime lords on the East Coast.

She pressed the tips of her fingers together. He was right; she was a nobody. And that was her secret weapon.

Nobodies were experts at hiding. Nobodies knew how to disappear. But it wouldn't be easy. If she married him, she'd have to kiss him. Let him touch her. Let him have sex with her.

A shiver formed deep inside. He already knew she was not who she pretended to be. Could she forget this marriage farce, and just ask him outright about Hanger?

She flattened her spine against the chair back and peered into his eyes. Despite his proclaimed love, the eyes looking back at her were hard and calculating.

No. If he did have Hanger, he would have another way to twist her to his will. She needed to catch him at a disadvantage. Marriage, or at least the prelude to marriage, might be the only way to do that.

Pharaoh had fallen asleep after sex. Maybe Shark Man did, too.

His hand snaked across the table and trapped her fingers in his. "I gave you time to think. You agreed to this dinner. You gave me hope. Now please don't embarrass me in front of all these people. Cole Tuccio is known for his amazing powers of persuasion."

She glanced out of the corner of her eye. People at the tables around them were gazing at them, smiles on their faces. The waiter stood to one side holding a white plate with four splashes of chocolate. She opened her mouth, but the words stuck.

He was a shark. She was a minnow. Could she really escape him?

Kiro's smile grew even larger. "Oh, my dear girl.

I'm offering you a life of wealth and privilege. I am gearing up my run for political office. I want you by my side. The people will love you—my little dark-skinned gypsy bride. My artist. My wife. My very grateful lover."

He turned her hand over, exposing her palm, and ran a finger along the lifeline. "Say yes or these beautiful hands will never paint another stroke. Alba Vargas, my little Miss Nobody, if you disappear, never to be seen again—who would know or care?"

Toro's heart stopped and then started up again, blood thrumming in her ears, thoughts racing through her head. She'd underestimated the man. Forgotten he was a cruel, ruthless killer.

She'd been so worried about Hanger, she'd neglected to protect herself.

She'd left the purse with all her defenses in it behind. She had no knife, no cherry bomb, no money. Still, she was not the innocent creature he thought she was.

El Toro could give him the slip. He'd never find her once she took to the roofs, dressed as a boy. She forced her lips up into a semblance of a smile. "Yes, I would love to marry you, Mr. Tuccio."

"Please call me Cole." He slipped the ring on her finger.

A smattering of applause filled the room. Still holding on to her, Kiro stood, tugging her to her feet. He held her beringed hand up over her head and gave a small bow. "Friends. Miss Vargas, winner of the Emerging Young Artists Competition, has made me the happiest of men. She has accepted my marriage proposal." He squeezed her fingers, pressing the ring into her flesh. "Let's make it a very short engagement. Now come eat your chocolate eclair."

Toro squeezed his hand back. "Yes, let's get married as soon as possible." The sooner they married, the sooner she'd know what happened to her brother.

Chapter 18

Pharaoh sipped his whiskey and placed his bet. Hanger was here. At Jax's. He was sure of it. All he needed to do was find out where they were holding him.

He nodded at the broken-nosed bruiser with eyes like a snake's and his hand around the waist of a slinky girl in a tiny skirt and crop top. "So, you caught a Deco Boy? What'd he do?"

The guy threw a wad of bills in the pot. "Messed up the Big Boss's Spyder."

Definitely Hanger. Pharaoh took another sip of his drink and pretended to study his cards. "Messed up—like with spray paint?"

"Yeah," Squash-Nose said. "Had me take the car in to be repainted."

"The whole car for a tag?"

"Not a tag, man. Deco Boy turned it into a shark. Teeth on the hood. Fin things. A tail. Kind of liked it myself. But Big Boss went all crybaby. Had me throw the kid down in one of the cells in the basement."

Pharaoh's stomach pinched tight. He didn't want to think about what the cellar in this place was like. He tossed another ten in the pot. "Cells?"

Across the table, Bear took a puff on his cigarette and gave him a close look. "Yeah. Used to be storerooms for the stash in Vernon's time. Now we use them to give people some time for a think. Worried, are you?"

Pharaoh forced himself to laugh. It sounded flat to his ears, like the laugh of a condemned man. He pushed aside the worry that he'd be dead before he could save Toro's brother and slapped his burly roommate on the back. "No, I'm on board. Jax is very convincing."

"That he is, Mr. Pharaoh. That he is."

The girl in Squash-Nose's lap gave a squeal and jumped up as if the man's lap had turned into a hot fire. "Jax."

The men's heads all turned toward the door.

Jax crooked his finger and signaled the girl to come to him. "Wrong floor, Annalee. Get. I will be visiting you later."

The girl turned white and slipped past him and out the door. Jax turned back to the group. "Sorry to break up the game. Big Boss Man wants to meet our newest recruit."

Kiro wanted to see him? Hell. Pharaoh tossed down his winning cards. "My takings, guys." He scooped up the bets.

Jax extended his hand. "No, mine."

"Huh?" He glanced behind him and saw the grins on the men's faces. There was a joke here. A nasty one. Using every bit of his willpower, he relaxed his body and put the money on Jax's outstretched palm. "Whatever."

Jax patted the gun-shaped bulge beneath his jacket. "Mr. Tat Man—consider me your personal banker from now on. All your earnings will be kept by mc until you prove your loyalty."

Despite all he'd drunk, Pharaoh's mouth went dry.

Jax had the power to do more than take his money. "Thought I already did. I'm here, aren't I?"

The men behind him laughed.

"*Here* is not enough. If you want our trust, we need to know you'll do anything I say on command. Lie, steal"—he slashed a finger across his neck—"kill. Until then, I hold your earnings, and Bear and Pitstop are your stuck-on companions. Now come along. Big Boss is waiting. Bear, guard your man."

Pharaoh followed Jax out the door into the bright morning light, head up, shoulders back, knees trembling. He had enough blood on his hands. No way could he murder someone on this bastard's say so.

He knew where Hanger was. It was time to escape. Get the info to Toro.

After that, Jax and his men could do what they wanted with him.

He glanced over his shoulder at Bear. The man seemed calm enough, no weapon in sight. But he had no doubt the guy was ready to jump him if he twitched the wrong way. Still, he had a longer reach and more athletic body than Mr. Hulk.

With luck, he could take him down. Then he'd need cover from Jax's gun.

He looked up and down the street for a place to get up the side of one of the buildings or an alley to slip through and clenched his hands into tight fists.

Forget escape. Jax had men stationed everywhere. They lounged in front of the hotel and in the doorways across the way. They leaned against parked cars and smoked cigs.

The deadliest-looking one of them stood beside a white panel truck, the bulge on his hip a gun for sure.

Despite the cool of early morning, sweat gathered on the back of Pharaoh's neck and under his arms. Running was a no-go. He wouldn't get as far as the gutter, and Toro would never know where his brother was being held.

He'd have to wait for another chance.

Jax stopped at the back of a white panel truck and threw open the doors. "In you go, Tat Man. Off to see the Wizard."

Despite the warnings shooting through his brain, he hauled himself up and in. There were no seats so he folded his legs and sat on the cold floor.

The truck bed tipped as Bear clambered in after him. His guardian stood and grasped the metal strut above his head.

The rear doors slammed closed. Small pinpricks of sunlight shone through tiny holes in the side panels and illuminated the interior. Pharaoh glanced at them and then at the brown stains on the floor.

A chill snaked through him. Bullet holes. Someone'd been murdered in here.

He braced himself against the side of the truck. Was he really being taken to see Kiro?

The truck jerked forward and took off, the metal floor vibrating beneath him. He knew he shouldn't ask, but he couldn't help himself. "Where we going?"

Bear grunted as the driver took a corner at too fast a speed. "Big Boss's place."

"Why?"

"He likes to impress new guys."

Sitting in the swaying truck as it swerved in and out of traffic gave Pharaoh too much time to think. Jax's words burned in his gut. Tatting the girl had nearly undone him. Next, he'd have to kill someone.

Was that why they were taking him to meet Kiro—to take someone down? Or was he hurtling to his own death?

****

The van slammed to a halt, and he cursed as his head hammered against the side panel. A garage door rumbled. The vehicle went up a ramp and then wrenched to a stop. Pharaoh let out a slow breath. He'd find out soon enough.

"We're here," Bear said, pulling him to his feet. "Now act nice." The working end of a pistol poked him in the kidney. "This will be pointing at you the whole time—and I know about your death wish, Tat Man. You step out of line, and I will not aim to kill. I'll aim to maim."

Pharaoh gave him his nastiest scowl. "You can try."

Bear shoved the muzzle into him harder. "Move, idiot."

Pharaoh had never been to the penthouse when Vernon had owned it. As Bear and the van driver escorted him through the garage past Kiro's snazzy car collection, Pharaoh couldn't help but be impressed by the security systems.

Remote cameras and sensors marked their progress. The elevator keypad required a finger swipe and a voice ID. The private, stainless steel elevator went only to the seventh-floor penthouse and opened into a bunker-type lobby manned by two uniformed guards. No way he'd be able to escape whatever fate Kiro and his men planned for him.

Shoved along by Bear, Pharaoh caught a glimpse

of fluffy wool rugs and overstuffed white leather sofas as he was hustled down a hall and into an office that could have come out of *Lives of the Rich and Famous*.

Valuable artifacts lined the shelving. Amazing paintings hung on the walls. But it was the man seated at the glass desk with a million-dollar view of Manhattan behind him who drew his focus.

Pharaoh had only seen Kiro from a distance a couple of times, but he knew the horror stories about him well enough. This was the man who'd kidnapped Bella and Hanger. Beaten Toro to a pulp.

The idea that the personable man sitting behind the desk in his elegant suit, expensive silk tie and perfect smile was the same person as the murderous Shark Man was disturbing. He dragged in a breath between his clamped teeth. "Nice digs."

"I think so, Mr. Fernando Pharaoh. Please sit." Kiro waved to a modern-looking, high-backed metal chair. Pharaoh's stomach writhed. Every muscle in his body burned to let loose and smash Shark Man right through that glorious window.

He struggled for control. This was not the time to go berserk. He needed to play cool and survive for Hanger's sake. He sat down, his hands fisted at his sides.

Kiro signaled Bear. "Handcuff him and then leave."

Pharaoh's hands were yanked behind his neck and cuffed high up on the top slat of the chair. The cuffs dug into his wrists. His shoulder muscles screamed in agony. But he refused to show weakness to this man. He concentrated on breathing in and out.

"I hate to make my recruits uncomfortable, but I

need your full attention." Kiro picked up a remote control, pointed it at the flat screen TV on the wall to the left of the desk, and flicked it on. "Now watch."

The TV lit up, and there he was tattooing Jax's girl. From the camera's angle, Pharaoh could see her face, glimpse the tears slipping down her cheeks, watch her grimace in pain. He squeezed his eyes closed.

"No. No. No. Open those eyes. The work is top-notch, Mr. Pharaoh. Top-notch. I think Jax's idea of having my own resident tattoo artist is brilliant. In fact, once Jax is secure in your loyalty, I plan to have you ink me. I want a shark on my back—something like Jaws, his mouth open ready to eat a big fish—if you know what I mean. Then make a small version to tattoo on all my men. You can start working on the sketches for me when you get back."

Pharaoh's stomach tightened even more. Shark Man wanted a tattoo? By him?

He peered at the man. Not a twitch of the lip or a blink of the eye. Hell, Kiro was serious.

He pictured having Shark Man at his mercy. Face down on the tat table. Purposely making a mistake. Causing the bastard pain. The thought was delicious and frightening as hell.

He tamped down his wild imaginings and focused on what he needed to do. Survive this encounter and get back and free Hanger. He tipped his head like a dutiful servant. "Uh—sure. An honor."

"But that's not why you're here." Kiro swung his chair to the left and clicked a button on the remote. The screen went black and then a photograph appeared. "I want you to tell me about this tattoo. Did you do it?"

Pharaoh stared at the small tat in the shape of a

crown. It wasn't an unusual tattoo, but it was a very familiar one. Toro had one like it on his inner arm. But so did the others, including Solo and Neto.

So did he.

It was T-Crew's logo—their tag. But he'd never tell Kiro that. Involving his former friends wouldn't help Hanger. It just might get them killed.

Luckily, at this moment, his crown tat was buried inside the complex Celtic cuff encircling his biceps. Still, ignoring the scraping of the cuffs, he turned his arm slightly inward before answering. "No, not mine. It's nothing special—found in all the tattoo source books. Could have been done by anyone."

Kiro pinched up the side of his mouth. "Too bad. Hoped you'd recognize it. Getting married, you see, and my fiancé has a tattoo like that on the inside of her arm, just above the elbow."

Pharaoh's pulse ratchetted up. No girl had a T-Crew tattoo. What was Kiro trying to pull? "You sure?"

Kiro gave him a sharp look. "Oh, quite." He squeezed his palms together. "The girl appeared full-blown on the art scene. Painting what I'm told are the most original, awe-inspiring artworks on the market. She's from around here, but my men haven't been able to find out anything about her background. Can't seem to track her down. She's a mystery woman."

Pharaoh pressed his lips together. A mystery, all right. "And you're going to marry her?"

"I like mysteries. I like creating them, I like solving them. This woman intrigues me. She radiates sexuality, but has this aura of innocence. It's most attractive. Besides, I find myself in need of a wife if I want to go into politics. At least that's what my political advisor

177

says. Thinking of running for senator, you know. She's young and malleable and seems to have no family. I think she'll work out fine. Here"—he leaned forward and clicked on the TV again—"maybe you'll recognize her."

A grainy, jumpy surveillance video appeared on the screen, the camera obviously intended to capture motion rather than detail. But despite the poor quality, Pharaoh recognized the place instantly. It was Ari's old rental—The Foundry. A huge painting, the details indistinct, hung on the far wall.

A woman came into view. She was wearing a filmy white dress that fluttered around her as she arranged paints and paintbrushes on a long table. She turned her head, her face a blur, but the glorious tumble of raven black ringlets unmistakable.

Pharaoh knew exactly what those curls felt like. Silk. He'd wrapped one around his finger when he'd made love to her on his bed. He bit hard into his lip until he tasted blood. Shark Man was marrying his angel.

Chapter 19

By the time Pharaoh arrived back at Kiro's lower Brooklyn headquarters, it was well past two in the afternoon.

Bear shuffled along behind him and deposited him in their room. "Now you stay put. In an hour, you get to do a job with us. Wiping out some guy Kiro's taken a dislike to. Some art nut over on Park Avenue. Need you all bright-eyed and bushy-tailed. You being our resident squirrel." He clamped a meaty hand on Pharaoh's shoulder and squeezed hard. "Just so you know. Some of us shoot squirrels for fun. Especially those who beat us at cards."

Bear closed the door and drew the deadbolt. It fell into place with a loud click. Pharaoh flopped down on the bed. In an hour, he'd be an accessory to murder. Hell, they might actually make him pull the trigger. His stomach sank to his knees.

He stood up and looked out the small window. He might be able to squeeze out, but he couldn't see any handholds and without a rope or even a knife to wedge in as a support, he could end up a sitting duck or a splat on the ground below.

Besides, Hanger was here—in the basement, according to his new buddies. He had to find him and get him out if at all possible. At least, let him know he had rescuers coming. And then he needed to tell Toro his girlfriend was in grave danger.

Pharaoh glanced out the window again. If only he'd brought some rope and harness. No one had even bothered to search his bags. Not that he had his gear anymore. He'd abandoned his fancy climbing paraphernalia at T-Crew's when he'd walked out on them and on street art a year ago.

He rubbed his hand across his chin and scalp, annoyed to feel rough stubble where before his skin had been smooth shaven. It had only been a few days, and already he was reverting to the scruffy tough he'd once been.

He dropped his hand. Who cared what he looked like? He needed to open the door and get past Bear before they came for him. Because if they tried to make him kill someone, he knew just what would happen. He'd be dead, not the target, and Toro would never find Hanger.

Pharaoh ran his hands over the door, knocking peeling paint flakes to the floor. It was one of those cheap, thin laminate jobs with a hollow core. With care, he should be able to burrow through to the dead bolt and flick it open. He crammed his ear against the wood panel and listened. Bear was definitely asleep, snoring with the gusto of a man who ate and drank too much. Loud gunfire roared from the TV cop show he'd been watching. The noise would be good cover for what he planned.

Pharaoh looked around for something to dig into the wood. A ceramic-base lamp stood on the makeshift nightstand next to the bed. He unplugged it, wrapped it in a pillowcase, and smashed it against the metal bedframe. The china broke into several large fragments.

He stopped and listened. Bear snored on.

He picked up the biggest piece and, ignoring the sharp edges cutting into his palm and the slow drip of blood from the resulting slashes, slowly chipped away in the area of the dead bolt.

Little by little a hole opened on his side.

He gave the door a rattle, estimated where the plates held the bolt and after choosing a smaller fragment, began to work through the other side of the door panel.

Bear would see the hole if he looked, but it didn't matter. Regardless of what happened next, he was getting out of this place. No way would he murder some art guy.

There. The shard broke through. Pharaoh pressed his eye to the hole but spied nothing but wall. He glanced at the clock on his nightstand. Fifteen minutes gone. He needed to hurry.

He scooped a pen out of his duffle, and grasping it between two fingers, poked it through the hole he'd made and searched for the bolt.

Yes. The pen tapped the end of something metal.

Sweat dripping down his neck, he pushed against it, met resistance, almost lost hope, and then heard it click. The door cracked open, and he was out.

Using his lightest footsteps, he slid past the sofa where Bear lolled, head back, mouth agape. Then he opened the hall door, and strolled as calmly as he could to the stairs. The guard at the end of the corridor pointed his gun at him. "What's the rush, Tat Man?"

He thought fast. "Big Boss called. Needs me to check that girl's tattoo. Think it's infected. Got to get it done before we go out on the job."

The thug lowered his gun. "Girl's up on five. Room 565."

"Thanks."

"No sampling, now," the guy said with a wink.

Pharaoh took the steps two at a time up to the fifth floor. This level was laid out differently than the guards' floor. In the hallway, the lights were bright. A faint hint of perfume and sex permeated the air.

He hadn't intended to check on the girl. But now he was here, he knew he had to see if she was all right. It would just take a minute—a precious minute, for sure. He glanced back. Then again, the girl might be able to help him get past the guard on the staircase.

Praying he was doing the right thing, Pharaoh walked down the corridor. Number 565 was at the far end. He considered knocking and then rejected the idea. Throwing back the bolt, he stepped inside.

After the brightness of the hall, the room was a dark haze, blinds drawn tight. The girl on the bed moaned and lifted her head from the pillow.

"I came to check out the tattoos. How you doing?"

"Been better, but I'll survive." The girl sat up and flicked on a table lamp. She'd removed the bandages, and he could see the redness around the tat lines. But nothing worrisome. She caught his once over and smoothed down the negligee she was wearing and pasted on a weary smile. "Jax send you?"

Hell, she thought he'd come to use her. Pharaoh held up a hand. "Just here to check there's no infection. Is there anywhere that hurts?"

She touched the tattoo on the inside of her wrist. "All of it hurts. Feels like a bad sunburn."

"Yeah, it would. That's normal. Try not to touch or

rub them. Wash with mild soap and take some aspirin."

"*Aspirin?* I'll tell Jax Baby when he gets up here to give me something stronger. He should be here any minute."

He stepped back. Damn it. Last thing he needed was for Jax to find him here. Time to move on.

Pharaoh backed to the door. But he couldn't help giving his sanitation spiel. The girl seemed clueless. "Listen. The burning sensation should decrease over the next few days, it may weep a bit, and then it will itch. That's a good sign—that they're healing. But if you notice any increasing redness, have Jax fetch me. If there's pus, get to a doctor pronto."

"Pus? Like the skin's all pimply like a boil and green goo comes out?"

"Yeah. That would be really bad."

"You checking the boy next?"

The boy? She had to mean Hanger. He blew out a puff of air. For once a good deed had paid off. "Yeah. Was just on my way to see him. He's in the cellar, the men said."

She lay back down, winced, and curled on her side. "No. They moved him to Cami's room. She used to be a nurse. Ladybell said he was burning up with fever."

Adrenaline flooded his body. *Fever?* Hanger's stupid self-inflicted tat must be infected. "What number is Cami in?"

She limply lifted her hand. "I don't know the numbers—three doors down."

He pushed the door ajar and checked the hall. Still empty. He leaned back in. "Which way, right or left?"

The girl flipped her hand to the right, and he took off, counted three doors, and knocked, praying it was the one she meant.

The small Asian woman who answered the door was a younger version of Bella's former landlady, Zeya Aung. She had the same feisty look in her eyes, and if she'd had a baseball bat, he was sure she'd be whacking him in the balls with it.

She scowled at him and rapidly waved her hands. "You go. No be here on this floor at this hour. Mr. Jax, he be coming."

"I need to see the boy."

"Go. Go." She gave the door a hard push.

Pharaoh wedged his foot in and grabbed the edge of the door. He could easily have knocked her over and forced his way in, but he didn't want to hurt her. Instead, he peered through the crack and whispered. "Please, I need to see the boy."

"Boy asleep. Not well."

"I'm here to help him escape—get him to a hospital."

Footsteps clomped up the stairs.

"*Please.*"

The woman opened the door, pulled him in, and shut it silently behind him. She crossed her arms in front of her. "Crazy fool. Hospital good but you must hide. Mr. Jax be coming in here to see boy. He will hurt you." The footsteps came down the hall. "In there." She shoved him into a narrow, dark adjoining bedroom. "Under bed."

Pharaoh fumbled in the shadowy blackness until he found the edge of the mattress. He could barely make out the lump that must be Hanger, but he could smell the sickly stink of the infection.

He moved to the head of the bed, put a hand on the

boy's face and yanked it back. The kid was burning up. Behind him, the door shook on its hinges as several men entered the adjoining room. Their muffled voices rose.

Pharaoh wiggled under the bed, the space so tight he had to suck in his stomach and bend his head to the side. But his comfort was the least of his problems. The important thing was no one caught sight of him.

The door opened, and light illuminated the room. Kiro's lawyer baritone filled the small space. "Well, let's see how our guest is doing. Wakey, wakey, Deco Boy."

Hanger shifted on the bed, pressing one of the wooden bed slats down against Pharaoh's ear. He bit his lip to keep from gasping. Then the boy moved again, and the pressure released.

"Huh?" Hanger's voice was weak.

"Time for another shot of penicillin. Cami, stick the kid and then leave."

The woman's tiny, red-slippered feet came into view on the far side of the bed. Pharaoh heard Hanger hiss as the needle went in. At least Kiro was treating the boy.

The woman padded away, and Kiro's highly polished shoes appeared on the other side of the bed. "Now, I came in person because I have exciting news for you. My marriage proposal has been accepted. In fact, she's right outside on the street below, sitting in my Spyder—the one you defaced—waiting for me to drive her home."

Hanger's voice quivered. "Don't believe you. She'd never have anything to do with a creep like you."

"Watch that tongue." There was a slap, and Hanger

screamed. "Still tender in that spot, it seems," Kiro said.

It was all Pharaoh could do to hold still and not bound up and take Kiro down. But acting without a plan wouldn't save Hanger nor the girl in the car below. Shark Man knew better than to slum alone. Pharaoh could see the boots of Kiro's guard standing behind him and hear more men talking in the other room.

Kiro's feet moved away from the bed. "Sleep well, Deco Boy."

The lights flicked off, the door opened and closed, and the men's footsteps faded away.

Pharaoh knew he should wait longer, but he had to make sure Hanger was okay. Hoping no guard remained behind, Pharaoh slid out from under the bed, and stood up.

"Pharaoh? That you?" Using one arm, Hanger eased up from the bed. The other was cuffed to the bedframe. "Forget me. Go. Check the window. Can you see a girl? Was Kiro telling the truth?"

Pharaoh dashed to the window and looked down. "Can't tell. Top's up."

He threw up the sash and leaned farther out. In the street below, Kiro's red sports car sat double parked by the entrance to the building. In the passenger seat, he caught a glimpse of black hair and an oval face.

If he could just see a little more. He thrust himself farther out. There. The girl leaned out the car window and looked towards the hotel entrance.

He slapped the windowsill, blood thundering in his ears. Hell, it was his angel. She'd agreed to marry the cur.

He pressed his forehead harder against the cold windowpane. Damn it. Did Kiro hold something over her, too?

The devil himself strolled out of the building and jumped into the driver's side. Then the car took off, taking Pharaoh's heart with it. He let the blind drop closed and spun around. "Yeah. There was a girl. Black hair."

"Oh." Hanger collapsed back down. "Well, glad you're here. You were right about the tattoo. It's gone rotten."

"Let me see." Pharaoh flicked on the light and then gently rolled up the sweat pant leg. The awkwardly-done, crown-shaped tattoo was raised up in pus-filled blisters, the whole thigh swollen and mottled. Worse, wicked-looking red lines spread outward from the wound. He choked down the bile rising up his throat. "Shit. It's bad. You need to be in a hospital."

Hanger wiped a tear off his cheek. "Am I gonna die? They gave me two shots of antibiotics."

"Maybe they were antibiotics—who can believe Shark Man? Why the hell did you go into Kiro's garage when I chased you?"

"Owed him for what he did to Bella and me."

"Toro's been crazy with worry."

"Yeah, sure."

Pharaoh gave him a sharp look. "Of course he is. Saw him at Bella's nearly out of his mind."

Hanger stuck out his lower lip. "If you say so."

"Well, I'm glad I found you. Though how I'm gonna get you out of here, I have no idea."

"I'm not leaving."

Pharaoh tugged down the cuff of the sweat pants. "What?"

"Got something to do." The boy straightened

slightly, swaying from the effort. "I'm working for Kiro now. Gonna be his messenger boy once the leg is better."

"That leg needs a hospital. A doctor. Antiseptics not bartered on the street. If that's MRSA, the skin-eating bacteria, you'll be lucky if they can save the leg."

Hanger's teeth chattered. "You can get me that stuff."

"What? No way. What you need is only available in hospitals." Pharaoh moved to the head of the bed and fluffed the pillows to relieve the pressure on the cuffed hand.

Hanger grasped Pharaoh by the wrist. "What are you doing here anyway? Thought you worked for Bella."

"Not anymore. Got trapped into being Kiro's resident tattoo artist."

Hanger let out a small wheeze. "So you're in as tight a jam as I am."

"Maybe. Maybe not." Pharaoh headed back to the window.

On this side of the building, there were no bars, and fancy moldings surrounded the windows. Better yet, two windows over—a fire escape. With luck, and nobody looking up, he could climb down.

It was coming on dark, this side of the building in shadow. Kiro's car was gone. He hated to leave Hanger behind in the condition he was in. But the timing was perfect, and if he could get away from Jax and his crew, he could call an ambulance, fetch the police. Get help. Find Toro.

Besides—he glanced at his watch—his hour was

about up. In a few minutes, Bear and his buddies would discover him missing and come looking for him.

He lifted the window sash, raised it as high as possible, stared at the narrow width of window frame he needed to land on, and glanced across at the brick wall for handholds and toeholds.

Plenty dicey. But if he didn't take the risk, Hanger would die, and Kiro would marry his angel.

"I'm going for help, Hanger. You hold on till I get back."

Hanger rolled his head to the side. "Don't worry about me. It's Toro who's in trouble."

"Toro?"

The kid raised his head. "Yeah. Kiro's gonna—"

He didn't want to hear it. "I know. I know." Kiro was going to marry Toro's girlfriend, his angel. Something clattered in the hall. "Got to go, kid. I'll be back. I promise."

Sucking in a deep breath, he threw himself over the window sill and found the top ledge of the window below with his toes. He compressed his body tight to the wall and worked at maintaining his balance.

With his weight on one foot, he flexed, then leaped across to the sill of the next window. From there, jumping over to the fire escape was a piece of cake. He landed with a thud and then took off down the treads and dropped down onto the street.

Now to get help.

He'd start with Toro.

Chapter 20

Toro slipped off Kiro's engagement ring and tucked it into her pocket. No way could she let her friends know what she had gone and done.

She pushed open the door to The Siren and slapped the useless report from the private detective she'd hired on the counter. "This was a waste of money. The PI hasn't found a single lead yet."

Bella closed the account book she been working on. "Oh, Toro. What are we going to do? The detective was our last hope. The cops are treating Hanger like he's some worthless street scum. He's been missing five days! If he were a middle-class kid from the suburbs there'd be an Amber Alert out for him. There'd be newspaper coverage. It would be on TV."

"Lunch time." Vernon hip-checked the door to The Siren open and set a bag of Chinese takeout and two coffees on the counter. He turned to Toro.

"You find the kid yet?"

Toro shook her head.

Bella came around the counter. "How about we hang up posters? Offer a reward?"

Toro bit her lip. Publicity wasn't going to save Hanger. More cops looking wasn't going to find him. And where would she get money for a reward? She barely had anything left from her thousand dollar check.

Deep in her heart, she wasn't even sure he was still alive. And if he were, all her bets were on Shark Man.

She glanced at Vernon. If he knew what she had gone and done—gotten engaged to his rotten brother—he'd be furious and disgusted. And Bella would do everything in her power to stop her.

Behind her, the door to The Siren slammed open. Toro's head jerked up.

Pharaoh.

She brought her fingers to her lips. She hadn't seen him since she'd left his bed after the most wonderful night of her life. But the person standing in front of her wasn't the same man she'd made love to. Wherever he'd been—whatever he'd been doing—it was eating Pharaoh from the inside out.

The overhead lights illuminated the harsh planes of his face, the dark circles under his eyes, and the slight twitch along his chin. Even worn with worry, he was the most beautiful man she'd ever seen, and the most infuriating.

"What are you doing here?" She stepped forward, ready to batter some sense into him, but Vernon slipped between them.

Vernon poked a finger into Pharaoh's chest. "How dare you set foot in this place? You disappear without a word. Leave Bella some scrap of paper saying you quit. Come to find out you are working for that crooked bastard G-Man. We all know what he does. Well, Bella forgave your betrayal once. She won't forgive you twice." He glanced at his wife. "For her sake, all I'm going to do is kick you out. You come back, I'll kill you." He went to seize Pharaoh by the shoulder.

Fisting his hands, Pharaoh spread his legs, and

glared at Vernon like a wrestler before a match. "Hold up. Listen. I know where Hanger is."

Toro's head spun as all the breath whooshed out of her. "He's alive?"

She lunged forward and slipped between the two men. She jammed her palm against Pharaoh's chest and forced him back. "Where?"

Pharaoh glared over Toro's head at Vernon. "Your rotten brother's got him. Holding him over at some decrepit place called the Sunset Palace Hotel in Red Hook. Fifth floor. Room 563. You'll know it. One of your former holdings, I assume." He looked back at Toro. "Thing is, Hanger's in a bad way. Idiot tatted himself. Got a hell of an infection raging. He needs medical care quick. He could lose his leg."

Toro thumped his chest with her fists. She'd been right. Shark Man did have her brother.

"Hell. And you left him there? How could you?" She hit him harder. "This is all your fault. You should have stopped him the day he ran from you. You should've dragged him from Kiro's garage if it was the last thing you ever did."

Vernon pulled Toro back. "Forget the conniving idiot. Let's go get your brother."

Pharaoh blocked the way. "No. Wait. You'll just get killed. The place is a fortress. Tons of guards, all heavily armed."

Vernon scowled at him. "You got out."

"I climbed down a brick wall. Hanger's weak. Burning up with fever. Handcuffed to his bed. Damn it, forget heroics. Call the cops and get an ambulance there."

Vernon grunted. "No cops. This is my brother's

doing. I will take care of it."

Toro grabbed Vernon by the arm. She couldn't let him get involved. "Please, you can't. Think of Bella and the baby."

"Enough," Bella said. "You listen to Toro, Vernon Newell. *You* are not going anywhere. You're not getting mixed up in that criminal mess again. You promised."

"But the kid—he needs our help."

Toro patted Vernon on the back. "Don't worry. I'll handle it. I can climb walls, too."

Pharaoh turned and headed to the door. "Cops are the better idea. But hey, do it your way. I told you where he is. Now I've got my own problems to solve."

"Yeah, at the bottom of a bottle," Vernon sneered, his whole face twisted with hate.

Pharaoh gave him the finger. "Whatever." He stepped outside and kicked the door shut behind him.

Toro's mouth dropped open. He was going to walk out on her and Hanger after she'd saved his freaking life? She should have let him jump.

Her hands fisted. No way was he getting away.

Ignoring the shouts behind her, she forged out the door and chased after him. He was already far down the block. But she'd always been the fastest of the graffiti crew.

Running full tilt, she swerved past the pedestrians, snaked through the traffic, and finally caught up to him as he ducked down the Bedford Avenue subway entrance.

Ignoring the flow of people tramping down the steps around them, she grabbed hold of his upper arm and yanked him around. "How dare you leave! We mean so little to you? My brother? T-Crew? Me? After all these years of watching each other's backs, you're gonna walk away? Again? Hanger idolizes you. I thought—I—"

"You thought what?"

She peered into his eyes and beneath the mask of world-weariness caught a glimpse of the man she'd kissed. The man she loved. "I thought you cared."

He glanced down at her hand on his arm. "Let go, Toro, before I do something you regret."

She loosened her hold as another wave of commuters came down the steps, pushing around them, cursing and shoving in their hurry to make the train rumbling into the station below. A student's book bag smacked her in the face, someone's knee hit her shin. Someone else bumped her from behind.

For a second, she wavered, searching for a foothold on the steps, and then she was smashing into Pharaoh with a whoosh.

"Damn it." He caught her in his arms and steadied her. Crushed against him, every nerve in her body came alight. He was warm and muscular and smelled like the night.

For a moment, she was all woman to his man. Her skin heated. Her body trembled. Her nipples peaked. Her brain shouted warnings. She had to get away before he became aware of what she was feeling. Before he remembered holding a very similar body in the shadow of a bridge and in a soft bed under a Williamsburg map.

She gave him a push and said in her nastiest Toro voice, "Let go. Got to move before we get trampled."

Pharaoh released his hold, seized her by the upper arm, and pulled her farther down the steps until they stood to the side, out of the foot traffic. A ray of dying sunlight sneaking down the stairwell illuminated his face.

He licked his lips. "Toro, let's get something straight. I care, damn it. I cared enough to risk my neck to find him. I cared enough to climb down a brick wall to get help. I cared enough to come and face the people I hurt and tell you where he was. I care enough to tell you, your girlfriend is in grave danger. She's—"

"What girlfriend?" Toro shook her head and took a step back. "I don't have a girlfriend."

He scanned her face, focused on her lips. His eyes widened. "*Hell, no.*" He shoved up her sleeve, turned her arm, and held it up to the light. "Wait a minute. That tattoo."

She yanked. "Let go." But Pharaoh's grip was like iron.

Toro's heart sped up. She prayed her face did not reveal her lie. "Huh. All T-Crew has one. Even you."

"Yes, we do. But so does somebody else."

"Who?"

"A *girl.* A girl who's marrying Shark Man. He showed me photos of her. Close ups of a tattoo. This tattoo."

Toro jerked her hand free and tugged down her sleeve. "It's just a crown. Nothing special. We got them so we'd be able to recognize each other's bodies, if—if we were killed."

"I remember. But you see—Kiro's desperate to find out who his mystery woman really is. It wasn't just a crown he showed me. He made me look very closely at a blown up picture of that arm. There was a scar too. A scar like this one."

With his other hand, he ran the pad of his index

finger over the tiny white line to the left of the crown. She had a number of scars from life on the streets. A fall on broken glass. A cut from barbed wire. She didn't even remember where she'd gotten the one he was touching.

His finger stopped and rested against the crooked line. Warmth spread through her body. Her breath came faster. Her pulse sped up.

She'd loved him so long. In her dreams, she'd imagined this moment—the second when the man she loved finally realized she was a woman.

She looked up into Pharaoh's eyes and watched them narrow in recognition. Would he kiss her?

His chin came up. His lips thinned. "*You.* You saved me on the bridge. *Twice.*" He dropped her hand and took a step back. His glance flickered over her. "I've been a fool. You're the angel."

Toro puffed a breath out and dipped her head. Time for the truth. "I pretended to be a boy to protect Hanger and myself in the shelters. Then later—I didn't know how to be a girl again. So I stayed El Toro."

"The woman on the bridge knew how to kiss."

She touched her lips. "It was my first kiss."

She waited for him to reach out and take her in his arms. Kiss her again. Tell her he loved her.

But he didn't.

Pharaoh stepped farther back, his face stone-hard. "Was it fun playing me for a fool all these years? Hell, I've been treating you like a jock. Regaling you with my exploits. Is that why you chose me to relieve you of your virginity?"

She clasped her arms in front of her. This was no pleasantly surprised lover. This was a man whose whole world had tilted upside down. He didn't love her. He was disgusted by her, just as she feared.

"No. No, Pharaoh. I love you."

He threw back his head and let out a raw laugh, torn from someplace deep inside. "Right, and that is why you are marrying Mr. Cole Tuccio. Otherwise known as Shark Man."

"No. I'm not—I told him I would but—I thought I could get him to tell me where Hanger was."

"Well, now you know where your brother is. So go back to The Siren and help your good friends get him out." He backed farther away. "Good luck breaking that engagement, too. Won't be as easy as you think. Someone will have to kill the bastard for you."

He turned away, then stopped, and called back. "Oh, by the way, the next time you see me about to jump from a bridge, *don't* stop me." He rushed down the platform and disappeared on to a waiting train.

Toro buried her face in her hands. She'd admitted she loved him, and he'd not even blinked. Solo and Neto were right. Pharaoh was a cold-hearted bastard. He didn't deserve her love. If only she could convince her heart of that fact.

She rubbed the tattoo on her arm and turned to go back to The Siren. She battled her way up through the oncoming commuters.

On the top step, she slowed. Wait a minute. Pharaoh said Kiro had a photo of her tattoo. And other pictures. He must have a hidden camera somewhere in the Foundry.

Hell. What could he have seen? She was pretty sure she'd never changed her clothes there. Certainly, she'd never had anyone else in the place, but Claude.

There was no way he could tie Toro and Alba together. She brushed her fingers over her crown tattoo. Or was there?

She glanced up and caught a glimpse of a security camera on the corner of the building above her. The city's surveillance cameras were the bane of street artists everywhere, and she knew how to stay out of view or disable one if needed.

How could she have been so stupid not to imagine Kiro would try to figure out who Alba Vargas really was?

He owned so many buildings he could have access to security cameras all over Brooklyn. Of course, he'd spy on her. Could he have found out where she lived? She tugged her ball cap lower over her eyes. Recognized her by her hair or skin coloring?

A chill ran down her spine. Hell, if he figured out who she really was, Hanger was in more trouble than anyone thought.

And so was she.

Chapter 21

Huddled in the shadow of the elevated train line, Pharaoh peered around the corner, surveyed the area in front of the hotel, and prayed Hanger's wound was no worse, and he was still in the same room. If he were caught rescuing Hanger, they'd kill him for sure.

And he was sure he'd be caught. He'd called 911 two minutes ago and told them they had a kid in critical condition at Sunset Palace.

He had no illusions they'd ever let the emergency guys up to see Hanger. The guards would say it was a prank and turn them away.

He couldn't let that happen. What he planned to do was probably foolish—run out into the street when the ambulance arrived and point to Hanger's window. Insist they get the boy. Make a very loud stink.

He glanced at the guards in the hotel entrance and on the opposite side of the street. It would save Hanger, but he'd never get away afterwards. Jax had too many men at his command.

Hell, his chances of surviving were nil anyway. So be it.

After the way he'd treated Toro, he deserved to die. But first, he'd do one good thing—he'd save Hanger's life.

Because he'd told Toro the truth. He did care. He cared too much.

Besides, Toro was right—Hanger was in too bad shape to wait.

He checked his watch, all his senses on high alert for the sirens. Soon. Soon he would do the most foolhardy, crazy thing in his life.

He'd do what he should have done all those years ago. Put himself between the gang's guns and his mother.

He touched the folded utility knife he'd hooked inside his waistband. Still, there was always a chance he'd be lucky. With enough commotion who knew what might happen? Commotion was a graffiti kid's best friend.

A car pulled up in front of the building, and Jax got out, a young girl by his side. Pharaoh banged his fist into the wall. Hell, he'd hoped the guards would be hesitant to hold firm, but that would be a no-go with the boss there.

He rested his chin in his hand. He couldn't remember when he last slept. Didn't matter. He could sleep long and hard and forever, once he retrieved Hanger.

He ran his hand over the knife again. If he survived this, his next task was to kill the Shark. It was the only way Toro would ever be safe.

Toro. He'd have never guessed she was a woman. He spent years in close contact with him—uh, her—and never suspected a thing.

Familiarity bred blindness, it seemed. He'd slapped him on the back. Punched him in the nose a couple of time for smart-mouthing, hoisted him up by his buttocks on innumerable occasions.

He pictured the curvy woman he'd held in his

arms. The woman who sent his blood drumming through his veins. The woman he loved. It was impossible to believe the wiry daredevil Toro and his angel were one and the same.

A siren sounded in the distance. Pharaoh lifted his head. Yes. They were coming—finally. He bit the inside of his cheek and peered around the corner of the building. In minutes, he'd put on the biggest show of his life.

"So what's the plan?"

He whirled around and came face to face with his angel. Her dark eyes met his, and all his resolve melted away.

He wanted to pull her close, kiss her every which way, and tell her he loved her, too. He wanted to grab her hand and run as far and as fast as he could and give her the life she deserved.

But he couldn't. Not now. Not with Hanger's life depending on him. So instead of welcoming her into his arms, he gave her a shove. "Toro. What the hell are you doing here?"

Her mouth quivered. "Rescuing my brother."

"But—it's too dangerous for a—"

"If you say 'for a girl,' I'll punch so hard in the nose you'll be seeing stars till next Sunday."

Pharaoh looked over her shoulder. "Vernon here?"

"No. But Solo and Neto are up there." She pointed to the roof of the building.

He followed her finger. His old buddies gave a wave. Something released inside him. He wasn't alone. He had T-Crew beside him.

Not that they could help much.

He shook his head. "You can't get down from

there. I already tried it."

She gave him the crooked-mouth, you're-an-idiot look. "Not bare-handed. They brought the climbing gear." Toro took out a cellphone. "Tell me which window is Hanger's. They'll rappel down and secure the room. Our job is to add to the distraction the EMTs make."

His heart pounded in his chest as he showed her Hanger's window. Toro was here helping him. She'd forgiven him for the way he'd treated her. He could see it in her eyes.

Boy? Girl? It didn't matter. It was his own fault for not being able to see what had been in front of him all these years.

The sirens roared up behind them. The King was a good person, and they had a sick kid to rescue. He whacked her arm like they were old friends. But they weren't. They were lovers. He swallowed hard. "How?"

Toro snapped the shoulder strap of T-Crew's paint-stained duffle bag. "By being annoying street kids."

"Huh. That's your plan? They know me."

"Yeah, I bet *your* plan was to go out there and get yourself killed. Tattooing has made you brain-dead. Here." She tossed him an old sweatshirt and a ski mask. "Even brought you this." She flipped an old ball cap at him.

Pharaoh pulled the sweatshirt over his head and tugged it down. Covered his head with the mask and tapped down the cap.

Then he reached in the duffle and pulled out a spray can. "I know exactly which car I'm going to tag."

Toro lifted her can and squinted. "Got my eye on the bruiser who keeps stepping in and out of the door.

Ready? Here comes the ambulance."

Sirens blared down the street.

Pharaoh gave her a high five. This was the way it used to be. Carefree. Fun. No fear. He let out a breath. They'd been friends. They'd had each other's backs. He'd loved Toro like a brother.

But now? He turned away, a small niggle running up his spine. He didn't want to think about how her lips tasted or how her body fit so perfectly against his. He still loved her, but not as a brother. Every fiber of his body was screaming she shouldn't be here. He should be keeping her safe.

He glanced back to make sure she was okay, just as all hell broke loose in front of him. The orange and white FDNY ambulance pulled up to the building, lights flashing, siren whooping, and stopped.

Jax and his guards rushed out into the street and surrounded the vehicle, yelling and banging the doors. Obviously trying to get it to leave.

Pharaoh raced forward and sprayed FUCKER on the hood of the yellow Lotus. Then he dodged down one side leaving behind a row of shark teeth. Out of the corner of his eye, he kept watch for Toro as she sprayed a huge hot pink dot on the backs of the men on the street side of the ambulance. She moved so fast the men's responses seemed to happen in slow motion. She was there, and then she was gone—out of sight—safe.

Good. Now to help the twins get Hanger. Pharaoh tucked the spray can in the back of his jeans, leaped up onto the roof of the Lotus, stretched for the fire escape ladder, and hauled himself up by his fingertips.

Before anyone below noticed, he was at the top of the fire escape and skittering across the bricks and window ledges to Hanger's window.

He entered the window feet first and got hit in the stomach with an elbow. He fell to the side.

"Get out of the way. You're too late." Neto swung out the window, his arm wrapped around the small Asian woman Kiro had called Cami. "He's gone."

"Hanger?"

Footsteps thundered down the hall.

"Yeah, Mini-Zeya here says the boy snuck out the window at dawn."

Pharaoh threw his head back. "*Idiota.* The kid's crazy. Amazing he didn't fall, weak as he was."

A loud crash sounded from the other room. Jax's men would be here any moment.

"Go." Pharaoh stepped away from the window. "Forget about me. Take her. I'll hold them off till you're safe away."

"Good choice. We did this for Toro. Not you." Neto and his burden disappeared from view.

Pharaoh yanked off his ski mask. Then he turned and, drawing himself up to his full height, spread his legs and raised his closed fists just as the inner door slammed open, and Jax and his guards tumbled in. In front of the scowling group stood Bear, tall, mean, and wearing knuckle busters on his fists. The guard grinned at him.

Jax shook his head. "Tat Boy. You've reached the end of the line. Nobody betrays me." Then he stepped back. "Take him out, men.

This was it. Hanger was safe. He'd go down fighting.

Bear lunged, and Pharaoh used his agility to sweep under and up, smashing his nose, crushing the cartilage, avoiding the knuckle busters. Blood spurted, and the man crumpled.

He swung again and another fell. But no matter how many punches he threw, more followed. Pain tore through him. But he kept hitting, until he could hit no more. Slowly, he sank down under a rain of blows and kicks, crushed like an unwanted fly.

The last thing he heard as the blows pounded into him and the men closed in was a high-pitched whistle—the signal T-Crew used to tell each other they were safe. At the sound, the fight went out of him. It was over. Done.

****

Toro's feet pounded on the pavement. She looked over her shoulder. "Where's Pharaoh? He's not with you?"

Solo gave her a little push as they turned the corner and raced up the street. "Behind us. Keep moving, King. You got a bunch of angry guys on your tail."

A motorcycle roared up the street. Solo gave her a shove. "Damn. Time to split up. I'll head to the river. Meet up at the Crown." With a wave, he dashed to the other side of the street and disappeared behind a jog in a building.

Toro dove to the left and cut across the cracked pavement of a car repair shop with three tired gas pumps out front. Turning sideways, she squeezed between the pumps, jostled past the old man pumping gas into his pickup, and ignoring his curses and the shouts of the guy on the motorcycle to stop, swung her arms out and took a flying leap to the lip of the half open industrial-size garbage bin sitting against the station's seven-foot cyclone fence.

Swaying slightly on her toes, she surveyed the yellow mini-school buses parked on the other side, made her choice, and bounded up and over the fence, landing on the roof of the nearest one with a perfect gymnast's stick.

Behind her, the motorcycle roared to a stop. She half-turned and peeked over her shoulder. The guy was off his machine and running toward her. *Fool.* She stuck out her tongue and then danced her way from van top to van top. No one could catch El Toro. She'd escaped a lot worse than an over-muscled thug with murder in mind.

After all, he couldn't shoot her in broad daylight in front of an audience. He'd have to get his hands on her and use a knife, and that wasn't happening—not today with the sun shining and the birds singing and the car repair guy storming out of the open bay of the garage and the man at the pumps yelling at her, and oh yeah—on the corner—one of New York's finest getting out of his shiny white police cruiser.

She turned all the way around and faced her pursuer. He was arguing with the car repairman who'd seized his shoulder and was pointing at his jacket and giving him a good old Brooklyn what-for. Well, that took care of him.

She couldn't resist. With a quick glance behind her, she backed up to the edge of the van roof. Then she doffed her ball cap and gave her unwilling fans a knee-sweeping bow ending with a back handspring somersaulting her off the roof and to the ground.

Just as she dropped down behind the bus, Mr. Thug's eyes met hers.

She gasped. She'd recognize those steel gray disks

anywhere. *Shark Man.* The guy she'd spray painted was Kiro, and he was furious.

Her feet hit the pavement, and she took off running blindly across the parking lot.

Estúpida. She'd taken off her cap. Had he recognized her?

She came up on a lopsided wooden fence. Beyond, lay a row of backyards, tiny patches of grass and scraggly bushes, each plot separated from the next by low fences. Here and there a smattering of spring bulbs was bursting into bloom. She leaped the first fence, and then the next, ducking under a clothesline, startling a dog chained to a post. The dog howled and snapped, and she sped up, twisting and thumping her way toward the end of the block, trampling daffodils and tulips beneath her feet.

This wasn't her neighborhood, but it didn't matter. Everything was based on the same basic grid. Somewhere a space would open between the houses leading out to the next street, or there would be something she could use to get up on a roof. Either way she'd soon disappear from Red Hook and with luck, she'd never come back.

At the far end of the row of houses, she found an opening through a driveway and took off, her sneakers slapping the pavement in the loose-kneed jog that could carry her for miles and miles without tiring.

All she needed was a nylon backpack and earplugs and she'd pass for another one of the idiots training for the New York marathon in November.

She knew she was fast. She'd always been tempted to enter the damn thing to find out how fast. But that wouldn't be happening now. Now she was running for her life—and Hanger's.

She'd make it to the Williamsburg Bridge and their emergency meeting spot beneath their crown tag. She just prayed all the rest of T-Crew and Pharaoh made it, too.

****

Two hours later, she swung down from the beam of the bridge where T-Crew's crown tag marked their territory and landed in front of Solo. He was alone.

"Neto?"

"He's stopped to drop off the woman he picked up at Zeya's place. Thinks the old lady will take her in."

Toro rocked back on her feet. Neto wasn't the kind to rescue a prostitute. He was more likely to haul her off to jail. Ever since he'd gotten involved in the local business groups, his politics had taken a right turn, and he'd become Mr. Law-and-Order. Even had aspirations of becoming a politician—running for city council, when he wasn't tagging with T-Crew "for old times' sake."

Neto was the reason Pharaoh had been kicked out of T-Crew's apartments. Didn't want a drunk and liar hanging around and giving the business a bad image.

Personally, she thought Neto full of baloney. But he had his thing, and she had hers. Still, taking the girl to Zeya? That was way out of character.

She whacked Solo on the shoulder. "What's the girl like to inspire such heroics?"

"Some tiny Asian thing. Cute. Been nursing Hanger."

"Oh." She peered down the pedestrian walkway. "Any sign of Pharaoh?"

Solo spit. "*Him?* He never came out. Stayed with

his friends, I guess."

A burning ball of acid congealed in her stomach. She grabbed his shoulder. "*What?* You said he was behind you."

"If I'd said he'd stayed, you would have gone back. Look, Toro, I know you feel a loyalty to all of us. It's what we admire about you. It's what makes you our King. But he's bad news. Bastard should have done more to get Hanger out when he first discovered him there. He's not T-Crew anymore. Hasn't been since he betrayed Bella. Admit it and move on. It's Hanger we've got to focus on here."

A shudder whipped through her. "They'll kill him."

"Oh, come on. Pharaoh's fine. He's with his own kind. Now think. Where would your brother go to hide?"

Toro clenched her teeth. She knew Pharaoh wasn't one of Kiro's men. She had to hope Solo was wrong, and Pharaoh had gotten away.

But her T-Crew buddy was right, Hanger came first. His infection could kill him.

She shrugged. The answer was obvious. "He'd come home."

"Not to a hospital?"

She shook her head. "He hates those places. Our mama was always in the emergency room for a beating or an overdose."

"Okay." Solo took out his cell. "So we need to have someone at the apartment at all times. That can be Neto's job. He's the workaholic." He tapped in a quick text and repocketed the phone. "But if he were weak and sick and not able to make it all the way—where would he go?"

"I'm not really sure. I know he has hiding places around the neighborhood. Since Ari's left, he's lost interest in school again. He's been truant a lot this month."

Solo rolled his shoulders. "It's spring. I know how he feels being cooped up in a classroom with all those kids bleeding hormones. Gets vicious."

"Vicious?"

"Look, he's strong and wiry, but he's small for his age and innocent in so many ways. Has no sense of fitting in. Dresses funny. Has a bit of a mouth on him. Smells like spray paint. Just the kind of target the would-be-gangsta kids like to bully."

"Bully?"

"Caught him one day down at the park playing hooky, and we had a heart-to-heart."

Toro fisted her hands. "He should have told me."

"Didn't want you to know he couldn't handle the other kids. Wants to be like you. *A leader of men.*" Solo tipped his chin and grinned at her. "That's a direct quote."

Toro moved to the outside fence and peered down at the strip of green running along the river. "Okay, so he hung out in the park. But he'll know the thugs will be after him and that's too exposed. He'd avoid stores and public places. Usually, I'd say one of the roofs we hang out on, but not with a bad leg. He'd stay have to stay on the ground and hide in the shadows. What about a parking garage or a construction site?"

"Good thinking." Solo took out his phone again and thumbed on his map app. "I'll see what locations like that I can find. Then we should call in the other graffiti teams and ask them to help check those out.

Let's go back to Big Bad and plan out where to search."
He took off toward the Brooklyn end of the bridge.

Toro kicked the fence, then pushed away and trailed after Solo.

Having a plan of action would help. But trying to find one hurt kid in an area covering hundreds of blocks would be like looking for a diamond in a heap of broken glass.

Especially a kid like her brother.

For all she knew, he was hiding from her because he didn't want to be scolded. *Mierda.* He hadn't even told her about being bullied.

She swerved around a pair of slow-walking lovebirds. Crazy kid. Taking off like that. Why couldn't Hanger have waited a few hours? They'd have gotten him out, and she could have whisked him away from this place.

She'd decided for sure they were going to flee to Greece. She'd liked it there. During her recuperative stay on Eudokia, she'd felt like she'd died and gone to heaven. The island air smelled like sun and sea and wild herbs—not overripe garbage and car exhaust. Gnarled olives and carobs hugged the terraced slopes, and if you climbed a hill, you could see the incredible blue water of the Mediterranean spreading out around you for miles and miles. It was better than any rooftop in Brooklyn.

She slowed to a walk, crossed through the small park at the end of the bridge, and headed north toward her neighborhood and home. They'd could have been on a plane tomorrow, if Hanger hadn't taken off on his own.

Not that she blamed him for running. He'd no idea

they'd come for him. At some level, that was Pharaoh's fault. He could have worked with T-Crew instead of setting out on his own. Maybe he could have slipped back in and warned Hanger.

Or maybe not.

Was Solo right about him being rotten?

She remembered Pharaoh's lips kissing her everywhere, their bodies touching and joining. It had been the most incredible experience of her life. It had made her happy she was a woman just so she could see the hunger and admiration in his eyes.

Could that man, the loving one who treated her like she was made of spun glass, be a cutthroat killer, a drug pusher, a pimp? She shook her head to rid it of the gross images.

No. She refused to believe he was one of Jax's men. He'd stayed behind for a reason. Had it been at the risk of his life?

Damn it. He'd do that—sacrifice himself. She knew he would. It would be another way of committing suicide. Had she saved him from one abyss only to lose him in another?

"You coming?" Solo called over his shoulder.

She gave him a wave. "I'm going to search along Bedford Avenue. Hanger's friends with all the shop owners."

"Yeah, right. All the food places," Solo yelled back. "Meet you back at Big Bad." With a nod, he took off up the street.

Toro crossed over to Bedford. She usually avoided this section. Down the block was where Bella had her first tattoo parlor. It was still a wreck from the bombing, the glassless windows boarded up with plywood, the door covered with corrugated sheet metal.

The destroyed building now belonged to Kiro. The man was a fool to let a prime location on Bedford Street sit unrepaired and empty so long. Toro scrunched up her nose. Showed how much money the bastard was awash in.

Toro slowed as she came abreast of the building. Above the door lintel, Hanger had painted one of his overly voluptuous mermaids. The silver sea siren's tail glittered in the late morning sun.

It was masterful. She'd been so inflamed by the breasts, she'd never really examined his street art pieces. There was no denying the kid was a gifted artist, almost as good as her, and he was five years younger.

She squeezed her hands into fists. Her brother had so much going for him, he couldn't die.

She walked past The Siren and headed for the bakery across the street. Hanger loved their chocolate chip muffins. She halted mid-street. This was stupid. Hanger wouldn't be noshing on bakery goodies. Pharaoh said he was feverish, infected, gravely ill.

A car horn honked, and she dashed back onto the sidewalk. Solo was right. They had to get the other graffiti kids together and start a block by block search. But it would take forever, with no guarantees of success. If Hanger was passed out or worse, he wouldn't hear them calling for him.

She rubbed her temples and forced herself to think like Hanger. She pictured the parking lots she'd cut through down in Red Hook. He'd not have stopped in one of them. He'd have wanted to get away from those men just as she had.

He would have passed through those yards with the

low fences, set on getting back to Williamsburg where he knew every inch of the ground.

He'd have had to walk several miles, what with zigging and zagging to throw off his pursuers. She'd just run it. But Hanger was tough. No matter how sick he was, she knew he'd make it this far.

She slapped her thigh. So where was he? Had he been recaptured?

She pictured Kiro staring up at her again in his damaged leather jacket. Damn. If Kiro had been at Jax's, then there was no more wondering on her part; he was knee-deep in all this shit. He was the one who'd captured Hanger.

And one thing was undeniable—Shark Man had far more manpower than T-Crew. If he was after Hanger, he'd find him.

She kicked a water bottle someone had dropped into the gutter and hurried down the street. Hanger was out here dying. She had to find him before Kiro did. She had to find him before it was too late.

Chapter 22

Hanger crept over to the opening in the wall and peered out. *Mouse turds*. Kiro's thug was still there.

He sat back and rubbed his leg. Three shots of antibiotics might have calmed the fever and dizziness enough to allow him to climb out the window and hoist himself down to the fire escape—he pressed a hand against his eyes—but now the blurred vision and pounding headache were back with a vengeance.

He might have managed to limp as far as the old Siren, but he wasn't going any farther. Not now. Not feeling so punky. He'd never outrun the guy on the corner. But he'd have to. He couldn't let his sister marry Shark Man.

He'd rest here awhile and wait for it to get darker.

Taking a deep breath, Hanger crept deeper into the ruins. He was glad Bella's old tattoo studio had not been repaired after last year's bombing. The blackened bricks and fallen tin ceiling made a warren of hidey holes perfect for a graffiti kid playing hooky or hiding from the neighborhood bullies.

He crawled beneath a beam and wiggled into his lair. With an old piece of foam on the floor for a cushion and Bella's dented-in file cabinet to lean against, this was the best hiding place in the whole world.

But not today. He rolled his shoulders. The foam

was damp and lumpy, and through a hole in the rusted tin, water dripped onto his neck and ran down his back, the trickle so cold on his fever-hot skin, it burned.

He shifted his thigh and let out a moan. The infected tat was a ball of fire, and his body throbbed with the pain of it. It was like having hundreds of tiny yellow jackets stinging him.

He leaned down and sniffed. It stank, too.

Pharaoh said he'd lose his leg. Right now, if a doctor asked him to give permission to cut it off, he'd say yes.

He had no knife or he might do it himself. It hurt that much.

Not that he wanted to be an amputee. He pictured the homeless veterans with their missing limbs. People looked at them with pity in their eyes, but also fear—like the guy would suddenly attack them or something.

He didn't want to be like that—deformed, different, handicapped. The kids already treated him bad. He'd be helpless if he couldn't run, couldn't climb up the side of buildings. He wouldn't be able to tag any more or go out at night with T-Crew to put up pieces or hit the subway cars.

Oh, what the hell. He sucked on a hard candy and ignored his thirst. At the rate he was going, he would die here in this burnt-out building and turn into a heap of bones, and nobody'd ever know what happened.

Someday workmen would find a skeleton, and it would be in all the newspapers. But no one would come to identify him. Toro would be married to creepo Shark Tooth or dead, and he'd be one of those cold cases the cops never got solved.

Damn it. He was just a kid. Fifteen. He squeezed

his eyes closed against the pain. He didn't want to die. He'd take living with one leg over being dead. And he had to warn Toro, even if it killed him.

A scampering and brushing sound came from deeper in the wreckage, and he went rigid. *Rats.* He hated the creatures. They ate people alive. He'd seen it. Homeless men missing noses. A woman with a piece torn from her lip. Too many chewed ears to count.

Laid up here, he was a sitting duck. He rubbed the scar on his finger where a rat had bitten him back in what Toro called their "wandering days," before Bella's brother Ari had taken them under his wing, and given them that great apartment building.

There was another rustle. He scrambled around for a brick to throw.

The swishing came again. Louder. Closer. He huddled farther back into his rickety cave, brick at the ready and waited.

In the opening, two eyes appeared and then two ears. Pointy ears.

Not a rat. A cat. He lowered the brick. Cats were all right. They ate rats. They liked people—the animal let out a low growl—sometimes.

"Sorry. Am I in your spot, old guy? Come, we can keep each other warm." He held out a hand and wiggled his fingers, hoping the creature didn't decide to take a bite. He wouldn't blame it if it did. The poor thing was all skin and bones and hunger.

But it didn't. Instead, the cat slunk closer, giving him a better look at the wreck of its body. It was gray with matted fur and ragged ears. One of its back legs was missing and one whole side was scarred and bare of fur.

The creature had had a rough time of it sometime in the past. The injuries were more than a feral cat would get in the normal course of things. He'd seen plenty of mauled toms.

Bella belonged to one of those spay and release groups. She'd had a regular cattery out back of this building before the bombing. He glanced around at the blackened timbers and warped metal. Burns? Scars? A missing leg?

"Hey, kitty, were you in The Siren when it was bombed?" He wracked his brain for the names of her cats. There'd been the nasty orange cat Pussyballs that bit. A black tom called Old Boy or something like that.

Wait. She'd had a gray kitten. He'd fed it when she went on vacation sometimes. A round little ball of fur, always purring, named Fishtail. Had the kitten survived the blast?

He studied the ratty creature. It seemed impossible such a small animal could have lived through an explosion. If it had, would it even remember its name after such a trauma?

Couldn't hurt to try. He wiggled his fingers again. "Fishtail. Are you Fishtail?"

The cat stretched out its neck and sniffed. Hanger held his breath as the little guy's cold nose brushed across the back of his hand. Hanger extended his hand. "Wow. You *are* Fishtail. I just know it. A real survivor, aren't you?

The world might be falling apart around him, his sister in danger, his body racked in pain, but in this moment, it was just him and this cat.

If he could win its trust, it would be a sign that maybe there was some hope—that things could turn out all right. If Fishtail could survive without a leg, despite the odds, then maybe he could, too.

The cat stood like a statue for what seemed like an eternity. Hanger's leg throbbed. The traffic outside hustled and bustled. Raindrops dripped down his neck. Somewhere in the distance, police sirens rose and fell.

Finally, just as he was losing interest, the cat took a slow-motion step toward him. Then another. "That's a boy," he whispered. "Come, Fishtail. I won't hurt you."

And then it was there, nuzzling up against him, stinking of garbage and who knew what shit. But then he did, too.

Hanger rubbed the cat under the chin and listened to it purr. "I wish I had food for you, Fishtail. If I ever get out of here, I'll bring some back, I promise.

"In fact—remember Bella?" He patted the cat's head with his lightest of touches. "She's gonna be real excited to see you again. She was over-the-top upset when she thought you died in the blast."

He bit his lip. "Only—she may not want to talk to me. Been making a fool of myself with her—putting her face on those throw-ups." He ran his hand down the cat's back, ignoring the fact it was sticky and matted and totally gross. At least it was warm and alive.

The cat purred louder. He worked at one of the tangles of fur. "I bet she's glad I'm gone and not messing with her. I bet they all are. Still—I should try to reach Toro. She's in danger." He shifted forward and peeked out the opening. "Getting dark, Fishtail. Time I moved on if I ever am going to. You want to come?"

He leaned over to pick up the cat. But it hunched away. He reached again. This time the cat hissed and scratched his hand. "I know. Can't trust anyone in this world. You stay. I'll come back for you. With kibble and treats."

Wiggling on his side, Hanger snaked his way forward, struggling to keep his bad leg from hitting anything. After what seemed like hours, he came out at the back of the shop and maneuvered into a sitting position.

He rubbed his leg. Up on the roofs, he would be home free, moving like a superhero.

But with this leg, he would have to act like a creepy, crawly toad, hopping from shadow to shadow, praying none of Kiro's goons were looking his way.

Chapter 23

Toro stuffed her brushes and paints into the wheeled suitcase and looked around the Foundry. It was time for Alba Vargas to disappear. She purposely avoided looking at the new painting she'd been working on—the one showing two lovers kissing on the Williamsburg Bridge.

She couldn't take it with her. It was too large. Kiro was welcome to it. But he wasn't going to have her. Now that Hanger had escaped, she didn't need anything more to do with Kiro and his stupid marriage proposal.

She looked down at the borrowed gypsy skirt and peasant blouse she had thrown on. It was one of Bella's favorite outfits, and she could see why. The clothing was loose and airy and made her feel like she could fly.

She imagined the look of male appreciation Pharaoh would give her if he saw her in the flirty skirt. She'd loved that look in his eyes and how he'd made love to her. It still sent shivers through her just thinking of his fingers and mouth touching her body, worshipping her.

Mierda. There she went again. Mooning over something she could never have. She'd never forget the look on his face when he realized his angel was the scruffy street kid he'd hung with for years.

She zipped up her suitcase and gave one last glance around. All the tables were clear. No trace left of art materials or fancy dinners. Done. Done. Done.

She grabbed the suitcase handle and started for the door.

"Going somewhere?"

Toro's heart jumped, and her stomach dropped. She came to an abrupt halt and looked up.

Kiro stood leaning over the railing of the second-floor suspended living area. He waved. "Been waiting for you to show up."

She grasped the suitcase tighter. "I have an appointment."

"To paint?"

Damn. He'd seen her collect up all her supplies. She needed an explanation, any explanation. She said the first thing to pop into her head. "Why yes. I've a commission to paint a mural."

He pointed his finger at her. "You signed a contract. All your work belongs to me. No outside jobs."

She thought fast. "It's for charity. A homeless shelter. It was arranged long before I met you." Toro gave him what she hoped was a brilliant smile. "I'll credit you with the donation."

"You're too kind." He started down the stairs. "May I come watch?"

Why not? Homeless shelters wouldn't turn away free art. And she knew which one she'd paint. The one where her hope had died. "Sure."

He reached the bottom of the steps. "But first I have a surprise for you."

"A surprise?" She hated surprises. They never turned out well.

He undid her fingers from the handle and moved

the suitcase to lean against the wall.

She glanced at the door and freedom. "But I really—"

"Hush, my love. Come and see. I've outdone myself." He looped his arm around hers and whispered in her ear. "It's upstairs."

There was no escaping his armlock without resorting to violence, and this close she was aware of his much larger size and well-muscled body. Surely, he was armed too.

Better she pretend to be enamored and wait till she could slither away. She'd take a quick look at his "surprise" and then bound down the stairs and out. He'd never catch her once she was on the street, no matter how many goons he had guarding the place.

Toro stepped up on the first step of the suspended staircase, the metal vibrating beneath the soles of her shoes, the supporting chain rattling.

"That's my girl." Kiro smiled like a man who'd won the lottery.

She really didn't think she was going to like his surprise.

Still, she took another step up. Kiro, on the outside, pressed against her—so close she could feel the rub of his clothes against her bare arm and smell his sharp, citrusy scent. Probably some expensive cologne.

On a different man, it might have been enticing. On Shark Man, it made her think of the fermenting oranges she and Hanger used to snag from the trash bins behind the wholesale food market.

She reached the top step. Kiro handed her up and then followed. For one second, she considered giving him a push. One shove with her elbow and he'd tumble fifteen feet to the metal-strewn floor below.

There was a high likelihood he'd die. If he didn't, she could end up in jail for assault. Hell, then who would take care of Hanger?

Still, it would solve a lot of their problems, and maybe she wouldn't be caught. Toro winged out her arm.

But she waited too long. Kiro stepped past her, swung around, and gave a sweeping bow. "Our love nest."

Her gaze swept across the apartment. It was completely refurnished. Hand-painted silk banners hung down, breaking the open-concept space into cozy intimate areas for two. In one corner sat an expensive leather loveseat with a fluffy white Greek flokati rug right in front of it.

By the window with the view of the river was a glass dining table and two well-cushioned chairs. The table was set with glittering crystal and black porcelain, illuminated by an overhead light made of thousands of pieces of rectangular glass. Beyond was the low wall that divided the bedroom from the rest of the space. She looked away. She didn't want to see what he'd done to the bed.

He tucked his hand under her elbow and to her relief guided her to the eating area, not the bedroom. "I have prepared a treat for us. Sit." He helped her into the chair.

In the center of the table was a tray of crackers with toppings she'd never seen before.

He sat down opposite her. "Arrayed before you is every aphrodisiac food known to man. Here"—he picked up one of the items and held it to her lips—"try one. Avocado spread."

Toro took a small nibble. Her mouth filled with a salty oily flavor, not unpleasant, but nothing she'd pay a fortune for either. She licked her lips and swallowed. "It's okay."

"No tingles? Then taste this one." He raised a seashell to her mouth. "Oysters Rockefeller."

She touched her tongue to it. This one tasted fishy, but seemed edible. She slurped the meat into her mouth and chewed. It was rubbery, hard to get down.

"Good girl. One more."

This one she recognized. It was a square of chocolate. But when it landed on her tongue the flavor was amazing. The chocolate melted in her mouth, rich, sweet, and heavenly. "Oh." She closed her eyes, savored the taste, and then regretfully swallowed.

"Open your eyes, darling."

She snapped her eyelids up, mortified to have shown such vulnerability before the man. She patted her mouth with the cloth napkin and peered down at the tray. "You said they were aphrodisiacs. Seems like funny tasting food to me. Liked the chocolate thing, though."

He reached out a finely-manicured finger and touched her lower lip. "So innocent. I am going to enjoy introducing you to the wonders of the world." He pushed away from the table. "Besides, I didn't say they would excite *you*, did I?" He stood up. "But I, on the other hand, am quite aroused by that gustatory display."

And he was. She could see the bulge in his pants and the lust in his eyes. She looked toward the stairs. "Well, I must be going. The mural—"

He corralled her with his arms. "Not yet. One more

surprise. This way."

Hell, he was taking her to the bedroom. She brushed her hand over the knife she had hidden in the waistband of her skirt. At this point all she wanted to do was leave and make Alba Vargas disappear forever. But she'd defend herself if she had to.

But it wasn't the bedroom Kiro had in mind. Instead, he guided her up the spiral steps that went to the roof.

It was the end of a beautiful spring day, and although the high rise to her left blocked some of the view, what she could see took her breath away. To the west, the city skyline was silhouetted against a sky streaked orange and yellow, rose and lavender.

Below, the inky East River flowed under the Williamsburg Bridge with its soaring towers—the bridge that defined her childhood, that marked the place where she'd saved the man she loved, and that sported the graffiti tags put up there by T-Crew.

Her fingers twitched as she imagined swirling ultramarine violet, rose madder, and gold ochre across her canvas and seeing T-Crew's jungle gym captured in all its glory. "I would love to paint this."

"And you will."

Her heart beat sped up. Damn, she'd said that aloud.

She glanced at Kiro. Confident bastard. Painting this view? Not likely. That would mean she'd married him, and that was never going to happen.

"This way." He drew her to a wrought iron bench on the edge of what appeared to be a rooftop garden. Earthenware containers full of green shoots and small trees lined a stone walkway, giving off a scent of dirt and growing things at odds with the fumes rising from the streets below.

She'd come upon a few gardens on rooftops in her travels. They'd always fascinated her. "You've put flowers up here? Must have cost a fortune."

He waved his hand. "Money well spent. Do you like it?"

"It's lovely. But it's only a temporary studio for me. Why waste your money?"

"It is not temporary." He drew a paper out of his jacket pocket. "You rented for only one month. Couldn't have that." He handed the paper to her.

She dragged her fingers over the legal-looking document. "What's this?"

"The deed."

"What?" She unfolded the paper. It was a deed to The Foundry, and it bore her name. "But why?"

He laughed. "It is so easy to surprise you." He shrugged. "My wedding present for you, of course. Your own studio and gallery. Prime location. Glorious view. Right next door to our main residence. A garden for you to rest in and sketch. It had been slated for demolition. But not anymore."

"But I—"

He closed her hand over the deed. "No buts. It is yours. Now come."

Stunned, she tucked the paper in the waistband of her skirt.

He guided her to the bench. "Sit, my dear."

Then he sat down next to her and snugged his arm around her shoulder. "Do you know how enticing you look with that filmy skirt floating around you and your skin tinted with the golden glow of the sunset?"

He brushed his fingers along the side of her neck.

She shivered, not because it was arousing, although she was surprised it felt pleasant, but because she was suddenly frightened. The man was wooing her. She'd never thought Kiro could be anything but cruel and nasty.

Vernon spoke so poorly of him. Hanger hated him. Bella feared him. But he was being gentle and that gentleness scared her more than if he'd held a switchblade to her neck.

He swirled his fingers beneath her chin. "You're so soft. Too delicate for this world of brick and concrete."

He kissed her behind the ear. "I love how you shiver and tremble when I touch you. Your back straightens right up like a newly adopted kitten not quite trusting its new owner." He stroked her again. "You're so different from the women I usually meet. Compared to you they all seem jaded—boring.

"Your inexperience and fear are so very, very attractive. I am looking forward to introducing you to new foods, dressing you in couture, showing you the wonders of the world. For our honeymoon, I've planned a trip to Europe. Think of the new sights and vistas you'll be able to paint."

"Paint?"

He wanted her to paint after they were married? She fingered the deed to the Foundry. Maybe marriage to him wouldn't be so bad.

She gave herself a shake. This was Kiro, the Shark Man. He'd kidnapped her brother, who was dying out there while she sat here and listened to sweet nothings from a monster. She put a hand on the bench seat and pushed up.

"Wait." He rose and pulled her around to face him. "I know it is hard to believe. I admit I know absolutely nothing about art. Thought it a stupid investment. Sold all my brother's collection. But you have opened my eyes. I look at your paintings on the walls of my living room, and I see this neighborhood with new eyes. Details of my empire I never noticed before."

He reached down and picked up both her hands in his. "I know I haven't been the best of men. Done things I am not proud of. But with you at my side, I feel like I can be a new person—a better person."

Toro nodded her agreement. She'd agree to anything if she could get out of his grasp. "I'm sure there is great goodness in you."

He laughed. "Not great. Not good. Look, before we go farther you need to know exactly who and what I am. There can be no secrets between man and wife."

He drew her around to face the city skyline and wrapped his arms about her. He nestled his chin in her hair. "My father was a cruel, abusive man. He beat my mother and cheated on her. I was just a kid, and there was no way I could protect her. She'd tell me to hide under the bed and I would, but I could still hear them screaming and yelling and then the slaps and punches and whimpers that followed. It was no way to grow up.

"My step-brother was older. A real tough. He knew how to fight. How to kill. He should have done something to stop it. Saved her. But he didn't. He walked out and abandoned us. I swore I would destroy him. And I did. Except, the plan went wrong, and my mother ended up dead." He let go and took a step away from her.

Toro was shocked to see tears in his eyes. "You

loved her?"

He wiped them away. "Yes. She wasn't perfect. But she took care of me. Kept me safe."

Toro felt a moment of sympathy for him. From what she knew, his mother had double-crossed him. Still, her own mother had been horrid, and still she loved her. Children grasped at the smallest thing.

But Kiro had gained control of himself. He faced her again. "I wrested my father's ill-gotten gains from my brother. Now it is time for me to make things right. I want to do good with what I have. I have big plans. I'm going to be mayor of the Big Apple or maybe a senator. I want you with all your mystery and passion by my side." He put both hands on either side of her head. "I never thought I'd feel this way. I think of you every minute of the day. My body wants you. But it's more than that. You make me feel alive. Needed. Like I can conquer the world. I love you, Alba Vargas. I know you don't trust me. I know you are frightened. But I swear I will never abuse you or hurt you. I will never cheat on you. I will not be my father. I will cherish you all my life. And I can't wait for the wedding day. In fact, there is no reason to wait. Let's get married tomorrow."

Toro swallowed hard. The words were perfect. They were just being said by the wrong man. "A wedding tomorrow?"

"Tomorrow." His mouth came down on hers, and for a moment, she thought he'd belie his promises and be rough and possessive. But he wasn't.

His kiss was gentle, tentative—she hated to say it—the kiss was loving. Hell. Maybe he really did love her.

She pulled her head back and broke the kiss. She peered into his eyes. They were soft and luminous in the glow of the sunset. Vulnerable.

The tough-guy façade was gone, and all she could see was a little boy hungry for love. Rejecting a man in lust was one thing, rejecting a man who wanted to possess and hurt was another, but rejecting a man in love—striking at his heart—was a level of cruelty she didn't want to own.

She'd seen the destruction that caused in Pharaoh's eyes when he learned who she really was.

She couldn't marry Kiro for all sorts of reasons. But the biggest one, the one thundering in her heart, was also the cruelest. She couldn't marry him because she loved someone else.

She pressed her hand against his chest. His warmth seeped through his shirt. His heart thumped against her palm. All sorts of things had happened to him to make him this—creature. He had her pity, but he'd have to find another woman to love.

"I can't marry you." She twisted the ring off her finger. "I—I—" Lies pounded around her brain, but only the truth would do. "I don't love you—"

Kiro glared at her, his face white with shock. "You can learn. I'll make it easy—"

She put the ring on his palm and closed his fingers over it. "I—I should never have let you think I was even interested. I love someone else."

Then she turned and ran. Behind her, she heard Kiro's shout, and then his feet thumping down the steps behind her. "Who—who do you love?"

She raced across the living room and throwing propriety and caution to the wind, grasped the suspension chain holding up the stairs and slid down. Grabbing her suitcase, she took one last look up.

Kiro glowered at her, his face a cold mask, his words turning her feet leaden. "I'm not giving you up, Alba Vargas. I just gave you my heart and soul. You can't reject it. I'll find out who you love, and when I do, you'll come back. Begging for his life. Begging to marry me. It's what my father would have done. Maybe he was smarter than I thought."

Chapter 24

By the time Toro got back to Big Bad, she was seething. How dare Shark Man make her feel sorry for him? He'd shown his true colors at the end.

She tore off the skirt and blouse and stuffed them in a black plastic bag. Then she whipped around the room, gathering up the frilly underwear and the dresses. This was all going back to Bella. She never wanted to be a girl again—to feel that vulnerable in the presence of a man.

She wrapped the elastic around her torso, ruthlessly crushing her breasts. Next, she pulled a spray-paint-stained sweat shirt over her head, snugged it down. Last, she yanked on a pair of jeans and put her hands on her hips. There. She felt like herself again.

The paper Kiro had given her lay on the floor. The deed to The Foundry. Wouldn't it be a scream if it she really owned it?

She picked it up and slapped it against her palm. If the paperwork was on the up and up, she could sell the place. Should bring in a pretty penny. And she needed it. Shark Man had never paid her the promised thirty thousand for her paintings.

And now he never would.

For a moment, she wondered what he thought when she'd slid down the chain like a street monkey and then tossed the thought aside. He could think what he liked. She was done with him.

She shoved the deed into the top drawer of her nightstand. She'd have Hanlin's law office check if it was authentic tomorrow.

If he said yes, she'd put it on the market. It was a prime location right on the river with a view of Manhattan. Worth hundreds of thousands of dollars. More than enough to escape to Greece—once she'd found Hanger. Eudokia was looking better by the minute.

There was a knock on the door. She opened it a crack. Solo handed her a brown envelope. "This was dropped off by courier just now. Addressed to you. Got a secret admirer? Never got mail here before with your surname on it."

A chill swept over her. "Not that I know of." No one knew Alba Vargas lived here. She'd used a post office box for her contest entries.

Toro took the envelope, hand shaking. A. Vargas was printed on the address label. "Thanks. Probably a bill."

Solo raised an eyebrow, disbelief written in his frown. "Pigeon piss. Bills don't come by courier, Toro. Could be something to do with Hanger."

"If it's trouble, I'll let you know."

Solo put a hand on the doorframe and regarded her. "About Hanger. Neto and I will start combing along the river after closing time. Check places he might hole up in. He's got to be close by now. It's been almost twenty-four hours since he escaped. The good news is the girl Neto rescued says he had three doses of antibiotic. Guess they weren't planning on killing him."

"Right." Toro rolled up her sleeves. "No leads

from the detective yet?"

"Cami gave the guy the lowdown. We'll find Hanger, Toro. I promise."

"I know. You guys are great. I was just changing and getting ready to go out and look. I'll check along Bedford again. He might head to Bella's."

"Sounds like a plan. Keep your phone on you so we can stay in touch."

She nodded. "Will do."

Solo left, and Toro pulled the door closed. She leaned against it and stared down at the envelope. No one she knew would send anything to her here. She poked at it. She had a feeling that if she opened it, all hell would break lose like in the story of Pandora's box.

She worked her fingernail beneath the flap and drew out the single sheet of paper inside. The grainy black and white photocopy showed her coming out of T-Crew's the night of the gala wearing the pickle dress.

Toro crumpled the picture and tossed it across the room. *Idiota.* How could she have been so stupid?

She yanked up the blind and scanned the façade of the building across the street. *There*—on the wall opposite the entrance to the apartments—the tell-tale glint of a red light from a surveillance camera disguised as a sconce.

She let the slats fall and retrieved the balled-up paper. The simple typewritten note at the bottom contained no identifying information. It didn't have too. This was Kiro's work, and it meant he'd known who she was long before the gala—long before his marriage proposal—long before his declaration of love.

How could she have thought she had the freedom to say no to a shark? Cole Kiro Tuccio had always been in control.

She stared at the note. His brief message gave her two choices. She could do what he asked and marry him tomorrow morning at eleven in the New Museum Skyroom in front of a select group of guests, or—although it would leave him heartbroken—she could choose not to and lose everyone she loved. He didn't specify, but she had a good idea who he meant.

The man controlled a criminal empire. One flick of his finger and Solo, Neto, Vernon, Bella and the baby would be dead, her brother and the man she loved lost forever.

Hanger might have escaped from Jax's, but the chances of finding him before the wedding were slim.

She slumped down on the bed. Why had she thought she could rise above the streets? Make a better life for Hanger and herself. Become a world-renowned artist.

Estúpida! She wished she'd never entered the competition. Never went to the awards ceremony. Never touched brush to canvas.

She smoothed out the note. Why was he so desperate to marry a nobody street brat anyway? He was a billionaire who could have any woman he desired. And if all he wanted to do was bed her, he didn't need a legal piece of paper.

She remembered the tender look in his eyes. He'd said he loved her. Could it be true?

She got up and looked out the window again. Shark Man in love? Preposterous.

Hell. If he loved her, he wouldn't be threatening her. He'd come wooing with flowers and chocolates. Something wasn't adding up.

But it didn't matter. She had no choice. She'd go through the sham of a marriage and find a way to escape him afterward—if she could.

So many things could go wrong. He could tie her up. Drug her. The thought of him taking from her what she'd so joyously given Pharaoh made her chest feel leaden. She should have knocked the bastard down the stairs when she had the chance.

She curled her hands into tight fists. It didn't matter what happened to her. She couldn't risk the lives of the people she loved.

Tugging on her baseball cap, she tossed the note in the wastebasket and picked up her sling shot. She gave it a practice pull. She hadn't used it in a long time. Not since she and Hanger had been homeless on the streets, and she'd needed a way to keep the rats and other vermin at bay.

Back then, she'd been deadly with it. She snapped it again. The surveillance camera was a lot bigger than a rat's eye. No matter how out of practice she was, she'd hit it.

Toro hustled out onto the stoop and stopped to pick up a small piece of broken concrete. Perfect. Then she took aim and let it fly.

The chunk hurtled through the air and made a satisfying smash as the plastic light cover splintered into a million pieces, and the intrusive red eye went dark.

Stuffing the sling in her pants pocket, she gave a nod of satisfaction. Then she set a course for The Siren. It was time to reveal all to her friends so they could protect themselves from her foolishness and along the way—she patted her pocket—take out every security camera.

****

Fifteen minutes later, Toro knew she'd made a mistake. Baring her soul hadn't protected her friends, only raised more problems. Vernon had already stormed out of the apartment. Across from her, Bella was giving her a look that hurt worse than a stab from a knife.

The tattoo artist put her hands on her hips. "What did you say to my husband to make him dash out of here after he's installed kitchens all day? Man's dead on his feet."

Toro looked down at the scuffed tips of her sneakers and said it again. "I told him I am marrying his brother. The wedding is tomorrow morning."

"You planning on ending up dead?"

"No, I'm gonna play the stupid loving wife and keep everyone safe."

"Right, and what fairy tale have you been reading?"

"I can do it."

"The man's a monster—he's vicious. The kind who would cut off a baby's toes just to hear it cry."

Toro pressed her lips together. Bella was right. The idea she could survive as Shark Man's wife was ludicrous. Didn't matter. She dumped the black plastic bag on the floor. "Just make me look like a bride."

Vernon came back into the apartment and slammed the door. "All right. I've gotten in touch with some of my old friends. The Siren and our apartment will be well guarded. The police are already watching Big Bad. And my brother's going to be majorly delayed getting to the church—"

"Museum," Toro corrected.

Vernon flipped his hand. "The whatever—on time."

Bella put a hand on his arm. "I told you—"

He clasped his over hers. "You want your friend here to end up dead or worse?"

"Can't you just talk to your brother?" Bella asked.

"Love, there's a time to gab and there's a time to take action. I warned Kiro if he threatened me and mine, I'd not sit back. And Toro is one of us. So's Hanger. He was the one who saved you from drowning in that cistern. I owe your life to him." He glared at Toro. "Word on the street is Jax has an army out there looking for your brother. You've got to find him first."

Toro looked from one to the other. "But the wedding—if I don't show?"

"Trust me," Vernon said. "My brother is not going to be thinking about weddings, brides, or street-smart scamps for at least the next twelve hours or more. He's got way more pressing problems to deal with at the moment. Deliveries are gonna show up in the wrong place. Debts are gonna be called in. Now get out of here and find your brother ASAP."

Toro turned to go.

"Wait." Bella put a hand on her arm. "Did you check out the old Siren? I caught him there a number of times when I went back to look for any strays still hanging around. I warned him away. All that debris could crash down any time." She rubbed her bulging belly. "It's been a while since I've walked that far, but boys like messing in places they've been forbidden."

Toro tipped her cap. "Good idea. I'll start there."

Chapter 25

Toro flicked off the flashlight and pulled her head out from under the sooty wooden beam that had once held up the ceiling of the old Siren. She sat back on her knees. Bella was right. Hanger hung out here.

Every rotting surface of the old Siren sported naked mermaids and his signature MV tag. Soggy old test papers, balled up truant slips, and irate notes from teachers tucked in every nook and cranny explained why she'd had the mistaken impression he'd been doing well at school.

She could find no sign he'd been here recently. But for some reason, she was sure he had. It was almost as if she could pick out his scent from all the other noxious smells.

The rubble creaked above her, and with a curse at Kiro for creating a kid-enticing-deathtrap by leaving the building derelict, she climbed out of the narrow space. She stood up and brushed off her jeans.

Hanger was damn lucky he'd not been crushed under there. But he was not going to be lucky when she found him.

Toro glanced above her and cursed again. Overhead, the sky was turning the silver color of predawn that warned all street kids to get into whatever safe place they could find. She'd hoped to find him before light. Her brother was smart enough to know not

240

to move during the day.

Toro slipped down the alley and came out on the side street. A man wearing a spray-painted jacket stood with his back to her. One of Jax's men. She pulled back into the alley and prayed her brother was nowhere close by.

A shout came from her right, and there he was. Hanger, face drawn, hair tangled, limping toward her from the opposite corner. She'd found him. But so had Jax's thug.

From the corner of her eye, she could see the man whirl and wave furiously at someone farther down the street.

Giving a whistle, she held up her hand to stop Hanger in his tracks. She yelled across, "Go. Go left."

Hanger turned, and she raced after him, running full out as she had so many times when the police and the night watchman and the social workers had come after them. No way was Kiro going to get his hands on her brother again.

Later, the intersection of events would seem like something only the devil could arrange, but at that moment, the lumbering New York City garbage truck with its squealing brakes and the upended trash can landing in her way and the streetlight turning red were simply obstacles to get around as she flew toward her brother as he limped along the other side of the street.

He stumbled, and she leaped in front of the oncoming traffic and, ignoring the horns blaring and the tires squealing and drivers cursing, kept going, reaching out, touching him, and then grasping nothing.

Whack. A hard fist struck her in the back, knocking the air out of her lungs and sending her skidding across the pavement. She landed up against a fire hydrant.

Pain ripped through her as every limb went numb, and her chest struggled to draw in the next breath. Not again. She couldn't be paralyzed. Not now.

Through blurred vision and throbbing silence, she watched two men grab her brother and yank him into a black car.

She'd lost him. Toro let her head fall

"You all right, son?" A gray-haired homeless man stooped over her, his clothes blanketing her with the mix of fermented sweat and excrement all street people wore as a badge of survival.

She knew it well, had worn it, too. In some strange way, it comforted her. And at the moment, his stink was doing her a big favor, because it gave the early morning pedestrians a reason to skirt around her and not look too closely. Probably thought her another bum.

She half-opened one eye. She knew most of the homeless in the neighborhood. Fed them regularly. Two rheumy eyes hazed with cataracts blinked at her. Combined with the four missing front teeth, he was instantly recognizable. "That you, Ernie?"

"Yes, sir, boyo," he said, his breath strong with alcohol despite the early hour. "I know you?"

Somewhere in the distance, an ambulance siren screamed. Some do-bee passerby had assuaged his or her conscience by calling for help. They were coming for her. "Yeah, you know me. Help me up, old man."

Ernie's tongue poked out through the space left by the missing teeth as he bent over closer. He touched her hand. His finger came away bloody. "Don't look good. Need doctoring."

She'd left a lot of flesh on the sidewalk. That

wasn't the major problem. It was her legs. "Later." She put her hand on his arm and by willpower alone pulled herself to her knees. She tipped her chin toward the trash cans lined up outside a flower shop. "Over there. Quick."

The guy's mouth opened and closed like a fish's. "Sandwiches."

"Huh? Oh yeah. I give you sandwiches." She leaned harder on him, prayed he didn't tumble too, pulled her feet under her, and amazingly, stood. *Gracias a dios*, she wasn't paralyzed.

Not being able to move, confined to a wheel chair for months, had been a nightmare. One she never wanted to repeat.

Her dazed rescuer finally got the idea and wrapped an arm over her shoulder to steady her. "Good job, Ernie. Now help me get off the street."

Ernie's daytime lair was behind a deli and reeked of spoiled meat and cat piss, a nose-burning combination, made worse by the emanating stink from a nearby sewer drain.

Getting her there had taken all Ernie's energy, or maybe the alcohol had finally kicked in. But whichever it was, he now lay snoring beside her, a newspaper over his head. Toro rubbed her calf muscles again, working the numbness out, and then rolled down the cuffs of her jeans. Time to go after her brother.

Chapter 26

For the thousandth time, Pharaoh ran his hand along the edges of the door, feeling for a place to wedge in the piece of plate metal he'd twisted off the piss bucket. The storage room they'd tossed him hadn't been intended as a cell. Amazingly, the door hinges were on the inside.

His prison was black as pitch, but from what he'd seen when the food and water were delivered, the hinge plates and screws were rusted from the damp. It wouldn't take much to bend or loosen them.

He fingered the rough-edged metal, found a space, and inserted the shim between the door and the frame as near the hinge as possible. With luck, the next time the door opened, he'd shove it in farther, and the plate would pull out.

Rubbing his ribs—they were surely broken—he sank back down against the wall to wait and think as he drew in each painful breath. He had to escape, and soon. If he stayed much longer in this stinking, dark hole, he'd go crazy.

From somewhere above came the steady banging from the water pipes. The rhythmic thumping mimicked the beating of a disembodied heart. *Thump. Thump. Thump.* He hated the sound.

He hadn't paid much attention in school. Hadn't even attended after tenth grade. But in some warped way, Poe's story of the "Tell-Tale Heart," which his eighth grade English teacher had read aloud to them one stormy Friday afternoon, had worked its way into his nightmares.

Funny that, because in real life, the nightmare had been pressing his ear to his mama's chest and hearing absolutely nothing.

He'd been such an idiot back then. Thinking himself a big man on the street, joining a gang, then having second thoughts. He'd done everything to get out of their reach. Paid bribes. Stayed away from their corners. Hid his face under a hoody. Carried a knife when he walked back and forth to school. Told his school counselor, hoping for protection.

But no one turned his back on the Boom Brothers and survived unscathed.

Their retribution for his desertion was swift and deadly. School bag on his back, he'd just reached the front stoop, and his mother had just stepped out the door, a smile on her face. Then it happened.

A car raced by, a gunshot popped, and his mother fell, her eyes turning in, her welcoming smile dying on her face, taking the bullet meant for him.

Didn't matter his mother had been an honored nurse or a self-sacrificing mother. A drive by shooting of a middle-aged woman in a poor black neighborhood didn't even make the evening news.

He left home that night and never went back. Somewhere in uptown Manhattan, he had a grandmother and aunts and a grown sister. But he'd never return home. No one else in his family would die because of him.

Pharaoh's head jerked up. Had he heard

something? Yes, there—a shuffling outside the door, a rusty bolt sliding. He gripped the jagged metal tighter. The door opened in with a squeal of the worn hinges. Blinding light flooded the small space. In went the metal wedge, and he threw himself forward.

"Out of the way, punk." Pitstop elbowed him in the side. Pain flamed through him. He bent over and took shallow breaths. The thug dropped a bundle at his feet. "Got company for you. Boss says he'll decide what to do with you two after the wedding."

The door slammed closed, and he was left in the dark with the thumping pipes and a companion. A very quiet one. Whoever it was hadn't made a sound or moved.

He called out. "Hey. You awake?" No answer. Damn, he hoped they hadn't locked him up with a dead stiff.

Pharaoh crawled forward, swiping his hand in front of him until he met cloth, then something harder. An palm. He gingerly slid his hand over. The chest beneath his hand rose and fell. Alive.

He let out the breath he hadn't realized he'd been holding and worked his way up until he touched skin— a neck, a small chin, a beardless cheek, a fevered hot brow.

A bad feeling smacked him in the gut. He pressed a hand on the burning forehead. "Hanger? That you?"

There was no answer. But he knew he was right. He gathered the limp body against him and rocked back and forth. Hanger hadn't gotten away, and the fever was back.

He had to escape. He had to save Hanger. He laid the boy down gently and crawled back in what he thought was the direction of the door. It took a few minutes to find it again in the dark.

When he did, a bolt of hope shot through him. The door was no longer flush. He stood and trailed his fingers up the frame. *Yes,* the wedge had worked.

The hinge at the top had pulled away from the wood. He wedged his fingers under the plate and began the slow, tedious process of extracting the screws from the door frame. It would take time.

Hanger moaned.

Time—the one thing they didn't have.

****

Toro stared at the Sunset Palace. She was running out of time. She glanced at the sky. The sun was well up, and the shadows shrinking. It couldn't be more than an hour or two until wedding bells were supposed to be ringing. She only had minutes left to find Hanger.

Across the street, the hotel entrance was quiet. One guy, smoking a cigarette, leaned in the doorway. But otherwise, there was no clue her brother was being held captive inside. Or that Jax was running a brothel.

She pulled off her baseball cap, shook out her hair, and picked up the backpack. She wasn't dressed all flirty and female, but hopefully, she would pass for a lost tourist—a Romanian one—an accent she knew well thanks to her long-gone papa—looking for a room.

She half-extracted her cellphone from her jeans' pocket. She should tell Solo and Neto where she was. But no. She shoved it back in. They'd come and put themselves in danger.

She slipped one arm and then the other into the backpack straps, checked that her knife was easy to reach, and set out across the street. This was her problem, and she was going to solve it.

The guard straightened up as she approached the door. She tossed her head and mimicked the broken English of a foreigner. "Vrooms?"

The guy, young, his sleeveless vest giving a good show of muscle and tats, held open the door. "Sure are, sweetheart. Check in at the desk."

Inside, the lobby was tiny, the narrow space filled with low-grade furnishings—a thin-cushioned sofa upholstered in orangey-brown fabric, a coffee table littered with paper cups and napkins and underfoot a nondescript brown wall-to-wall carpet. Cheap prints on the wall and pots of plastic flowers provided what passed for ambiance.

A half-asleep clerk with slicked-back hair and a potbelly watched a monitor hanging over the check-in counter. He looked up and gave her a grin that would look better on a hungry rat.

Toro held up one finger. "Vroom. One night. How you say. No—" She mimed puffing a cigarette.

The clerk shrugged. "Forty dollars. Paid up front."

Thank heavens for the prize money. A week ago, she couldn't have afforded even a flea bag place like this. She put her pack on the floor, hustled out the cash, and slapped it on the counter.

"Floor three. Room 310. Shared bath." He handed her a key with a plastic tag that looked like it had been chewed by that self-same rat. "To the right and up the stairs. You want food, there's a burger place next door."

Toro squeezed the key in her hand and headed off in the direction he'd pointed. Great. She'd made it inside. Now she had to figure out how to find her brother. Knocking on doors didn't seem to be the best idea. Perhaps she could question a maid.

She reached the third floor and walked down the hallway looking for her room number. For now, she'd play the lost tourist and see what happened.

Her room, when she found it, matched the rest of the place—worn, washed out, and smelling of old cigarette smoke. But considering what went on in this place, it did a good imitation of an up-and-up hotel.

The bed occupied most of the room. A nightstand and a sink filled the rest. An air conditioner in the window blocked her view outside and turned the sunny day to a bare glow of light, but it worked. Cool air blew into the room.

A neatly folded stack of clean towels sat on the bed, topped with a paper-wrapped bar of soap. The sheets looked freshly laundered. Someone at least cared that the customers had a few amenities. Nothing she or the cops could really complain about. Jax was a smart business man, it seemed.

She spied the two glasses on the sink. Ah, water. She could wander around looking for the ice machine. She seized a glass, hitched her knapsack higher on her shoulder and set out to find her brother.

Three floors and a utility closet later, Toro was ready to give up. She'd found the maids to be unable or unwilling to speak English, and the few customers at this early hour in the morning hardly gave her a glance as she padded up to each door and called Hanger's name.

On the fourth floor, she ran into a drunk who'd wanted to know if she was looking for a good time, but who thought her unattractive enough or unisex enough to point her to the ice machine when she demurred.

On the fifth floor, where Hanger had been before, she saw no one and heard nothing. No TVs blaring. No water splashing in a sink. Most likely all Jax's girls were asleep.

She trudged back down to her room. Hanger could be anywhere in the place. Would he even be capable of answering her by this point, or would he be delirious with fever? He'd been barely able to walk.

An expensively suited man stepped out of the room next to hers. He gave her a considering glance. "Looking for someone?"

Toro came to a halt. She held up the glass. "Ice, *please*?"

"Of course, this way."

Broad-chested with dark, darting eyes that seemed to see right into the core of her, the man exuded menace but there was no other choice but to maintain her cover.

A knot of fear curled up in her stomach. He could be leading her anywhere. Toro tucked one hand along her side, ready to draw her knife if she had to.

The gentleman stopped and opened a door. "Here you are. Ice machine and soda and snacks, too." The closet was narrow with a door at the other end. He stood back to make room for her to enter.

"*Mersi.*" It was one of the few Romanian words she remembered. Toro tucked her head down lower— Mr. Suit gave her the willies—and pushed past him to get to the ice machine. She shoved the glass under the spigot. The machine grumbled. Ice clanked into the glass.

"You visiting here in the city?"

Toro nodded her head.

He gave her a hard look. "Girl or boy?"

"Boy." It seemed the safer answer.

"I think not." He reached out as if to touch her face. She jerked back. His hand dropped. "Not that it matters. You are very desirable." He reached into his breast pocket and took out a business card. "I run a modeling agency. Call or stop in any time. I pay well. Very well. I will make you rich. Very rich."

Toro took the card and pinched it between her fingers. "*Da*. Yes."

The man ran his hands down his lapels. "I'll be downstairs if you want to talk. Ask the clerk to show you to my office."

He turned and left, the soles of his highly polished shoes squeaking down the hall.

Modeling agency? Sure. Mr. Shiny Shoes was a pimp if she ever met one. Just being near him made her feel dirty. She glanced down at the card. Jax Wheeler. So this was the man Pharaoh was working for. Ugh.

She picked up her glass and started back to her room. Then stopped. Strange. Where did the door at the other end of this tiny room lead to? Probably a storage closet. But it wouldn't hurt to check.

Putting down her glass of ice, she released the latch, and opened the door a crack, then opened it wider and peered into an unlit stairwell. Obviously, it had originally been built back in the hotel's heyday as a way for the maids to move from floor to floor without meeting guests—a secret way in and out. She stepped out on the landing and let the door close behind her, leaving her in the dark.

Could it also lead to where they were keeping Hanger?

Here was her chance to explore the place. But

which way. Up or down?

She waited for her eyes to adjust. She had a flashlight in her pack, but didn't want to clue anyone she was there.

Besides, it wasn't completely black. Light escaped from under the doors at each level. Down below, it seemed a bit lighter. It would be easier going, and if there were a basement, it would be in that direction. She shivered at the old memory of being trapped in a cold and dark cellar totally at Kiro's mercies.

Shark Man liked those kinds of places. She wouldn't put it past him to have Hanger locked up in a subterranean room.

Down then. She reached out, found the wall and carefully slipped one foot down a step and then another, all the while trying not to think what Kiro would do when she didn't show up on time for the wedding.

Chapter 27

Pharaoh laid Hanger under the staircase and looked up. Overhead, footsteps echoed in the stairwell. Somebody was on the way down. He looked over his shoulder at the way they'd come. They couldn't go back. Not with the storeroom door hanging crazily on its hinges.

The minute the lights came on they'd be bigger than targets at a shooting gallery. And the guns would have real bullets. The best thing would be to hope it was only one person, and he could overpower the creep before he knew what hit him.

He hoped it wasn't Bear. In the condition he was in, he'd never bring down that hulk.

Drawing his jagged piece of metal, he tucked himself under the stairs and waited.

The footsteps grew closer. Step. Pause. Step. Pause. Whoever it was, wasn't in a hurry. Pharaoh adjusted his crouch, his bruised muscles screaming, his broken-rib breath shallow.

Step.

Now. He leaped up and seized the person by the leg. The limb was small and sinewy. Definitely not Bear, thank heavens.

He tugged, and they tumbled together to the floor. An elbow whacked him in the ribs, and he saw stars. He grabbed a hank of hair and held on. He clawed upwards, aiming his sad imitation of a knife for the neck.

Two hands wrapped around his arm, pushing and pressing. Fingers digging in. "Stop, Pharaoh. It's me."

The adrenaline flooding through him turned to ice. He dropped the shiv. "Toro?"

The familiar curves and concavities of her body, soft and vulnerable, pushed tight to his body. Her imprinted scent rose around him. How could he have mistaken her for anyone else? He held on despite the pain.

He wanted to cry. He wanted to kiss her. He wanted to tell her he loved her no matter who she really was. He said nothing. How could he? He'd almost killed her.

A door slammed above them. Voices came and went. Then silence.

Pharaoh pushed her aside and stood, pressing a hand against his throbbing ribs. He offered her his other hand and yanked her up.

He needed to be kind. He needed to be gentle. Instead, all his anger at finding her here in Jax's den whipped out. "What the hell are you doing in this shit hole?"

"Looking for my brother."

He was glad he couldn't see her face in the dark. It was tantalizing enough he could smell her. That he could feel her body against his. He pulled her under the stairs. "Hanger's over here. He's bad, Toro. Got to get him out. Now."

Toro squeezed his wrist. "I knew you didn't abandon us."

He shook off her hand. "Come, I was heading up

the stairs when you came on us. The next visitor won't be on our side."

He hefted Hanger, pain racking through him, sucked in as much air as he could, and spat out the words. "Up. Next. Level. Street."

She brushed against him again. "You can barely stand. Let me help."

He nudged her away with his hip, the contact filling his traitorous body with heat. "Got him. Go." He couldn't see more than the gray shadow of her as she dashed up the steps before him. He was slower, dragged down by the limp weight of the boy and the inability to draw a deep breath.

By the time they reached the top of the stairs, his legs were trembling, and the pain unbearable. He lowered Hanger to the landing and bent over, sucking air into his lungs, every muscle and bone screaming from the exertion. He had no idea how they would get the kid away from Jax's and to safety.

Toro opened the street level door slightly. Pharaoh glanced out. After hours in blackness, all he could see was blinding sunlight. He blinked and then looked again. The hotel backed up against a narrow alley. He could make out walls, trash cans, and little else. Toro looked back at him. "*Mierda*, your poor face. What'd they do to you?" She brushed her hand over his split lip.

"Nothing I didn't deserve. Now get going."

Toro thrust the door open wider. "Looks clear. Know where the alley goes?"

"To the side street. Got folks waiting?"

"No."

His head thundered. "You came alone? Into this pit? They eat girls like you."

"I'm not alone. I have you, don't I?"

This was his chance to apologize. "Yeah, I—"

Hanger moaned. Toro turned away and laid a hand on her brother's back. "We'll get you safe."

"Toro?" Hanger's eyes fluttered.

"Yeah, I'm here."

"Don't—"

"Don't what?"

"Marry Shark Man. You have to go. Hide."

Toro pushed his hair off his brow. "First, we need to get you to a hospital, kid. Then we'll both leave. Go somewhere no one will ever find us."

Pharaoh pulled away. They were going to leave? But of course they would. They needed to get away to somewhere safe. He'd known there was no future for him and Toro. Hell, she thought the idea she was a girl disgusted him—but it still hurt.

Above them came the pounding of feet coming down the steps. Time to move.

Gathering all his strength, Pharaoh pulled Hanger into his arms, kicked the door open, and pushed Toro ahead of him.

He stumbled out into the glare of the sun and glanced at the building opposite them. He wished he could climb up to the roof, but no convenient garbage bin or fire escape stood at the ready and besides, he'd never make it with his broken body and the kid in his arms.

But Toro could. He grasped her by the arm. "Go. Climb up to the roof and wait for me. Call for help. I'll find a place to stash Hanger. Then when it's safe, we can get him to the hospital."

Without checking to see if she obeyed, he threw

Hanger over his shoulder and, moving as fast as he could, he whipped down the narrow alley, searching for an alcove or pile of garbage they could hide behind.

At the end of the alley, he pulled up. Directly in front of him stood Kiro, blocking the only way out.

Kiro smiled, his filed teeth brilliant white in the sun. "Why thank you, Pharaoh. Saved me so much worry and mess. Stick the boy in my car, and I'll see he gets the medical attention he needs." He held out his hand. "Alba, come. We have wedding guests waiting for us."

Alba? Pharaoh spun his head around. Toro stood behind him. "Why didn't you—"

Toro put her hand on Pharaoh's arm. "Put Hanger in the car like he says."

No. He couldn't turn her brother over to that bastard. He'd kill him for sure.

Kiro signaled with his hand. Feet thudded toward him as Jax's men filled the alley from both ends.

Pharaoh gripped Hanger more tightly. There was no room in the narrow alley to fight. No way to escape. He was a goner. Hanger was too, probably. But Toro could still get away. She could scamper up any wall. "You can't marry him. Climb, Toro. Climb. I'll—" But the words died as Bear wrapped his arm around his neck and squeezed.

Pharaoh kicked and flailed and grabbed and scratched at the arm. He didn't care if he died, but he couldn't let Kiro marry his angel. Yet no matter how he twisted and punched he couldn't escape the relentless pressure. The man was like a garbage compactor.

Pharaoh's vision blurred. His limbs weakened. He lost his grip on Hanger. But before he could drop him, the kid was lifted from his arms.

The last thing he glimpsed through the tunnel of blackness closing in on him was Toro, her face drawn and pale, climbing into Kiro's car. He wanted to scream. Tell her he loved her.

But what would be the use? He was a dead man, and she had another battle before her. One she'd have to win by herself.

Chapter 28

Toro scrunched the satin and toile skirt of the wedding dress with her sweaty palms. It had cost a fortune. The woman at the bridal shop who helped zip her into it had looked like all her money troubles had been solved when Kiro pulled it off the rack.

It had tiny crystals all the way down the very low front, long lace sleeves, and layers of skirts that floated around her ankles. She wanted to tear it off and rip it to pieces.

She blew the netting of the filmy veil out of her face and peered out the window as the limo sped across the Williamsburg Bridge. If the door hadn't been child-locked, she'd have jumped out. Instead, she searched for T-Crew's tags. But they were going too fast.

Her groom was in a hurry.

She twisted the engagement ring around her finger. Married. She was freaking getting married to Shark Man.

"Relax. I don't bite."

She squeezed closer to the door. "Oh, yes, you do."

He reached across and touched the bite mark on her neck. "A love nip, sweetheart. I had to have a taste."

"I'll never be yours."

He folded his arms behind his head. "But you will. You are going to say 'I do' in front of the mayor, the police chief, and my law partners. In"—he checked his watch—"thirty minutes." He patted the pocket. "Have the marriage license right here. Went to a lot of trouble to get it. Had to have one of Jax's girls double for you. And then there was getting a birth certificate. Been off the grid a long time, haven't you?"

"You're a lawyer. I'm sure you had no trouble doctoring everything up."

"It was your real birth certificate."

She wrinkled her nose at him. "Yeah. Just like those are your real teeth."

He fumbled in his mouth and pulled off the plastic mold. "You like these better?" He bared his filed teeth at her. "I hope so. It's what you'll see every morning when you wake up next to me."

"Not happening." She glanced toward the front seat where Hanger lay so still she feared he was already dead. "My brother?"

"He's fine. My driver's given him a dose of antibiotic. He'll get another—after we consummate this marriage."

"He needs to be in a hospital. Not getting some half-assed treatment from your chauffeur."

"Sweetheart, I've been more than patient. I have courted you and treated you with respect and honor. I know you don't believe this, but I love you."

"Love me? You have no idea what love is. People who love someone don't threaten them. They don't risk the lives of people that person loves. What kind of marriage do you imagine we could possibly have? I hate you."

He reached across and grabbed her hand. She gave it a jerk, but he only squeezed tighter. "I am going to enjoy taming you. And in a few hours, you and I will be alone, and I am going to show you what true passion is."

Toro glanced out the window. True passion? True passion was going to be her stabbing her new husband to death. But first she had to get Hanger to safety. And that was looking pretty much impossible.

Hanger's head lolled farther to the side until it was bumping against the window. Even if she could escape, her wounded brother couldn't.

Pharaoh had tried so hard to save him. She didn't even want to think about what had happened to the man she loved. They hadn't even gotten to kiss again.

Choked to death in broad daylight just yards from hundreds of people zipping past in their cars, shopping in the stores. It seemed impossible—but true. Kiro had made sure she watched long enough to see him collapse and lie still on the ground.

She pressed her fingers over her mouth and struggled to keep from crying. She couldn't let grief overwhelm her. Not now. She had to save her brother.

****

By the time the limo pulled up at the museum, Toro was desperate. Nothing she could think of doing would stop Kiro from getting his way and making her his wife. She was like one of Bella's stray cats being taken to the pound. She could scratch. She could bite. But in the end her captor would win.

She glanced at the entrance to the museum where Kiro's buddies and political climbers milled about dressed in tuxes and gowns. Not one of them cared about her, some nobody. A dress-up doll hanging on the arm of the billionaire she'd caught. A poor girl who'd gotten lucky. No one would believe her if she said she was being coerced into marriage by one of the city's up-and-coming politicos.

The limo stopped. The driver got out to open the door for her. Kiro tightened his grip on her hand. "No taking off now. Your brother is going to stay and have a nice rest in the car. You make one twitch the wrong way, and I call up my driver here and swish, your brother is going to lose that leg of his. Pretty rotten anyway. Might die. Then it'd be just you and me, sweetheart."

Right then, a city bus drew up beside the limo, stopping for a red light. Hanger's door snapped open, and he tipped out and disappeared under the bus.

"*Hanger.*" Toro yanked and twisted her hand, but Kiro didn't let go.

Instead, he wrestled her out the car door and wrapped an arm around her. "Forget him. My driver will round him up. He's not going far on a bum leg." He signaled his driver, who took off in pursuit. Then he shoved her forward. "Now don't you embarrass me in front of our guests. Remember they are your future art patrons."

Toro glanced back over her shoulder. The light changed, and the bus moved on. But there was no sign of her brother, lying in the street. Clever boy. Pretending to be unconscious, using the bus as cover.

He'd done the impossible. He'd gotten away. And given her a chance to escape.

She prayed Hanger knew enough to lie low until she could come after him. She turned back and faced the entranceway. "You win. Let's go get married."

Kiro smiled and kissed her cheek, but he didn't let go. Then, whistling the wedding march, he escorted her into the museum.

Just inside the entrance stood Vernon, wearing an Armani suit and a clenched-jawed scowl. Toro blinked. Compared to his brother he looked like the real crime boss.

Kiro drew to a halt. "What are you doing here?"

Vernon moved to face his brother. "Calling off the wedding."

"Ha. You have nothing to say about it."

Toro looked back and forth between the two men.

"I think I do. I'm this woman's legal guardian, and you need my permission to marry."

Kiro's eyes narrowed, his lips quivered. "Really? Sounds like something out of the medieval days."

Vernon rocked back on his heels. "I'm very medieval."

"Let me see the papers."

Vernon withdrew a folded paper from his inner suit pocket and handed it over.

Kiro gave the document a quick once over. He waved the last page in Toro's face. "This your signature?"

It wasn't. But it was close enough. "Yep. Alba Marie Vargas. That's me."

"Fine." He stuffed the papers into his pocket and let go of her. He turned on Vernon. "You were supposed to stay out of my way. That was the agreement."

"You're getting loud, brother. Let's step outside."

Toro wanted to do a little dance. She was loving the way Vernon had deflated his brother like a poked balloon.

Vernon put a hand on his brother's back and

nudged him out the door.

Toro followed. She couldn't wait to get out of the dress and take off after Hanger. But as she stepped out behind the two men, a burst of wind caught her veil. She reached out to catch it just as Kiro whipped out a razor-thin knife and drove it into Vernon's midsection with a whispered, "For Mother."

Vernon crumbled to the pavement, a blossom of red blood staining the front of his shirt. People around them gasped.

Toro jerked back in shock. "What the—"

"Shut your mouth. You're coming with me." His expression fierce, Kiro grabbed hold of her arm and dragged her like a shark with its prey down the street toward the parked limo. She kicked and punched and screamed her head off. It did no good. Kiro was unstoppable.

"My bride has cold feet," he hissed at a man stepping into his path. The man held up his hands and backed away. The few pedestrians close enough to do something fell back as if from a madman.

He *was* a madman.

At the curb, she set her feet and yanked against his hold. To get in the limo was to be trapped with no escape. She'd be at his mercy, and now she knew for sure he had none. He'd stabbed his own brother.

Hampered by the dress, she attacked with every weapon she had. Teeth, nails, knees and elbows, and he didn't even grunt. He might be smaller than his brother, but he was bigger and stronger than she was.

She glanced back to where Vernon lay on the street surrounded by passersby. Some taking photos, others calling on their phones. At least Vernon was getting help. Bella would kill her if he died.

Cielos, Bella's baby! It would have no father, and she wouldn't wish that fate on anyone. She yanked again. "Your brother. You've killed him."

"Got what he deserved. But he isn't dead. Now move it." He picked her up like she was a bag of garbage and tossed her into the back seat. She landed in a tumble of satin, her head throbbing where it had smashed against the door opening.

Then he climbed in after her and slammed the door. For a second, she hoped the driver was still searching for Hanger. But he wasn't.

"Penthouse."

"Yes, sir."

The chauffeur stepped on the gas, and they flew forward, speeding through a red light, spinning around the corner.

She gathered up the skirt and scrambled for the door.

"It's locked." Kiro leaned over her, his breath hot on her bare back.

She was in trouble, and she knew it. But she wasn't going to make it easy for him. No way.

Toro twisted to punch him, and he pushed her down on the seat, pressed his weight against her, and caught her by the wrist. Twisting her arm behind her back, he snapped on a handcuff. He grappled for her other one, found it and snapped on the other cuff.

"There." He bent down and nuzzled the nape of her neck. "Very nice. I may just keep you this way from now on."

"You can wish." She wiggled beneath him and then stopped. The man was aroused. Definitely not the reaction she wanted.

"That's my girl." He sat up, and gripping her arms, pulled her up with him.

Toro bit her lip and looked for some way to hurt him. But with her hands behind her back and her legs twisted in all the layers of satin, she might as well have been a mummy.

He tucked her up against him. "Now relax, sweetheart."

Relax? The man was crazy.

The driver tipped his head back. "Sorry the kid got away. But the guys will find him. The tracker you put on him is sending out a nice clear signal."

Toro gaped at Kiro. "What tracker?"

"Nothing to worry your little head over. There's one on you, too. Have you forgotten I have access to the highest level of technology or were you tricked by that dump of a hotel? So don't think you will ever get away from me again, sweetheart."

Hell. She'd spent her life under cover, out of sight. Yet, she'd been tracked and manipulated from the moment she'd met this man. The idea she was visible on some surveillance device drove her crazy. "Where—where is it? On this stupid dress?"

"Now why would I tell you? But here"—he pulled his cell out of his pocket—"let's find out where your brother is." He flicked on the phone and selected an icon. "Now let's see—yes, right there."

He held the phone in front of her face. "See—the blinking red dot. Looks to be inside the building across from the muscum—a doughnut shop, I believe." He nudged her with his elbow. "Think he's scoffing down a jelly-filled delight?"

"I think he's long gone." At least, she hoped he was.

"Yeah, might be dead. Wouldn't matter. I don't really need him anymore. I have you just where I want you."

Toro yanked on her cuffed hands. The metal dug into the skin of her wrists. "You don't really love me, do you?"

Kiro threw back his head. "Ha. I convinced you? I must be a better actor than I thought. No, my dear. I don't love you, but I *do* want to be married to you. And I am looking forward to having you in my bed. A nice perk."

Toro slumped in the seat. That sounded ominous.

He brushed a finger across the top of her breasts. "You don't know how attractive you are. But I will teach you."

She tried to draw away but there was nowhere to go. She shook off the slimy sensation of his touch. He seemed to be talkative. Maybe she could find out what his plans were. "I'm a perk? So what are you really after?"

"You don't know who you are, do you?"

"I know exactly who I am and what I am capable of, and I warn you. Never underestimate me. I'm going to slit your throat. Count on it."

"Fcisty. Feisty. You really are delightful. Cuffed. Bound. In my possession. And still making threats. My guest is going to be most pleased."

"Guest?"

"He's waiting at the penthouse for us. He is expecting the marriage to have taken place. But that's not a deal breaker. We'll take care of the paperwork

267

when we get there."

He put a hand on either side of her head, clamped it in position, and lowered his mouth.

She waited until his lips touched hers, and then she bit as hard as she could. He pulled back and wiped away the blood.

She spat. "I bite, too."

"So you do, sweetheart. So you do." He laughed again and tousled her hair. She snapped her teeth at him. "We're made for each other. Don't you think?"

Chapter 29

Pharaoh rubbed his neck where Bear had choked him. He'd been lucky to get away. If a police car hadn't turned the corner at the moment Bear had started to drag him back inside the hotel, he'd be a goner.

It was the first time in his life he'd been glad to see the cops. He'd flailed and kicked and stirred up enough disturbance that the patrol car had actually slowed to check them out.

Bear and the goons behind him disappeared, leaving him gagging on the sidewalk. Pretty much dead. But not dead enough to be caught.

He'd managed to stagger to his feet, give the scowling officer a silly grin, make the okay sign, and amble off toward the elevated subway as if being choked by a mammoth man happened to him daily.

By the time he reached Manhattan, the red dots in front of his eyes had settled, and he was starting to see normally again. He dropped his hand from his throat and forced himself to focus on what he had to do—stop a wedding. But public transportation wasn't fast, and it wasn't reliable

He had arrived too late.

Pharaoh stood on the opposite side of the street from the New Museum and watched Kiro follow a trail of satin into the back of a limo. Near the entrance, a crowd gathered around a fallen man.

He blew out a breath and scuffed his foot on the pavement. *Qué diablo!* Where to now? She was married. Hooked to Shark Man for life.

He gazed down the street. They'd go to the penthouse. Should he follow? Try to save her? Would she want him to? He'd already let her down too many times.

"Pssst, Fur Tree."

There was only one person who still called him by his graffiti handle—*Hanger.*

Pharaoh spun around.

"Pssst. Down here."

He peered under a white van. "Hanger?"

"Yeah. Hey, man. Gotta get me out of here. I'm bad—can't walk."

He could hear the boy's gasps, each breath torn from a pit of pain. The kid needed medical care—fast.

Pharaoh glanced around. He didn't see any of Kiro's men. He leaned against the van and pretended to clean his nails like any street hood might when casing out a joint. "Anyone after you?"

"Yeah. Shark Man put a tracker...on me...got rid of it."

The sound of sirens echoed down the street. An ambulance pulled up in front of the museum.

Pharaoh squinted across the way. "Who's injured?"

"Don't know. Escaped. Hid under here—good as any place to die."

"You're not gonna die." Pharaoh watched the EMTs get out of the ambulance. He checked the other onlookers. All eyes were focused on the commotion across the street. This was their chance. "Can you roll out?"

"Yeah." An arm appeared. And then a leg, and then Hanger was half-crouching at his feet, his face a torment of pain, his infected thigh a mess of filthy bandages. Hanger gave him a wavering grin. "Leg. Gonna explode."

"Yeah. I get that." Pharaoh bent down. "Wrap your arm around and hold on. Gotta get you some medical help. Then I'll rescue Toro somehow."

"Toro?"

He helped the boy up. "She'll kill me if I let you die, kid."

Hanger wriggled against him. "She? You know?"

"Sure do." Oh yeah, he knew she was a girl all right. A woman really. He pictured her lying next to him with her perfect breasts and luscious mouth.

Hanger rolled his head. "My sister—don't get no ideas about her, hey?"

Yeah, right. He had plenty of *ideas* about her. But right now, he needed to get Hanger medical care.

Pharaoh hefted the frail body up into his arms and dashed across the street toward the ambulance, ignoring the cars honking their horns and swerving to avoid the ones that refused to slow down. He tucked the boy tighter against him. "She's married—to Shark Man."

"No," Hanger gasped. "You got to save her."

Pharaoh choked in a breath. His throat burned, his ribs throbbed. But Hanger was right. He had to save Toro from Shark Man, married or not. "Plan to. Now let your head droop and act half-unconscious."

"No acting needed." Hanger went limp.

"Don't give them your name, either."

An EMT carrying an emergency bag came around the side of the ambulance. Behind him, two others rolled a stretcher.

Pharaoh gave a call, "*Here.* Over here."

The EMT looked up from stowing his gear, his frown deepening.

Barely avoiding a motorcycle, Pharaoh and his burden stumbled closer. "Injury. Kid's hurt."

The man took one look at Hanger and hurried over.

The man knelt down and gently lifted a bit of the stained bandage. Where the tattoo had been was now a gaping wound, red and foul smelling, the edges surrounded by pus.

The EMT stood up. "Whoa. This needs treatment immediately." He gave a wave and another EMT came over. "Got another to transport." He turned back to Pharaoh. "Know who he is?"

Pharaoh hated to abandon the kid to the mercy of the medical system as an indigent, but if he gave Hanger's name, Kiro's men could track him down to the hospital. "No idea. Found him. Over there in the gutter. Saw you guys."

There was a hint of suspicion in the man's eyes. "And you are?"

Pharaoh clutched onto Hanger, wincing from the effort as pain cut across his chest. He adjusted his grip. "A good Samaritan."

Hanger's head rolled to the side, and he moaned. The two men caught him under the arms and lifted him. Pharaoh backed away. "Take good care of him."

Then he was running. Running to save the woman he loved. Running even though every breath was like a knife stab. Running even though the boy he'd left behind might die with no one ever knowing who he was.

****

By the time he reached Kiro's place, Pharaoh's strength was failing. He grasped his side and peered up at the condo. Somehow, he'd made it across the bridge and to Kiro's despite traffic and an almost run-in with one of Jax's thugs.

The black-jacketed guy on the motorbike had been searching for either him or Hanger. But Hanger was safely off to Bellevue. He'd made sure to find out what hospital so he could tell Toro—if he ever saw her again. He prayed the kid wouldn't lose his leg.

Now for the hard part—getting inside the heavily secured building. Kiro's penthouse was at the very top, on the seventh floor. But he had a plan.

For starters, he no longer looked like a down-and-out tattoo artist.

A quick swipe off the back of an open panel truck had resulted in him now wearing a janitor's white coveralls and carrying a broom.

It wasn't much of a disguise. Unfortunately, the coveralls were for someone a bit shorter and his high-top sneakers were not sweeper wear. But one thing you learned on the streets was that people usually saw only what they expected to see.

He surveyed the building again. Toro was up there. The idea she was married to Kiro made his gut burn. Was the bastard making love to her right now? The thought sent chills radiating through his body.

But Toro wouldn't be subdued easily. Knowing her, she'd fight the man until he hurt her or even killed her.

He clenched his teeth and stood up straighter. Somehow, he would get through the guards, through the protective steel entryway, and rescue her. He just hoped he wasn't too late.

Chapter 30

Kiro punched the keypad, and the elevator whooshed upward. Hands cuffed behind her back, Toro was at his mercy in the small confined space. Trying to kick him wearing ballet slippers and yards of satin was futile.

But she refused to be intimidated. No matter what happened, it wouldn't be because she gave up. She used the only weapon she had—her tongue. "I'm going to kill you."

He bent over her, his fermented citrus scent assaulting her nose. Toro held her breath. If she ever got free, she'd never eat an orange again. He grinned. He was wearing the plastic tooth-covers again.

He leaned over and arranged Toro's hair so it hung down over the front of her dress in a cascade of ringlets. His fingers brushed the bare skin along the top edge of the low-cut neckline, sending icy chills down to her toes.

She pulled back and shook her head to muss up her hair again.

He pursed his lips. "Don't you want to look nice for our guest?"

She pressed her head against the wall of the elevator, wishing it would suck her in. "Why should I?"

"Why?" His eyes widened as if in surprise. In the bluish light, his pupils were the color of worn nickels.

"Because he is someone very important to you."

"Bah. No one who knows me would go near you, Shark Man."

The elevator came to a halt, but he didn't open the door. He seized her by the chin. "Now while I would have preferred some semblance of a love match, it's a dead issue. So this is the way it's going to be. You will do exactly what I tell you, or everyone you care about will be dead."

He pulled out his phone and held it up to her face. "I made it easy. All I have to do is press this icon, and the kill text message will go out. I have men stationed at Bellevue to take out Vernon and your brother."

Toro gasped. Hanger had survived. "They're at Bellevue? Vernon's alive? My brother is getting medical treatment?"

"Yes, and totally helpless and right under my men's noses. Now let me finish, sweetheart. I have more men ready to shoot up Big Bad and wipe out those pains in the neck of yours, Solo and Neto.

"My best man is stationed outside The Siren waiting to do in your bosom buddy Bella and her unborn child. It would be a shame about my brother's kid, but"—he squeezed her chin harder—"then my sons will inherit without any competition from a cousin. And that is the way it's going to be. You and me are going to rule the world, whether you like it or not." He let go.

"Never!" She head-butted him against the elevator wall, knocking the air out of him. "You're crazy. Why should I do what you want, when you're going to kill everyone anyway? You basically just said so. Why am I so important—a nameless street kid?"

He whipped back up and came at her, all furious

male. "Because you are not nameless, sweetheart."

Cursing the handcuffs, Toro dove for the elevator control panel, and aimed for the down button with her shoulder. But he beat her to it. "Oh, no you don't. Not when we are this close to the payout."

Toro yanked herself free, but there was nowhere to run in the tiny space of the elevator cab. It only took a second for him to overpower her and shove her face first against the smooth stainless wall. Her cheek hit the metal with a slap that jarred her teeth and made her ears ring.

Shark Man wheezed in a breath of air and then thrust his entire body against her back, trapping her legs between his own. His voice, husky from the effort, penetrated her ringing head. "Don't even think of moving."

With one hand, he forced her head even harder against the cold steel. The other rucked up her dress and found the top of her panties. In the blurred reflection, she could see his face looming over her, his gray eyes as emotionless as a shark's.

"I didn't want to do this. My guest really deserves to meet you in full color, but you're too wild, uncivilized. I truly think you'd let all those people die before you'd cooperate. Can't risk it."

He leaned in, pressed his body against hers, and whispered against her neck. "So little bride, welcome to the world of feeling oh-so-good. Soon you'll do anything to feel this again."

A needle jabbed her in the butt. She jerked and twisted to no avail. Kiro was much bigger and stronger, and with her hands still in cuffs, he had all the leverage.

He spoke against her cheek, his breathing faster.

"Stand still or I'll break off the needle and leave it in that pretty little butt."

She stopped moving, and then the needle prick was gone.

The stuck-pig pain faded, leaving only a burning sensation. For a moment, it was all she could feel—the spot where the drug waited to do its nasty work.

He dropped the skirt and rubbed his hand over the injection site. Back and forth. Until whatever he'd given her rushed into her bloodstream like a warm wave. Under the onslaught, her muscles melted, and her lungs grew heavy. Every breath became an effort, the air so thick she could swallow it.

He leaned against her. "There, you're already feeling calmer, aren't you, sweetheart?" Behind her, he fumbled with the handcuffs. They snapped open, the sound a distant click like the release of a mouse trap.

Blood rushed into her fingers, but there was no pain, only a tingling sensation that said *look, you have fingers*. She spread out her hands, marveling at the way they cast shadows around her.

She peered up. The overhead light above her glowed brighter than any star she'd ever seen. Her heart pounded somewhere high in her chest. Her vision blurred around the edges. Her body swayed, weightless.

She put out an arm to keep herself upright. "What's happening to me? Am I in space?"

"The drug is taking effect as it should. Now come, darling." The voice echoed as if from a tunnel, but the words pummeled her brain, driving out the lethargy blanketing her.

An arm snugged around her. A voice called down to her from some distant place. "Come, my love.

Come."

Still, the lights overhead were so beautiful. So peaceful. She peered up at them and swayed back and forth.

"This way."

Toro tore her eyes from the swirling lights and let herself be tugged to the elevator door. The heavy steel slid open with a whirr. Holding on tight to the doorframe to keep from floating away, she entered a hallway lined with glistening metal that matched the interior of the elevator.

Everything was clean and smooth and endless. She reached out and touched the shiny surface. What looked like cold metal was surprisingly warm.

A guard dressed all in black stood up from where he'd been sitting and said something. But his bass-toned words dragged out like a recording played at slow speed, and she could make no sense of them. She turned to get a better look at the man and tripped on her skirt. The guard sprang forward, and pulling the fabric up and away, straightened the train. "Welcome, Mrs. Tuccio."

Who was Mrs. Tuccio? She swung her head around, looking for her. All she saw was a distorted reflection of a small person in yards of white satin with a crazy mop of dark hair. Poor girl.

Toro stared at the face, the features blurred and broken like a reflection on a wind-stirred puddle.

The guard moved at her feet. She bent over and took a closer look. Who did she know who was so dark all over? Dark skin. Black eyes set deep into the skull. Soft looking lips the color of plums. He looked so familiar.

She thought she knew his name. "Are you…?" She

pinched her lips together. It couldn't be him. That man was dead. This face was rounder, and sadder. She sniffed. And he smelled wrong. Too clean. Too much like disinfectant and floor cleaner.

"Return to your station." Kiro ordered. The guard stepped back. Her sidekick pulled her upright. "Tippled too much champagne at the wedding."

There was a wrongness somewhere in that sentence. She clasped her guide's arm. "I like champagne?"

"Of course." He patted her hand. His touch sent icy prickles creeping through her.

She glanced up at the man supporting her. Through the drugged mush that was her brain, this man she knew—Shark Man. But he'd lost his pointed teeth.

Goosebumps rose on the back of her neck. What would happen when he found them? The thought magnified the coldness growing inside her.

He led her across the way to another door, tapped a number into the keypad, and laid his thumb on the glowing blue button. The inner door glided open soundlessly, and Toro stepped into the one place she'd sworn never to be—the Shark's lair.

She gazed around, fascinated by the gilded walls and terrazzo on the floor. The interior wasn't what she expected. The penthouse was spectacular. Golden candelabras glittered. Oriental rugs cushioned her feet. Vases full of calla lilies filled the room with a light, fruity scent.

Through her drug-fogged eyes, it was like a castle out of a fairy tale.

Kiro put his hand on the small of her back and nudged her farther inside.

The foyer opened into an expansive living room with a glass wall framing the Manhattan skyline, the buildings blue-gray against a pale ochre sky.

A short, but broad-shouldered man stood in the middle of the room, facing the view. He wore the trappings of a former soldier, an old army green jacket and camo pants. On his head was a green knit ski cap at odds with the spring weather, a few black curls escaping around the edges. He looked totally out of place in the sleek marble and gilt room.

Kiro gave her another shove. "Here she is."

The man spun around. "*Finally.* The deed done, Tuccio?" The tone was irritated, a perfect match for the scowl lining his harsh face. Deep creases cut from his nose to the tips of his lips and ridged his brow. Squint lines fanned out from the corners of his eyes. This was a man who'd lived a hard life and done hard things.

Toro halted, sensation rushing back in and dispelling the fogginess of whatever drug Kiro had given her. This was a man she knew. A ghost. Someone who'd haunted her dreams for years. Someone her mother had insisted did not exist.

She stretched out her hand. "You're real?"

He laughed, the sound loud and jarring and dream-shattering. "Very real, Alba. Very real."

Her feet floated her to him. "Father?"

The man talked over her head. "See, she remembers, Cole. A true Vargas."

The drug might slow her thinking and her reflexes, but it wasn't strong enough to make her forget this man.

The last time she'd seen him, he was stuffing things in a suitcase. Cursing at her mother in some Romanian dialect. Kissing her small self on the top of her head and leaving in a flurry of thrown objects, broken glass, and spilled perfume.

After he left was when all the bad things started to happen. Hunger. Pain. Always being cold. Fear.

Her hand dropped to her side. "You left us." Her voice was weak as a child's.

She backed away on shaking limbs. Whatever Shark Man had given her was slowly wearing off or being driven away by the adrenaline flooding her body. Her muscles still didn't respond right and her breathing was off, but she could feel her brain clearing.

The man who had once been her father pushed past her as if she hadn't spoken. "So hand over the marriage license, and we deal." His accent was heavy and his English broken.

Behind her, Shark Man shuffled. "There was a slight contretemps at the museum. Judge Yeats, a friend of mine, is arriving shortly. We will hold the ceremony here. He'll complete the certificate of marriage and voila, we will be the happiest of couples." He stepped forward and twined his arm around hers. "Right, sweetheart?" He patted the pocket where he'd stowed his cellphone.

His threats came thundering back. Would he really kill all her friends? Her brother? Bella's unborn child—his own kin? She glanced between the two men and knew he would.

Something big was happening here. Something so big, Kiro was willing to do anything for it. Besides, he was scared, too. His body trembled where he pressed against her. And if she had learned anything on the streets, it was that frightened people did crazy things. They screamed at shadows. They killed without looking. They pushed others between them and death.

Better to play along. Wait for a chance to do something. What was the saying her mother always said, that had sounded so strange coming from a woman who'd lived her whole life in the city? Her brain scrambled for the words. Ah yes. *Wait long enough and even a scared rabbit will twitch.*

Toro studied the two men. She was obviously a pawn. Maybe if she disappeared into the background, they'd forget she was even here. She sagged against Kiro's arm. "I need to sit."

He caught her and kept her on her feet. "Of course. You must be exhausted." Hand clamped to her waist, he assisted her to the white leather sofa and set her down.

Kiro plumped a throw pillow and slipped it behind her head. "You rest. Nap if you want. The judge will be here in about fifteen minutes."

Toro flopped back on the sofa and sank into the cushions. The leather was soft and smooth. With the drug still ebbing through her, sucking away at her strength, she could easily fall asleep.

But she wanted to play dead, not be dead.

She curled up in the corner of the sofa and focused on the bit of tattoo peeking above the collar of her father's jacket. Hopefully, puzzling the design out would keep her from dozing off.

Kiro unfolded the marriage license and laid it on the large white coffee table that looked like a slice of a Greek column. He took out a pen and set it atop the papers. "There—everything's ready." He checked his watch. "Ten minutes at the most. A drink, Iancu—while we wait?"

Toro's father frowned. "I do not like this. The

ship—it must sail."

"A few minutes. That's all." Kiro crossed the room and opened a cabinet, revealing a well-stocked, built-in bar. He took out two tumblers and poured a finger of whiskey into each. He offered one to his guest. "A drink to seal the deal."

Her father put the glass to his lips, threw back his head and drained the golden liquor down, his Adam's apple bobbing as he swallowed. He slammed the glass down on a side table, and in the process, his collar moved.

Toro gasped. The tattoo. It was a crown. Like the one on her inner arm. Her fingers found the mark she'd worn since infancy. The mark she'd turned into T-Crew's signature tag.

Her father turned at the sound of her gasp. He tipped his head, his eyes softened. "You look like her."

"Mama?" Still dizzy, Toro could barely get the words out. "I look nothing like her. Besides, she's dead."

He wiped his mouth with the back of his hand. "Didn't know. Who you live with?"

"I live by myself."

He stiffened slightly. "Not your aunt?'

Toro shifted on the cushion. Now she was going to get answers just when her poor brain had gone all bubbly. She rubbed her hand against the side of her aching head. "What aunt?"

"Your fucking rich vampire of an aunt, my sister Maria."

"Never heard of her."

"Of course you have. Princess Maria, descendent of Romanian royalty. She took you away from me. Said

I married like a fool. Wrong woman. Could not trust me to raise you as royal princess."

Princess? Toro blinked and then burst out laughing. She was a princess? She laughed harder. Now she knew what Alice felt like when she fell through the rabbit hole.

She glared at this stranger in his pretend military uniform. "You're a funny man, Papa. Sorry you left us. Life would have been a lot more fun." She peered into those dark brown eyes and caught a hint of her own. "To be honest, Papa darling—I've spent the last six years of my life living on the street. Before that I spent my days and nights huddling in a closet while Mama got beat by whatever druggy boyfriend was having her at the time."

"No, this is not true. You have the mark on your arm. I can see it." He stepped up to her and fingered her pendant. "You wear the royal medallion. You are my daughter. Your aunt, Princess Maria, she swore to take care of you if I left."

Toro broke into laughter again. Hell, she never laughed so hard in her life. Even her stomach hurt. "I guess the *Princess's* promises were as good as yours."

Her father was staring at her, a weird tilt to his mouth. "Stop it."

The command in his voice drove the laughter out.

She placed her hands on her stomach. "Sorry, must be the drug." She caught Kiro's scowl. "Oops. I think I'm supposed to say—the champagne my would-be groom has so generously provided." She wiped the tears from her eyes.

"He drugged you?" Her long-lost father fisted his hands, widened his stance, and suddenly he no longer looked like a down-and-out seaman in an old military jacket.

Hey, maybe this papa guy was gonna be her hero after all. She peeked over at Kiro who was frantically searching his pockets. Toro grinned and pressed her hip tighter into the cushions.

The hard rectangle of his cellphone pressed back. She stifled the laugh that came welling up. You learned a lot living on the streets—things like pickpocketing.

She exhaled all the air in her lungs. Somehow, she had a feeling she'd come to the climax of her story. She had Kiro off-stride, his kill button under her control, and her papa's full attention.

She glanced around the room. Time for the truth. "You think I'd marry that bastard of my own free will?"

Papa Iancu glanced over at Kiro. Shark Man stopped twitching and carefully set his glass down on the counter. Her father tipped his head and studied her as if she had no sense in her head. "Why not? He's rich, powerful, good-looking. He make good deal for your land. He fund our uprising. Smooth the politics here in U.S."

"I'm funding an uprising?" Toro stared pointedly at Kiro's groin. And here she'd thought she'd caused a different kind of uprising. She swallowed down another laugh. Hell, if she died in the next few minutes, she'd die laughing.

"Yes, to restore the Romanian monarchy to full power."

"Never finished school so my Romanian history's foggy. But the plan sounds a bit far out. Like something I might read in a romance novel."

His brow wrinkled into deeper folds. "So yes. You

marry him. Your holdings become his. He helps us. See, we all scratch each other's backs. Works nice."

Toro readjusted the throw pillow behind her neck. "It's not my back getting scratched."

Kiro moved closer to her. "I'll scratch you wherever I want."

A buzzing sound filled the room. "The judge." Kiro dashed over to the entry and hit the button on the intercom. "Yes, send him up." Kiro opened the door and crossed over to the elevator. The door slid closed behind him.

Papa Iancu sat down on the sofa. The fug of long days on a ship washed over her. "You don't want to marry him?" he asked.

"He's a murdering bastard. He'll kill me."

"No. I think not. Yes, he is criminal. Yes, he does bad things. But you are too valuable. You are in line for the throne."

Toro looked at her father. Did he really think in such simplistic terms or was his control of English just very poor? "Look, I will be his prisoner. A slave. To me that is the same as being dead."

"No, you see this wrong. You will be rich lady. Do as you please." He thumbed his finger at the painting over the sofa. "Tuccio says you paint this masterpiece. Be great artist if you like." All will make up for what happened."

"Nothing can make up for what happened. Besides, I love someone else."

"Love. Pah. Later, you take him as lover."

"You're a bastard, you know."

He settled his hand on top of hers. "I wish your life could have been different."

She yanked her hand away. "Tell my brother that. He's the one who really suffered. Still is."

Iancu jerked to his feet. "*Brother?* What brother?"

Toro had to pinch her lips together to stop another burst of laughter. "Mr. Tuccio forget to mention him?"

"How old?"

"Fifteen. Think he's yours?"

"Doesn't matter. He'd still be a prince. I never divorced her."

"And a prince is better than a princess any day?"

"A prince is a good thing. He will inspire the rebels. But the land is yours."

"Poor Hanger. Lucky me."

Iancu huffed. "Hanger? What name is that?"

"He hates his real name—Mircea."

A flash of something like regret flashed across the man's hard features. "She remembered that much. So where is your brother?"

"You'll have to ask him." She pointed at Kiro, who was escorting a tall, elegantly suited man through the entry. As he entered the living room the last rays of sunlight struck the visitor full on the face.

It couldn't be, but was. Another ghost from her childhood. And not a welcome one. It was all she could do not to jump up and dive through the glass window to her death. But acting a crazy fool would not save Hanger.

Instead, she dropped her head and fingered the crystals on the bodice of the gown like some ingénue embarrassed to be caught with a *Playboy* magazine.

She buried her hands in the satin skirt. The day couldn't get more bizarre. What were the chances this judge, of all judges, was Kiro's choice.

This was the man who'd abused her mother the worst. Had hit her baby brother because he was crying. But then again, one shouldn't be surprised two nasty sharks would know each other.

The judge glanced around the room, then took the glass of scotch Kiro handed to him.

He held up the tumbler in toast. "To the bride."

She sat up straighter and smoothed down her skirts. Time for action. "Despite appearances, there is no bride."

Next to her, her father shifted. "But you must. I need Tuccio's power behind me. He will provide many guns."

She gave him a look as hard and unyielding as his. "I have no interest in your little war. I have no interest in you. I have no interest in being a princess."

"But you will be a wealthy woman."

"Don't need the money."

"But Tuccio says you're poor."

"Did he?"

"Enough, you two," Kiro butted in. "The judge is waiting."

Toro nodded. "I'm sure he is." She rose from the sofa and carefully rested her hands on her hips. "Let me put this in terms you all can understand. I am not your pawn. You, Kiro, take the land. I gift it to you. Send the deed to my lawyer to sign over. You, long-lost-good-for-nothing Papa, crawl back on to whatever stinking freighter you hitched a ride on. And you, Supreme Court Judge Yeats. You, I am going to kill. For what you did to my mother." With that, she pointed the knife she'd lifted from Kiro and charged the man who'd beaten her mother to a pulp more than once and made her childhood a misery.

Unfortunately, she miscalculated the length of her skirts and the speed of Shark Man. His hands wrapped around her neck, and she missed.

Well, not completely. Blood blossomed very satisfactorily from beneath the bastard's jaw. But he wasn't dead, and tangled in satin and weak from the drug, she could not loosen Kiro's hands from her throat and finish the job. She sucked in what air she could and fought Kiro with all the strength she had left.

How fitting. She was going to die the same way Pharaoh had.

As she struggled to breathe, she tore at Kiro's wrists, futilely digging her nails into his flesh. As colors swirled behind her eyes, as her body went numb, she did something she never thought she'd do. She prayed there really was a heaven, and that Pharaoh would be waiting there for his joke-of-a-princess.

Chapter 31

Pharaoh crouched inside the doorway, stunned by what he was hearing and seeing. Toro was a princess—a real princess—a rich princess. That battered hulk of a man was her father and some kind of mercenary. And wonders of wonders, she was not married to Kiro.

He tightened his grip on his knife. His angel princess needed rescuing, but he hadn't the foggiest idea how he could help her.

He surveyed the room. Toro was in the farthest corner with the three men between her and him. Thankfully, she was not looking his way.

She'd almost recognized him out in the corridor, but she'd been drugged, and Kiro had proved the cliché that all black men look alike to rich white guys. Some toilet paper wadded in his cheeks and up his nose had helped. He had to laugh. It was amazing how far a black man could get carrying a bucket and a mop.

Getting inside the penthouse had been a little harder. Luckily, the judge guy was so self-important he didn't notice the helpful guard who'd pretended to hold an automatic door open for him.

So now he was in and helpless. Or was he?

Toro had stood. He saw the silvery flash of the knife in her hand. She'd go for Kiro, he was sure. He rose slightly, ready to take down the supposed father. He doubted the judge was armed.

There was a whirl of white, and then she was slashing not at Kiro, but the idiot judge, leaving Kiro free to grab her from behind and catch her in a choke hold.

No. Pharaoh knew how having your breath cut off felt. His neck still ached from Bear's rough hug. He half-rose, looking for an opening.

Toro scrabbled with her hands, kicking her feet towards Kiro's groin, scratching at his eyes, fighting dirty—being El Toro—the kid who never gave up. But she'd never win. A diminutive gypsy had no leverage against a furious man who towered over her.

She needed help. She needed him.

He flew forward, his eyes still on the father who was rising from the sofa, a gun in his hand. Pharaoh ignored him. He was going to kill Kiro dead and save his angel if it was the last thing he did.

Bang.

The gunshot deadened his ears. A small red hole appeared in Kiro's forehead. In slow motion, Kiro's face went slack, his arm dropped away from Toro's neck, and his body fell back against the bar, sending glasses and bottles tumbling to the floor in a shatter of breaking glass. The pungent scent of whiskey and vodka filled the room.

Pharaoh turned and faced the hulk in green. The man still held the gun. The lethal weapon pointed directly at him. He dropped the knife and threw his hands up. "I'm a friend. Toro's friend."

The man wrinkled up one side of his mouth and kept the gun on him. "My daughter—she coming with me. Stay back or I kill."

No way was he letting Toro out of his sight. "I can

help carry her."

Her father leaned over and hooked an arm under Toro's limp body. He lifted her up and over his shoulder in one smooth move. "She light. I can do." He moved around Kiro's body and gave the judge a kick in the knife wound. The man groaned. "You will die here slow for what you did to my wife." He tipped his head. "You, boy. You get the keys for car from dead man's pocket."

"Sure." Pharaoh tore off the stupid uniform jacket and strode across the room. "But I'm not one of Kiro's men. I came to rescue Toro. *I love her*." The words echoed in the deep silent room. He did. He loved her, and he wasn't going to let this supposed father take her away.

The man huffed. The pointed gun did not move. "Get keys."

Pharaoh knelt down and dug in Kiro's pockets. His fingers hit the key fob. A thought struck him. "I could drive you where you need to go. I know the city." He stood suddenly hopeful. He *did* know the city—a lot better than this foreigner. "She's going to wake up soon, and she's not going to be happy. How will you drive and handle her?"

The man glanced at Toro and then waved the gun at him. "All right. You come. Lead the way."

****

Twenty minutes later, they were out of the garage and driving the silver SUV that had once been Vernon's toward the South Park Terminal.

Doing his best to avoid a collision, Pharaoh kept one eye on the road and the other on the grim face of his captor, peering at him in the rearview mirror.

He couldn't see Toro where the man had laid her down on the seat. But he knew she had to be conscious by now. It didn't take long to recover from a partial choke hold, as long as nothing vital was damaged, and he was praying nothing was. She had to be playing possum. He turned his head to check on her.

The gun jabbed the back of his head. "Eyes on road."

Pharaoh straightened up. The man might talk like a fool, but he was as alert as a feral cat. The muzzle of the gun dug into his skull. "Drive faster, boy."

It was going on dusk and commuter traffic lumbered around them as people headed home from work. He avoided the Gowanus Parkway and stuck to the busy thoroughfares lined with double-parked cars, diesel-spewing city buses, and New York pedestrians who crossed against traffic as if they were made of steel and not flesh and blood. He was in no hurry to get to Toro's papa's ship.

He pulled up at a red light and glanced in the rearview mirror again. The hard-lined face looking back was Toro's father for sure. He might be worn and wrinkled, but there was no mistaking the set of the eyes and the point of the chin. Time to get friendly and let Toro know what was happening. "Where're you from?"

"Not your business."

Okay. Man's got his secrets. He needed another approach. The light changed, and he started up the SUV. "What are you going to do with Toro?"

The gun shifted against his head. He was pretty sure the man wouldn't kill him while he was driving—he had to have some measure of self-preservation. Still, he wished the weapon gone. Having a loaded weapon held to his head was making him twitchy.

"Who's Toro?

"Your daughter. She's known as *El Toro*—The Bull in Spanish. She's been living as a boy for years. Did you know that?"

"A boy? She smart. I know streets. It's not safe if you're a beautiful girl."

Pharaoh squeezed the steering wheel. Fool. He'd accused her of tricking him. Even this ass of man understood Toro's life better than he did.

The gun pressed a little harder. "You love her?"

Toro had to be awake by now. Here was his chance to make his last plea. "Yeah, I love her. I've loved her for years. She's my soul mate."

"Good." The gun dropped away.

There was a movement in the back, and Toro sat up. Her eyes met his in the rearview mirror. "Hey, you." It was the greeting they'd always given each other, followed by a high five. She rubbed her head. "I thought you were dead." Her voice had the hoarseness of the recently strangled. He sympathized. If he wasn't trying to avoid hitting a city bus, they could compare bruises.

"Yeah, well, people keep trying to kill me. Including your father there."

The gun was back, this time poking into the nape of his neck. There was another movement in the back, a swish of skirts, a slight breath. The gun wavered. "*Da*, Papa. Put the gun down. Pharaoh's driving in heavy traffic, and you're making him nervous."

"You want him alive?"

"I love him, Papa."

The gun didn't move. "How long you know my

daughter, boy?"

Cielos, the man was interviewing him like he was a prospective son-in-law or something. Hell, maybe he was. "Six years."

"You know who she is?"

He'd overheard crazy talk about princesses and wealth back at the penthouse. Surely some fantasy spun by this erstwhile ragamuffin father to win money and guns from Kiro.

Besides, that wasn't who Toro was. He raised his voice. "She's the best street artist in Williamsburg. She's the most loving and caring person I know. She's cared for her brother better than any mother." He hesitated, and then decided it wouldn't hurt to say it again. The gun was still pointing at his neck after all. He turned a corner on to a side street. They'd be at the Red Hook terminal in a few minutes. "She's the woman I want to marry."

"Good answer." This time, Toro's father tucked the gun back in his jacket.

Pharaoh snuffed in a breath and drove down the street paralleling the East River. It was past sunset, and they were getting into an area of factories, parking lots, and construction zones—T-Crew's favorite type of playground.

A fine mist rose off the river and swaddled the warehouses. Pharaoh surveyed his surroundings. A smart street kid or two could disappear in seconds in this neighborhood.

He drove slowly past a likely spot and checked to make sure the car doors were unlocked. If he could catch Toro's eye again, she could be out of the SUV and gone in an instant. He glanced in the mirror and met papa's eyes instead of Toro's.

The man grasped him by the shoulder. "My daughter trust you. I trust you."

Even in broken English, the tone of his voice carried weight. Pharaoh could almost believe the man was royalty. Then he gave a roll of his shoulders and shook the thought off. The man was a murdering thug.

Still he couldn't help saying it. He had a death wish after all. "Thank you, *Prince*."

Toro's father grunted. "Don't matter who I am. You take care of her. Yes?"

"Yes."

The car door snapped open, but Toro didn't jump out. Her father did.

The man climbed the adjacent cyclone fence with the agility of any street kid hightailing it away from a night watchman and, without looking back, disappeared into the fog.

Pharaoh let the SUV roll to a stop along the curb. He turned around and stared into the back seat. There was no trace of the boy he'd known as Toro. The girl sitting in the glare of the streetlamp looked like a broken doll in her yards of wrinkled, blood-stained satin. Her hands rested in her lap. Head bent forward, her glorious hair curtained her face. Her shoulders rose and fell as if her heart would break.

How could her father have broken her heart like that? He hadn't even said goodbye.

Pharaoh let go of the steering wheel and got out of the SUV. He opened the rear door and leaned in. "Don't cry. The man's a bastard."

Toro raised her head and feathered her hair out of her eyes. Not a tear streaked her cheeks. Not a frown marred her brow. Instead, her eyes were bright with laughter. A huge smile spread across her face. "Pharaoh, I'm a freaking princess."

He crawled over to sit beside her and took her hands into his. "No, you're my angel." Then he was kissing her, and she was kissing him back.

Chapter 32

Pharaoh pulled back and studied the woman he loved. The streetlight illuminated her face and gave her hair an angelic glow. Her lips glistened from their kiss. Her eyes glowed with what had to be happiness or maybe just overwhelming mirth.

He wanted to kiss her, make love to her, take her home, and cherish her for the rest of his life. Fulfill his promise to her father. But how could you kiss someone who kept breaking out in hysterical laughter?

Not only that, but Toro's laughter was catching. He hadn't laughed in a very long time. But every time she broke into an outburst of laughing, he did too. His damaged ribs ached. He was lightheaded. Or perhaps what he felt was merely the adrenaline surge letting go.

Damn, but the whole thing was ridiculous. He wrapped an arm around Toro and absorbed the peals of laughter rising up and bubbling out of her.

Between laughs, he touched her, amazed she was uninjured, fascinated she was his. That she loved him. He tangled his hand in the silk of her hair and gently kissed her on her forehead. On the tip of each ear.

Kiss by kiss he worked his way down the smooth curve of her jawline. His hands followed. He avoided the bruised throat and spread his palms across her bare shoulders, found the thin ridge of her clavicle and ran his thumbs along it. "So—he was really your father?"

"Mmm. I sort of remember him." She tilted her head back, exposing the rounded tops of her breasts. The soft swells rested in the glittering crystal bodice like a jeweled offering. Her breasts rose and fell, tantalizing him. All laughter fled. Blood whooshed through him and settled in his groin.

What was he doing? He lifted his hands off her. This was not the time and place for loving. Toro deserved fine sheets, a soft bed, and a gentle lover—not the cramped back seat of a stolen SUV, the dead fish stink of the port, and—well—him.

She gazed into his eyes. "Don't stop. Take me to heaven again."

Hell, how could he refuse her? All his good intentions fled. "You wish is my command, your Majesty."

Pharaoh settled on the seat and lifted the woman he loved into his lap as he feathered kisses along the plunging neckline. Her scent, rich, spicy, and all Toro, filled his nostrils and intoxicated him. His cock lengthened and hardened. He had to have more.

Trembling, he reached around to unzip the dress and stopped. If she were really a princess, he had no right to be touching her. "Your father—he's royalty?"

She nested her head against his chest and gave a laugh. "A gypsy king with delusions of grandeur."

Pharaoh pictured the man in his worn foreign army jacket with its reek of a freighter's bilge. "No, a filthy mercenary looking for guns and support."

"That too."

"He fooled Kiro."

"He—he killed Kiro."

She shivered, and he drew her closer. "That he did.

And—think me bloodthirsty, but I'm glad of it."

He clasped her against him. "It's over. Your brother's safe. You're safe. Whatever your father said, forget it. His crazy plans have nothing to do with us."

She worked her hand between them and reached up and under his tee shirt. Her hand was cool against his heated skin. "You're right. The man's utterly forgettable." She captured one of his nipples between her fingers and squeezed. He let out a short breath. "But you are not. Make love to me, Pharaoh. To me—Toro—not some mysterious girl in the night." She ran her hands down his torso and worked at undoing his fly. "Take me to heaven. Now."

His cock quivered in eagerness, and he groaned. The time for conversation was over. When Toro wanted something, she acted—whether it was doing a whole car challenge, spray painting bad guys, or making love with an unworthy bastard like him who brought nothing but pain to those he loved.

She touched him, and his self-control fizzled away to nothing.

He breathed out the answer she wanted. "Yes." And with that word he resolved to do everything in his power to bring joy to the woman he loved—despite being cramped in the backseat of a car, despite being in full public view beneath the streetlight, despite being a Jonah who'd ruined everything good in his life.

He drew her to him. Despite the painful ribs and aching bruises, this time he was going to do right.

Nuzzling his nose in the silk of her hair, Pharaoh found the tab at the back of the dress and slowly unzipped it. The cloth separated, exposing the supple spine, and the warmth of her skin to his touch.

Released, her enticing scent emanated into the air and filled the car's interior. He inhaled deeply, and as gently as he could slipped one sleeve and then the other over her shoulders.

With shaking fingers, he pushed the gown down revealing the breasts she'd managed to keep hidden for so long.

He gathered them in his hands, felt the warm, round weight of them. They filled his palms perfectly. He flicked the nipples as he peered into her eyes. He expected to see pleasure.

Instead, a small worry line crossed her brow. Wary eyes met his. "Are they—pleasing? Am I woman enough for you?"

As much as he ached to be inside her, she needed to hear the words first.

Hard as it was, he moved back and ran his gaze up and down the incredible woman before him. "Oh Toro. You are so beautiful to look at my heart hurts. All these years, I have been blind. Never seeing you as you truly are." He ran his palms down the swells of her breasts. "Everything about you is pure perfection. You are a man's fantasy. My fantasy. Let me see all of you. Touch all of you."

She nodded and he slipped the wedding dress past her waist, over her hips. Then he lifted her slightly and yanked the satin off.

He blinked his eyes, struggling to believe she was real. The streetlight shining in the car window highlighted her strong lithe muscles, her velvety skin, the feminine roundness of her hips and buttocks.

He spread her thighs so she straddled his lap facing him, and let out a long, slow breath. The woman peering back at him was an amazing combination of femininity and strength. She had the powerful legs of a trapeze artist, the elegant posture of a dancer, and the controlled musculature of a gymnast, all wrapped up in a body that curved in just the right places.

It was the sexiest thing he'd ever seen. He rested his hands on her waist. "Believe me. You would please any man."

"I don't want to please any man." She rubbed her nose against his. "*Only you.*"

He smiled. "Oh. You will."

He moved his hands lower. She had on the most adorable panties—white lace embroidered with tiny blue roses. But he wanted them gone. He found the elastic band and finagled them down her legs and over each high-arched foot.

With a wink, he held them to his nose and then wadded them up and tossed them over the seat back. With his most gentle touch, he brushed his hand back up her calves and along the inside of her thighs, whispering the words she needed to hear. "So soft. So smooth. All woman." She shifted on his lap, and he could scent her arousal, feel her wetness.

He cupped her between the legs, his fingers searching for the tender nub. "You are female from head to toe, angel. Made for pleasure. Made for loving." He grinned and moved his finger back and forth, up and down. He slipped one into her heat. Then the next. Her muscles clenched around them. "I have to be inside you."

****

Toro's head fell back. Waves of heat rippled through her. She'd waited so long to hear those words.

To be claimed by the man she'd desired for six long years. To be seen as woman to his man.

All her attention focused in on that one spot where Pharaoh touched her so knowingly, moving softly, gently, relentlessly. Over and over until her whole body throbbed. Until her breath came in little gasps. Until her arms and legs trembled and shook.

Inside her, pressure built to the point of pain and then exploded into convulsions of pleasure that left her heart pounding and her limbs weak. She sagged against Pharaoh, only his strong hands keeping her from falling to the side.

She caught her breath and peeked up at him. "I—I thought women didn't—"

"What?" Pharaoh smoothed her hair out of her face.

"Have as much pleasure as men." She laid her cheek against his chest, surprised to find it sweaty, his breath coming fast.

"Oh, Toro. Have you been jealous of men all this time?" Pharaoh gave a small laugh. "Women are more sensitive everywhere, far more gifted with sensual power, and the ability to make love. You can orgasm over and over for hours. I, on the other hand, am a weak little man capable of rising to the occasion, perhaps— twice—before I collapse."

She wrinkled her nose. "*Twice?* I think you exaggerate. You fell asleep last time after only once."

"Oh, Toro. That was the biggest mistake of my life."

"You are so right." She yanked his T-shirt up and over his head. "So did you say *twice*?"

The tee brushed the roof of the SUV and dropped

down on top of the satin gown. And there he was—her prince with his richly muscled body, bruised in places, cut and scraped in others. Blue-black marks marred his throat. He'd almost died trying to save her brother.

Avoiding his wounds and using her lightest touch, she traced the wings of the hawk tattoo that spread across his chest from collar bone to collar bone. She lowered her lips and kissed the hawk's beak where it lay over his heart. His skin quivered beneath her touch.

"I've watched you for years. Always wanting to touch. Always wanting to do this." She reached down and found his erection where it lay hard and upright between them.

Her small hand wrapped around his thickness, and the muscles of his abdomen flexed in response. She slid farther back on his legs and ran her hand up and down the length of him. He collapsed back against the seat and closed his eyes.

She slid her hand up and down faster. "I've seen lots of penises. Being a boy and all."

His chest rose, fell, and stopped. One eye popped opened.

"But I think I like this one the best." She moved her hand again and marveled how his already stiff cock hardened even more. It twitched in her hand. Then she bent over and kissed the tip.

Pharaoh groaned.

"You like that?"

"As much—as you liked—my—kisses."

"Ah." She lowered her head and took him in her mouth. He was huge and hard and silky. She ran her tongue up and down the length of him. He tasted like he smelled—rich and strong and all male. He was right.

She would never forget the taste and smell of him.

His hands clasped her waist, and he lifted her up. *"That's it.* You've had your fun. No more. Not if you want *twice."*

He shucked off his jeans, and then resting back against the seat, settled her atop him with his big strong hands. She could feel the tip of his cock at her opening.

Pharaoh stilled. "It won't hurt you this time. I promise. But you will have to be careful not to hurt me. The ribs are real sore. Take it slow and easy on this battered body of mine."

He pulled her down and slipped inside in one long, smooth stroke. For a moment, it was too much, and then he lifted her and slid her down again, and her body opened and wrapped around him and it felt wonderful. His hands clasped her around her waist. "Now—you—do it."

She drew herself up on her knees, and then down until he was deep inside her. At first, she moved slowly. Careful not to put pressure on his ribs. Testing. Watching the changing expressions on Pharaoh's face. Then she lost herself in the ancient dance. A swirl this way. A lean forward. A lean back. Finding and rubbing that spot that sent sparks snapping through her.

She felt powerful. Ripples of incandescent pleasure shot through her. She took him harder and deeper. Her limbs trembled. Her skin flamed.

Beneath her, Pharaoh matched her thrust for thrust until their breath synchronized and they melded into one. There was no him and no her. No male. No female. Only perfect union.

Through blurred vision she peered down at her lover. Sweat glistened on Pharaoh's shoulders. His breath came in uneven bursts. His whole body shook.

He tightened his grip on her, drew her against him, and whispered in her ear. "Come with me, Toro. Come."

Then he pulled her down hard, hitting some magic spot inside her, and she burst into a quivering ball of pure joy. He thrust one last time and his head tipped back, his chest rising and falling as he gasped for breath.

Toro curled over him, little ripples running through her, her heart pounding, the confined air sticky with their mingled scents and the car windows dripping with condensation from their body heat.

He was still inside her. Still hard. Her inner muscles fluttered.

She bent over and kissed him on his lips, then sat up again and gave a wiggle. *"Once."*

This time it was going to be all her. Slow, steady, no hurry. She was going to bind him to her so he would never leave her. She rose on her knees and then lowered herself down. Beneath her, he shuddered. His cock stiffened even more.

Pharaoh smiled up at her. "Go, dancing girl."

****

Later, more sated than he'd ever been in his life and all his pains and bruises forgotten for the moment, Pharaoh lifted his head slightly and peered through his eyelashes at the woman lying beside him on the seat. Even with her hair tangled, and her sweat-covered body glued to his side—Toro was glorious.

Nipples swollen from his kisses and bites, the long narrow torso flaring out into wide feminine hips. Her body screamed woman. How could he have not seen her for who she was?

Everything about her was the opposite of him. His huge hands totally encircled her tiny waist. Her unmarred olive-tan skin stood out against his battle-scarred brown. Her fine-boned, long muscled arms and legs were those of a dancer or acrobat, not a street tough. And her scent with its undertones of ginger and peaches could only be that of a woman.

Yet, for six years, he'd worked beside her, hefted her up walls, hidden from night watchmen with her, and even, on occasion, arm wrestled with her, and never suspected.

Fool. He'd been a fool. He'd seen what he wanted to see. He'd known Toro was small and delicate for a boy. A natural leader, yes. But no match for the other street kids. He'd always been aware it was up to him to protect Toro and Hanger. And he had. He'd taken on the role of enforcer. Kept the other crews away from their turf. Beat up the bullies who came after them. Gone to jail so they could escape the cops.

But now—he kissed the delicate whorl of her ear—she was more than a friend. She was part of him—the only part that mattered.

He'd do anything for her. Protect her. Die for her. He felt like a knight in one of those fairy tales she was always spouting off about.

If he could, he would lock her away in some castle and let no one else discover her secret—their secret. He kissed her on the tip of her nose.

Toro's hand captured his. "You awake?"

"Yeah."

"What are we going to do?"

"Been thinking. We need to go to the hospital and

see how Vernon is and Hanger. Then we should—"

She raised her fingers to his lips. "No. Let's see how they are, and then we can make plans. You're mine, you know. Don't you ever leave me."

He caught her hand and kissed her fingers. "You stole my line."

She batted him on the side of his head. "No, that was Richard Burton's line in *Camelot.*"

"Yeah, well, royal folk can be rather domineering, I find."

****

It took a while to untangle their clothes and work them over their sweaty bodies.

Pharaoh got in the driver's seat, flicked on the engine, and opened all the windows. Damp night air wafted in from the river. He glanced over as Toro joined him up front, a very satisfied-looking bride in a mass of wrinkled satin.

It had been damn hard getting her to put the gown on, but he refused to drive around with a naked woman in the car. It would be impossible to explain to police if they were stopped. "We should get married."

"What?"

"Well, you're dressed for it and, I hate to say this, but we didn't use a condom—might have made a little prince or princess."

Her face went colorless. "Find me some sweats, and maybe I'll forget you asked."

The pain in his ribs was back. He sucked in a swallow breath, wrapped his fingers around the steering wheel, and focused on the line down the center of the street. He'd bared his soul to her. Told her he loved her. Promised to never leave her.

But she didn't think him trustworthy enough to be her husband.

He gripped the steering wheel tighter. "I'm serious."

"So *am* I. Let's go get Hanger."

Chapter 33

Just before the entrance to the Brooklyn Bridge, they stopped at a row of stores, bustling with late night shoppers. Pharaoh doubled parked like everyone else and ran into a small clothing store to get Toro some sweats. Waiting in line, he had plenty of time to curse himself for not using a condom. It wasn't like he'd totally forgot.

He was a guy. He always had a couple tucked tight in the back pocket of his jeans. He just hadn't been thinking clearly.

The baby in the arms of the woman standing front of him gave him a toothless smile. Hell, how could he have done that to her?

Of course, Toro had no wish to marry him. She had her art. She had Hanger. She had friends—T-Crew and Vernon and Bella.

She didn't need a baby to care for. She didn't need a husband she couldn't trust.

He was no prize. Unless he wanted to go back and work for Jax, who'd surely kill him, he was not only unemployed, but had lost his entire tattoo kit. What legit tat parlor would take him on after working for G-Man?

Like that mattered. Hell, he probably end up in jail—framed for that poor girl's murder.

He paid for the sweats, stormed back outside, and

stopped dead. A police cruiser was behind Kiro's SUV, lights flashing.

"Psst. Pharaoh"

He turned. Toro stood in the doorway of the next store looking for all the world like a runaway bride.

She cupped her hand around her mouth and half-whispered. "Got the duds?"

He held up the plastic bag. For his own selfish reasons, he was going to hate seeing her back in boy's clothes.

"Then let's go." She took off like one of the sea gulls that hung out on the bridge, white skirts billowing around her like wings.

One block down, Toro pulled between a brick wall and a parked truck. "Think anyone saw?"

Pharaoh held his aching side and looked back the way they'd come. "Nah. It's Brooklyn. Probably thought we were eloping."

She gave him the no-nonsense-tolerated-Toro look. The one she used when a member of T-Crew suggested tagging in No Man's Land. "Get your brain in gear. I'm not marrying you or anyone else, for that matter."

Well, that answered that question. Pharaoh held out his purchases.

She grabbed the bag, pulled out the sweat bottoms and slipped them on under the dress. The sweatshirt went over her head. "I have plans."

He let out a breath of air. Of course, she did. And they didn't include him.

She tipped her chin at him. "Got your knife?"

"Yeah."

Satin was a lot tougher than it looked. Toro had to work like a fury to slash her way out of the dress.

Finally, it fell to the sidewalk. She kicked the satin aside. "That was a four-thousand-dollar dress. What a waste. Could have fed the homeless for weeks."

He couldn't help it. Pharaoh picked up the bodice and half-cut, half-tore off a piece. "It wasn't wasted on me." He stuffed the jeweled cloth in his pocket, and then glanced down. "What about your feet? We're still over a mile from the hospital."

She daintily pointed one ballet-slipper-clad foot. "Started out on the streets wearing these. I'll manage. Let's go."

They took off again, this time jogging side-by-side, Toro doing a good job pretending to be a health-conscious hipster out for her evening constitutional—him, just barely keeping up with all the endorphins from their love-making long gone, and steadily increasing pain shooting through his side with every breath.

After two blocks of silence, Pharaoh had enough. "Not talking to me?"

Toro shrugged. "Did you know I wanted to be a ballet dancer? "

She was a dancer, all right. He reached out and patted her bum. "You move like one."

She tossed back her head and sped up. "No, really. I was attending the Performing Arts High School—before Mama died. I was very good."

"You can dance for me anytime."

She glanced over her shoulder. "I'll take you up on that someday."

She pulled ahead and turned down the street leading to the Williamsburg Bridge pedestrian path. She turned and jogged backwards, facing him. "Remember when we painted the cars at Bedford Street Station with Ari?"

Pharaoh grinned. The All-Car Challenge had been the high point of T-Crew's time together. "Yeah. He took a big risk painting that subway car."

Toro gave him a long look. "I miss him."

"Who? Ari?"

"He took good care of Hanger and me when I was injured. I've been thinking—once Hanger's better, I plan to go back and live on Eudokia. It's an incredible place—a true paradise."

Pharaoh's heart did a tailspin. She was going to leave. No wonder she refused his marriage proposal. He caught up to her. "You want to live in *Greece*? What about your art?"

"I can paint anywhere."

"But you paint Brooklyn—"

She jogged across the street. "Kiro did make one good point amidst all his sputtering. There's a whole world out there for me to paint. And now Shark Man's gone, I should be able to make a good living as an artist—what with my award and all." She faced forward and settled into a steady pace.

Pharaoh let her pull ahead. She was right. There was a whole world out there waiting, not for him, but for her. She was going to be a great painter. Become rich and famous and live a life of elegance like the princess her father claimed she was.

Hard as it was to believe, maybe her old man hadn't lied. She probably was royalty.

He laughed. Not that she looked very royal at the moment. Not with her hair flying every which way, her gorgeous curves hidden beneath loose baggy sweats, her feet shod in scruffy ballet shoes.

But he knew what was under them. He knew what she smelled like when she was aroused. He knew how silky her skin felt to his touch. He knew what she sounded like when she came. He'd been her first. For him, she would always be a real princess.

He gulped a breath of air into his aching lungs and ignored the burning pain in his side. Whether she was royalty or not, she didn't belong married to a broken-up tattoo artist who would almost certainly end up in prison.

Ahead of him, the Williamsburg Bridge loomed. Sure, he promised her crazy father to take care of her. But Toro was well capable of taking care of herself. The King had been doing it for years.

They turned on to the ramp and then raced along the walkway toward Manhattan. Pharaoh let himself fall farther back.

Ahead of him, Toro ran with a lightness of being, her ballet slippers barely touching the pavement. She deserved hope and joy and a bright future.

What need did she have for him?

He gazed down at the cold, watery grave she'd saved him from too many times. He should let her go. Let her become the woman she was meant to be.

He took out the tattered piece of her wedding dress. He should do the right thing, the generous thing—set his angel free.

He crushed the cloth in his hand. But how could he? He loved her with every part of his being.

He'd die without her.

****

By the time, they arrived at Bellevue Hospital,

Pharaoh was wheezing, his battered ribs sending waves of stabbing pain up his side. He cupped his hand against the most painful spot.

He needed a doctor himself, but he would not leave Toro. Not now. He'd assured her Hanger was going to be all right. He hoped he had told the truth.

Bella met them in the hallway outside Hanger's room, face pale, hands supporting her huge belly, her eyes red-rimmed.

Toro rushed toward her. "Vernon?"

"He's going to be okay. Nothing major damaged. Bastard of a brother missed all the vitals. They'll release him tomorrow. But…"

Pharaoh stilled. She hadn't been crying for Vernon.

Toro's voice wavered. "Hanger?"

Bella rested a hand on Toro's arm. "He's alive. But he lost the leg. They just brought him up from the recovery room. He doesn't know."

"Hell." Toro disappeared into the room.

Behind her, Pharaoh smashed his fist into the wall. They'd been making love while her brother suffered alone. What kind of a selfish bastard was he?

But he knew what kind he was—the kind who let his mother die in front of his eyes. The kind who tattooed garbage on perfect skin to save his own measly life. The kind who took an innocent girl's virginity while her brother lost his ability to scale buildings. The kind who would drag the woman he loved into the hell that was his life.

Bella put a hand on his sleeve. "The police are looking for you." She glanced over her shoulder. "They were here—maybe ten minutes ago.

Pharaoh's breath caught in his throat. "The

police?"

"For the murder of Kiro. They've been to see Vernon twice. Wanted to know if he knew you. Apparently, your prints were all over the penthouse." Tiny wrinkles formed across her brow. "It's not true—is it?"

"I didn't kill him."

"Then turn yourself in. Vernon will get you a lawyer."

But he was already stepping away. Toro had been there, but she'd been Kiro's fiancée. She'd get off. The gun used in the killing was gone, along with the murderer who seemed to have left no fingerprints.

He, on the other hand, had snuck into the building illegally. Knocked out the guard. Stolen an SUV. All in front of those security cameras. He had an arrest record. Had worked for Jax. Somewhere there was a tell-tale gun with his fingerprints on it.

They'd never believe he hadn't shot Kiro or knifed the judge.

He glanced into the hospital room. Toro was bent over her brother, a shattered angel in gray sweats. She had her work cut out for her. Fifteen and an amputee. The boy would need therapy. Help dealing with the loss of his leg.

Hell, Hanger lived for his street art. How would a kid who'd conquered the rooftops of Brooklyn adjust to limping his way through life?

And it was all his fault. If he had just stopped Hanger from going into Kiro's garage all those days ago, none of this would have happened.

"You okay?" Bella asked.

Her husband was wounded, and here she was

offering him kindness. He struggled to draw air into his lungs. He couldn't look into the eyes of the woman he'd hurt so much.

He took another step back. The best thing he could do was to leave. "Got to go."

He turned so fast he stumbled over his own feet, and then he was running down the corridor, leaping down the steps two at a time and flying out into the street, heading for the bridge and a watery grave.

****

When he reached the middle of the bridge, he came to an abrupt stop. This was what he'd always done. Run. Run from his problems.

Toro deserved more. He might not deserve to live, but he had to—for her sake. She might not think him husband material, but if her rescues of him proved anything, they showed she didn't want him dead. If he jumped, she'd blame herself.

He tipped back his head and stared up at the sky. Time to stop running. Time to turn himself in to the cops and face his punishment.

He turned toward Brooklyn and headed for T-Crew's.

There was one thing he had to do first.

Chapter 34

Toro glanced up at the bridge. Empty. He wasn't there.

Ever since she'd stepped from Hanger's hospital room and found Pharaoh gone, her heart had been pounding in her chest so hard she could barely draw breath.

She'd feared he'd planned to jump. But his favorite roost was empty. And there'd been no reports of suicides.

She set her baseball cap more firmly on her head and clambered over the red fencing, swung across to the diagonal beam, and then like a tightrope walker, jauntily worked her way up above the roadway.

Someone down below bellowed at her. It was stupid climbing the bridge in broad daylight—a sure way to draw the authorities. She didn't care. The yell came again. She ignored it.

She reached the horizontal beam spanning the width of the bridge, sat down, and dangled her ballet-slippered feet over the side.

She was wearing a boy's tee, rolled up skinny jeans, and a frayed denim sleeveless vest with a small can of spray paint in the pocket. She'd compromised. Not girl clothes. Not boy clothes. Just comfortable clothes a person could move in. She took a minute to take in the view and say goodbye.

She shielded her eyes from the sun with her hand and gazed around her. It was one of those rare New York City days when the air was clean, and the temperature perfect—some magical thermal point between spring and summer.

Down below, cars whizzed and trains rumbled their way to Manhattan. To either side, the East River glittered in the sunlight like the bodice of her abandoned wedding dress, and above her, sea gulls swooped and squawked, complaining in their coarse voices at being disturbed.

She stared up at the web of steel that had been T-Crew's rallying place. Across from her and to the left was Hanger's first tag—the one that had led to all that nonsense with Kiro in the first place.

Above that hung T-Crew's crown tag, the red and silver landmark riding high, only slightly weathered. Her artist mentor, Ari Stavros, had been the last person to touch it up.

She fingered the note in her pocket. As soon as Hanger was stable, they were leaving for Eudokia. Ari and his wife, Melissa, had encouraged them to come and stay at the villa. It was the perfect solution.

She needed to get Hanger away from the buildings he'd never climb again. The warmth and sun of the Greek island would help him regain his strength as it had her when she'd broken her neck the year past. And he'd get the best therapy in the world, the best prosthesis, plus tutors to prep him for college.

Money was no longer a problem. In the biggest joke of all, Shark Man had named her his beneficiary. For some crazy reason—or more likely because her father had demanded it as a condition of marriage to a "princess," all of Kiro's wealth was hers.

She was now a fabulously wealthy woman. She owned blocks and blocks of Brooklyn real estate, several factories, a mansion and three shopping malls in New Jersey, even a pseudo-castle in the Catskills, plus a bunch of disreputable places like Jax's brothel, which she, with the help of Vernon and Daniela's Mercy House staff, had already started to dismantle.

She even owned the red Spyder Hanger had turned into Jaws. She'd promised him he could paint his masterpiece on it again. Then she was giving the car to Bella. She deserved it.

It had been Vernon's wedding present to her before Kiro had stolen everything from them. Besides, a shark car would be the perfect vehicle for a mermaid.

Everything was falling into place except one. Pharaoh was missing and apparently intended to stay missing. He'd sent a note. It was why she was here.

She lifted her legs and turned to face the other way, toward Manhattan. She peered up at the west tower. In beautiful calligraphy was Pharaoh's message: "My Dancing Angel. Dreams Live."

She swiped the hair from her eyes and blinked to clear her vision. This wasn't the way it was supposed to end.

In books, fairy tales came true.

But he was wanted by the police, so he could never come to Greece with them. He either had to face the justice system or live in hiding the rest of his life. She knew which he had chosen.

She stood, ready to climb down, and stopped. All the way here she kept thinking she'd turn around, and he'd be there. Was he watching now?

She scanned the row of windows at the top of the bridge towers. Many times, she'd caught Pharaoh sneaking up to the off-limits observation deck. Called it his "Watching and Waiting Place."

She hoped he still did.

Taking a deep breath, she stood up on the girder, planted her feet and took the first position in ballet. Then, hands extended in perfect symmetry, she moved smoothly into the next four stances, ending with a *pas de bourrée*. From down below came a smattering of applause and a distinctive whistle.

She couldn't get down fast enough. But only strangers, an angry police officer, and a trampled and torn piece of her wedding gown waited for her.

Chapter 35

The tattoo shop was small and out of the way, but well-known for its quality of work. At least, that's what the sign on the pole proclaimed. Alba drove the rental car into the gravel lot and parked facing the building.

Still, no matter the quality, this far out of town in the middle of nowhere—why would anyone come here for a tat? She glanced around. Judging from the one other car in the lot, few people did.

She shut off the engine and waited a moment in the cool of the air-conditioned car, studying the building. The shop had once been a house—a small ranch with blue plastic siding long ago faded in the southern sun to a swamp gray. The windows had tattoo designs with black backgrounds painted on them. Every design featured a crown.

That alone told her she was in the right place.

She opened the car door and climbed out of the seat into the steam-furnace heat of a Florida day. Greece could get hot, but not like this. One day in Orlando, and she was ready to fly home.

Her phone beeped. She scanned the incoming text and then shoved the cell back in her purse. So what if the dignitaries were waiting for her at the gallery in town. So what if she missed the opening cocktail party. So what if her agent thought she was crazy.

She slammed the car door. Well, they could all

wait a little longer. She headed to the door. She had a missing brother to find.

A bell tinkled as she stepped inside, the room dark, her eyes sun-blind. It was like walking into a grotto. A mechanically-cool breath of air, scented with incense, settled around her and raised goosebumps up and down her bare arms.

Little by little, brilliantly colored tattoo flash became clear as her eyes adjusted to the intermittent glow of thousands of twinkling white string lights draped across the walls and ceiling.

There was a movement to her side. She spun around.

"Welcome to the Crown. Lookin' to be inked, little lady?" The voice was heavy, gruff, and straight out of a bayou, or at least it sounded like she thought a bayou accent would sound: long-voweled, clipped endings, a slowness of words, a length of breath.

Toro's heart stuttered. She faced the speaker. The man was tall and broad with dreadlocks spread over his shoulders and down his back. Tattoos ran up and down his arms, around his neck, and disappeared under his sleeveless tank top.

His skin was almost as black as the ink on his arms, his face heavily scarred down one side. Not a man you wanted to meet alone in the dark.

Not the man she hoped for.

She'd worn a dress today because of the heat, something light and cottony and cool. A lot of her skin showed. It still made her uncomfortable. So did the way the guy glared at her. Like she was something he wanted to chew up and spit out and sweep out the door.

She really didn't want to be alone with this man.

But the private investigator she'd hired had been sure. "Tell my brother I'm here."

"Brother?"

"Yes, Hanger. I know he's working here."

He slowly shook his head back and forth. "Don't know any Hanger."

"Mircea, then. Or Mic."

The guy rolled his shoulders. "No one by that name. So are you here for a tat?"

Had the detective she'd hired gotten it wrong? She glanced to the back where the tat stations sat dark and empty, studied the tattoo designs on the wall.

No, she was in the right place. Her brother was here using a different name, or Bayou Man was lying. Well, she could lie too.

She held out her arm and twisted it. "I hear crowns are your specialty. I would like this tattoo on my other arm. So they match."

The man put down his pencil and stepped out from behind the counter. He had to be over six and a half feet tall with hands that could go around her biceps twice. But he picked up her arm as gently as if he were handling a baby bird, and examined the tiny blue shape on the underside of her upper arm.

He squinted at her. "Very old, this tat."

"It was done when I was a baby."

"Unusual."

He wasn't referring to the tattoo. Crowns were a dime a dozen. Baby tats, on the other hand, were cruel and unusual punishment. "I come from an unconventional family."

He tipped her arm one way and then the other. "Very intricate." With a grunt, he flicked on a high intensity lamp, then fingered her skin, and studied the crown. "Got words on it."

"Designs. Meaningless squiggles."

He extracted a jeweler's loupe from under the counter and inserted it in his eye. "*Printesa*."

She snatched her arm back and stared at the crown. "You made that up."

He tilted the lamp toward her and handed her the loupe. "You look."

Alba shook her head and handed him back the magnifier. "Doesn't matter. I have a different word in mind for the new tat."

"Whatever. It's your arm." He opened the appointment book. "Nando does the girls. He's off today. Come back tomorrow. Around nine." He switched off the light.

Nando? Was that the name Hanger was going by? She leaned on the old Formica counter top. "Place is empty. I'll wait. Call him."

"Come back tomorrow." He turned his back to her and flopped down on a folding chair.

"I said I'd wait. I'm busy tomorrow."

The guy's face wrinkled up on the unscarred side like a brown paper bag. "Suit yourself. I'll buzz him. But no guarantee he'll come."

She licked her lips, then despite the turmoil in her stomach, sent the only message she knew would work. "Tell him Ballet Slippers wants a crown tat."

The old guy pushed up from the chair, leaned over the counter, and peered down at her feet. He shrugged. "Right."

She took out her cell, texted her apologies to her agent, and sat down on the cracked leather sofa.

Books of tattoo designs littered the side table. She picked up one and thumbed through looking for a tell-tale crown. She hoped she wasn't making a mistake.

It didn't take long. Outside, car wheels crunched on the gravel and braked to a stop.

Bayou Man's head went up like a gator catching a scent. "Your lucky day. Nando's back. Must not have been a good day for surfing. He'll take care of you." He picked up a comic book and settled back into his chair.

Toro tossed down the sketchbook and stood. Please let this be her brother.

The door opened.

"Got you here a customer." Bayou Man nodded at her.

"So I see."

Toro stared. Not her brother.

The man filling the doorway had dreads, too. But no scar. And his skin was the color of burnt umber. He looked older. Wiser. Tiny wrinkles gathered at the corners of his eyes—maybe from the Florida sun. Maybe from worry.

Of course, it had been five years.

The twinkling lights flickered over skin covered in a riot of tattoos. But the wingtips of the hawk were still there, peeking out from under his sleeveless leather vest.

She released her breath. "Pharaoh."

Bayou Man called across. "Lady wants a tat to match the one she has."

Pharaoh shaded his eyes. "Does she?"

He bent down and scooped up the three-legged gray cat that had bounded in from the back of the shop. He cuddled it against his chest and stroked the top of its head.

She remembered those gentle fingers touching her, exploring every part of her, bringing her to the heights of ecstasy. A shiver skittered down her back. Damn, she still loved him. Still wanted him.

But that wasn't why she was here. Ignoring the pounding of her heart, the heat flooding her body, she took a step forward. "Where are you hiding my brother?"

"Not hiding him. He's apprenticing with me." He looked over his shoulder. "Get in here, kid. Your sister's here." He stepped aside.

Hanger, wearing swim trunks and a smile, stuck his head in the doorway. "What you doing here, Toro?"

She hadn't seen him since he'd graduated college ten months ago. He'd grown, filled out, the way twenty-year-olds did.

He'd never be tall, but he definitely would turn girls' heads with his midnight black hair, broad shoulders, and gypsy smile—as long as they didn't look down and see the dull metal of his prosthesis.

She rushed to him and threw her arms around him. His skin carried the scent of sand and salt and sun. "*Idiota.* You drop out of graduate school and don't tell me? I had to hire a private investigator to find you."

"I didn't want to be found."

"Why?"

"Gonna be a tattoo artist."

"Hell no. I didn't send you to college to get an engineering degree so you could waste your life in dumps like this. Thought you wanted to build bridges?"

"This ain't a dump, and yeah, I'll build bridges someday. Just not right now. Taking a break. Building other kinds of bridges." He put a hand on her shoulder and turned her slightly. "Aren't you going to say hi to Pharaoh?"

She glared at him. "Why should I? He left."

Pharaoh shrugged and kept petting the cat. "You said no."

She looked away. Pharaoh was right. She'd turned him down.

Hanger glanced from one to the other. "Uh, Fishtail and I have better things to do." He lifted the cat from Pharaoh's arms and headed for the door.

On the threshold, he stopped and grinned at them over his shoulder. "Don't kill each other." Then he was gone.

Despite the air conditioning, perspiration broke out on the back of her neck and trickled down her back. Damn her brother. This was the conversation she'd never wanted to have.

She could run. Go after her brother and drag him home. But she didn't. She peered into Pharaoh's eyes. "I had to. I had to go to Greece. Take care of Hanger."

"And become a big name artist." There was twist in his voice that made the words sound like a curse.

"That too. So?"

"So—a world famous artist deserves more than an ex-felon."

She bit the inside of her lip. He would think that. "They didn't charge you with murder."

"No, breaking and entering. Ratted on Jax and his buddies. Took the plea deal. But you must know all that. Spending Kiro's fortune and all on a lawyer for me. You did do that, didn't you?"

"I thought…Oh, never mind. You've been out over

a year and never got in touch. Stayed in communication with my brother, though. Wait. Is that the problem—Kiro's fortune?"

He rolled his shoulders. "Couldn't have gone to a nicer princess."

She wanted to give the man an earthquake of a shake. His face was blank. His posture rigid. Being Mr. Iceman. Wasn't he feeling what she was?

She glanced down at his hands. They were fisted at his sides, the knuckles bloodless. On the back of each hand was a crown inside a heart and her name.

That was all she needed to see. He might keep everything within, but his skin didn't lie.

"Enough being stupid. I love you, you crazy man." She took a leap and wrapped her hands around his neck.

"And I love you." His mouth came down on hers. His strong hands caught her under her rear end and lifted her off her feet.

He spun her around like a princess in a Cinderella movie, all the years and crimes and fears fading away, the twinkling lights whirling above her like thousands of stars.

He smelled of the sea he'd swum in. His lips were warm and soft and hot and spicy. His tongue found hers and twisted around in greeting. He shifted her against his hardness and deepened the kiss. He inhaled, and she inhaled with him. Their hearts thundered together.

It was the kiss she'd been dreaming of. She wanted it to go on forever. But there was something she had to say first. She flattened her hands against his chest as if holding down the hawk's wings would keep him from flying away again and separated her lips from his. "Yes."

"Yes what?"

"Yes, I'll marry you if that's what it takes to pin you down."

"That's all I needed to hear. I love you, princess." Then he spun her around again. And kissed her.

This time she knew. Sometimes, fairy tales did come true.

Zara West

A word about the author…

Zara West loves all things dark, scary, and heart-stopping as long as they lead to true love.

Born in Williamsburg, Brooklyn, Zara spends winters in New York where the streets hum with life, summers in Maritimes where the sea can be cruel, and the rest of the year anywhere inspiration for tales of suspense, mystery, and romance are plentiful.

An accomplished artist by training and passion, she brings a love of art to every book she writes.

A fan of handcrafted and ethically produced clothing, Zara's original clothing designs and artistic creations have been sold in numerous venues including Bloomingdales, Putumayo, and the Museum of American Folk Art.

In a life full of misadventures, she has had sunstroke on the top of a Greek mountain while doing ethnographic research with shepherds, been stranded on the banks of the Rhine with no money and one chocolate bar, and while she has never been kidnapped, she has been abandoned on an uninhabited island in the middle of the wilderness for longer than she wants to remember.

In her spare time, when not writing award-winning books, magazine articles, and flash fiction stories, Zara tends her organic herb garden, travels widely, and whips up ethnic dishes for friends and family.

A member of RWA, Zara is a published author of both fiction and non-fiction. Her short stories have appeared in several anthologies, and have received awards from Women on Writing, Stone Thread Publishing, Tryst Literary Magazine, and Winning

Writers. Her novels have placed first in the Romance Through the Ages contest, second in the Touch of Love Contest and long listed for the Myslexia Award. http://zarawest.wordpress.com

Thank you for purchasing
this publication of The Wild Rose Press, Inc.
For other wonderful stories of romance,
please visit our on-line bookstore at
www.thewildrosepress.com.

For questions or more information
contact us at
info@thewildrosepress.com.

The Wild Rose Press, Inc.
www.thewildrosepress.com

To visit with authors of
The Wild Rose Press, Inc.
join our yahoo loop at
http://groups.yahoo.com/group/thewildrosepress/

www.ingramcontent.com/pod-product-compliance
Lightning Source LLC
Chambersburg PA
CBHW071523260626
47170CB00002B/488